BER

ENDC

James Baddock

Andrews UK Limited

Contents

BERLIN ENDGAME

Prologue

Hannover, Germany: October, 1948

Somewhere in the distance a church clock struck two, the bell pealing out mournfully into the night. The sound made McCluskey check his watch absently, but he did not look up; he was standing on the canal towpath, his hands pushed deep into the pockets of his trench coat, his attention seemingly focused on the distorted reflection of the moon bobbing up and down in the dark water below him. Slowly, he drew in a deep breath, then turned to face the man standing in the shadows five yards away from him. 'You're sure about this, Easton?' he asked quietly.

'I didn't say I was sure, sir,' Easton replied; like McCluskey, his accent revealed him to be an American. 'I'm just telling you what I saw in that document. It could be a purely theoretical exercise, for all I know, but if it isn't...' His voice trailed away meaningfully.

'Yeah. I know what you mean,' McCluskey replied quietly. He turned back to face Easton. 'You've got photos?'

'Yes, sir. Two of each sheet.'

'Good, good.' McCluskey said absently. Suddenly, he shook his head. 'This really will stir things up - if it's kosher. I can't honestly believe they'd carry it out. They could start another war if they did, for Chrissake.'

'Maybe that's what they want, sir. Given what some of them think about the Reds...'

'True, true,' McCluskey agreed, still with that preoccupied air, then shook his head again. 'Jee-sus,' he said softly, then began walking slowly back towards Easton. 'You could be right, Easton, I'm afraid.'

'I hope not, sir,'

'Amen to that, pal. Amen to that.' McCluskey stared across the canal for a moment, then said, his voice suddenly brisk,

1

businesslike, 'OK, let's get this sorted out. You're sure nobody knows you've seen those documents?'

'I didn't see anyone at all, either on the way in or out.'

McCluskey nodded approvingly. 'And you got straight in touch with me?'

'Of course, sir,' Easton replied, a note of bewilderment in his voice: who else would he contact? The next moment, his eyes widened in stunned surprise as McCluskey's right hand came out of the coat pocket holding a silenced pistol. Easton began to react, to throw himself to one side, but he had barely begun to shift his weight when the gun coughed three times in rapid succession. The impact of the bullets threw Easton backwards, his chest a sudden mass of blood: he fell heavily onto his back, arms outflung. For a moment, his eyes focused on McCluskey and his mouth opened as if to ask one last question - *why?* - then his head lolled to one side and he lay utterly still.

McCluskey stood looking down at the motionless body for perhaps three or four seconds, then walked over to it, bent down and quickly searched it, taking a Walther pistol from a jacket pocket and spinning it out into the canal. As he straightened up, a man emerged from the shadows further along the towpath and walked towards him. The newcomer also looked down at Easton.

'Do you believe him? You're sure nobody else knows?' His accent was unmistakeably British.

'He won't have told anyone else,' McCluskey said firmly. 'He is - *was* a pro. I was his field officer - he'd only report to me.'

'Pity you didn't have a better idea what he was up to, then, wasn't it?'

McCluskey glared at the Englishman, then shook his head. 'Easton was an independent bastard at the best of times. But, like I said, he was a pro. He would only have reported to me,' he repeated.

'So the leak's plugged?'

'Yes.'

'Just as well, for both our sakes.' The Englishman nodded. 'Very well. I'll notify them that there has been no breach of security. "Carronade" can still go ahead.'

Part I

Chapter 1

Berlin, November, 1948

'Hallo,' the pilot said suddenly, bringing Cormack awake with a start; he looked around the Dakota's cockpit, a startled expression on his face as if this were the first time he had been aware of being on an aircraft at all. He was just about to stretch and yawn hugely when the pilot craned his head round - Cormack was sitting in the spare seat behind the Flight Engineer - and continued, 'Looks like trouble.' He nodded to his left and Cormack looked out of the side perspex window, following the direction of the pilot's gesture.

A Soviet fighter plane was paralleling their course, seemingly almost touching the Dakota's port wingtip, but Cormack guessed - hoped - that it wasn't as close as it seemed. All the same, he could still see the pale blur of the Russian pilot's face staring back at him - the other plane was not that far away either... 'What's he doing?' Cormack demanded; he had to shout to make himself heard above the constant roar of the engines.

'Playing silly buggers,' the young Flying Officer yelled back. 'They do that from time to time,' he explained. 'More to put the wind up us than anything else - although this one is closer than most,' he added. He grinned across at Cormack as if in reassurance. 'Don't worry, sir. I don't think he'll try anything really daft. They've just about given up buzzing us these days. This is about all they do, sit on one wingtip, which cramps your style a bit, but he'll probably peel off when we get lower.'

'Still looks too bloody close to me.'

'Don't worry, sir - the RAF will see you to your destination in style and comfort,' the pilot said, grinning boyishly. 'Well, maybe not in comfort,' he added, then looked briefly around the cockpit interior. 'Not very much in the way of style either,' he finished, switching his attention back to the Soviet fighter, which was still keeping station on them. 'Silly sod,' he commented. 'He must be damn near stalling that thing.'

'Aren't you going to report it?' Cormack asked, vaguely surprised.

'Not much point, old boy,' the pilot replied, in an RAF drawl that Cormack was convinced was carefully cultivated. 'Nothing the Ground Controllers can do, is there? I'll let them know when we get down. All that'll happen will be another protest to the Russkies, which they'll ignore, and we'll all carry on as normal.'

Cormack stifled a grin. 'As normal' - Jesus Christ, that was an expression that could never be applied to the present situation in Berlin, not after four and a half months of the Blockade. He looked at the pilot, who could not have been more than twenty-two or three, yet whose face was gaunt and hollow-eyed, clearly on the edge of exhaustion - but he was still keeping going. How many times had he carried out this flight now? And how many more times would he have to do it before this was all over?

'There he goes,' the pilot said, with a note of evident satisfaction in his voice as the Soviet plane tipped over to port and dived away. 'We're almost there,' he added, as if in explanation.

Cormack looked out through the windscreen and saw the city sprawled out ahead of him. Berlin. Hitler's capital, that had been devastated firstly by RAF and American bombers, then by the savage assault of the Soviet Red Army; large areas of it, he knew, were still in ruins, but none of that was visible at this height or distance. He could just make out a grey expanse of water that had to be the Havel See; their destination, the airfield at Gatow, was just short of that.

The pilot was saying something to Gatow Tower, but Cormack hardly heard him; he was totally absorbed in the view of the approaching city. He must have come in along virtually the same route, three and a half years ago, he realised, only it had been night time then, of course... It was probably round about here that the Soviet fighter had damn nearly shot them out of the sky, for Christ's sake...

With an effort, Cormack wrenched his mind back to the present as the pilot made his descent, his languid air belied by the way his eyes kept flickering from the gauges to the runway ahead in total concentration. Then, with only a moderate jolt, they were down and taxi-ing almost to a halt at the end of the runway before the Dakota turned and headed towards the unloading area. Four overalled men were waiting on the concrete apron, directing the plane to its berth.

Almost before the Dakota had come to a halt, a lorry had been backed up to the cargo hatch and, as soon as the hatch was opened, six men jumped into the plane to begin unloading the crates of tinned food, dried milk and medical supplies. The men worked rapidly, efficiently, with only a minimum of conversation; it was evident to Cormack that they knew their business. Mind you, he thought as he jumped down from the cockpit hatch, they ought to by now...

'Thanks,' he called out to the pilot, who was watching the unloading with an undeniably proprietorial air.

'Any time, old boy,' the pilot grinned nonchalantly, then spoilt the effect by having to stifle a yawn. 'See you around.'

Cormack nodded and headed towards the Control Tower. A stocky, uniformed Lieutenant was standing by the door that led into the Administration Block; as soon as he saw Cormack, he stepped forward and saluted smartly.

'Captain Cormack? I'm Lieutenant Galvin, your assistant. Colonel Pallister told me to meet you.'

'Galvin,' Cormack said absently, shaking the other's hand. Galvin was no more than twenty-five, with the innocent air of a choirboy - how the hell had he found his way into Intelligence Corps?

'I've got a jeep, sir. I've to take you direct to HQ.'

'Right. Carry on, Lieutenant.' Cormack said awkwardly, wondering if he would ever get used to issuing orders. *Or taking them*, he thought suddenly, suppressing a grin.

Inside the Administration Block was a scene of scarcely controlled chaos. There were about a dozen trestle tables crammed into a room that was no more than thirty feet square and, at each one, a harassed looking clerk was taking down details of cargoes and manifests from equally impatient looking pilots or flight crew. Beyond was a second, similar room - Cormack remembered hearing somewhere that Gatow was now the busiest airport in the world, with three times the daily traffic of La Guardia, the previous record holder. Seeing this frenzied, but purposeful activity (not to mention the rows of aircraft on the concrete apron outside), he could well believe it. He followed Galvin across this sea of bureaucracy and was just about to go out through the door at the far end when a familiar voice called out:

'Alan! Alan Cormack! What the hell are you doing here?'

Cormack spun round, his face creasing into a broad grin as he saw a tall, brown-haired man in a leather flying jacket striding towards him. 'Tony Woodward! Where did you spring from, you old bugger?'

'Less of the old.' Woodward grinned, taking Cormack's hand in a firm clasp. 'Good to see you, old boy.' Unlike the pilot, Woodward's use of 'old boy' was entirely unaffected; he came from a minor aristocratic background - one day, he would be *Sir* Anthony Woodward - and his accent, refined, cultured, the product of a public school, was normally the sort that set Cormack's teeth on edge, but he and Woodward had been through so much in the war together that he scarcely noticed it.

'And you, old son,' Cormack replied, his own accent, that held more than a trace of his East End origins, contrasting markedly with Woodward's. He tapped the front of Woodward's flying jacket. 'So they roped you into all this as well, did they?'

'Afraid so. Couldn't really not get involved, now, could I?'

'Suppose not. You never could say no, could you, Tony?'
Cormack agreed, looking intently at Woodward. Wild horses
would not have prevented him from taking part in the Airlift
- even if he had been bombing hell out of Berlin four years ago.

'Not really, no. And what about you?' Woodward asked,
looking meaningfully at Cormack's uniform. 'You were back in
civvy street, the same as me, the last time I saw you. Did they
rope you in as well?'

'It's a long story, Tony.' Cormack felt suddenly awkward:
he ought to be reporting to Colonel Pallister, not standing
around chatting, even if it was with Tony Woodward - but then
somebody called Woodward's name from across the room.

'Yes?' Woodward replied, looking over at the man who had
called to him.

'Your plane will be ready in ten minutes.'

'Right. I'll be along in a minute.' Woodward turned back
to Cormack. 'Sorry, old boy. Have to dash, I'm afraid - they
don't like us being on the ground at this end any longer than
necessary. Look, are you going to be in Berlin long?'

'I've been posted here.'

'Good! What say we get together for a drink or three? I can
arrange to have the kite serviced overnight - she's about due for
one, anyway - and we can get disgustingly drunk and reminisce
about old times. How's that sound?'

'Sounds pretty good to me.'

'You can contact me here, or I'll give you a ring at your HQ
- OK?'

'OK.'

Woodward turned to go, then hesitated momentarily. He
stared at Cormack, then said gruffly, 'Look after yourself, right?'

'And you, Tony.'

Woodward nodded and strode away. Cormack watched
him go, then pushed the door open and stepped outside, where
Galvin was waiting for him with a jeep. Cormack threw his

bag into the back and jumped into the passenger seat, barely noticing as Galvin drove away.

Bloody hell - fancy seeing Tony Woodward again... It had been - how long? Two years? Three? Early '46, that had been it - nearly three years. He hadn't changed, not really, although there had been the shadows under the eyes that seemed almost *de rigeur* for the Airlift pilots, yet they still held the alert enthusiasm that Cormack remembered, the almost boyish innocence that would make Woodward volunteer for almost suicidal operations behind enemy lines simply because it was the done thing to do... Just like he'd probably volunteered for the Airlift, offering his considerable flying skills for way below what other civilian pilots would be asking - and he'd be loving every minute of it. He should have been born six hundred years ago, Cormack decided, idly - he'd have been a natural as a knight in shining armour. One of the best, though - they'd broken the mould when they'd made him...

A jolt as the jeep hit a pothole brought him out of his reverie and he looked round, suddenly seeing the bomb-damaged streets and buildings for the first time. He remembered reading somewhere that the bombing raids throughout the War had accounted for over fourteen per cent of Germany's total war damage - indeed, during a raid in February, 1945, one and a half square miles of the city centre had been wiped out in a single hour - but, despite this knowledge, he was unprepared for what he saw all around him. He had spent the last year in Hamburg and so, unfortunately, he was used to the skeletal remains of buildings, the piles of rubble and the general air of hopeless squalor, but, as the jeep drove past block after block of devastation, he became aware of a subtle difference. OK, so Hamburg was still in a hell of a mess, but at least there were signs of recovery there, in that some reconstruction was beginning to take place, but there was little indication here of any attempts to repair the damage. Hardly surprising, of course, given the extreme privations caused by the Blockade, but it was depressing, all the same. This was what the Soviets had done to the city...

The Berlin Blockade, as it had come to be called, had started nearly five months before, on the 24th of June, when the Soviet authorities had cut off all road and rail links between Berlin and the Trizone, the part of Germany which was administered by the British, American and French Occupying Powers. The object was to drive the Western Allies out of their respective sectors in Berlin so that the entire city would fall under Soviet control; it was seen as a valuable prize, both from the propaganda viewpoint, but also as a test of how determined the United States would be to maintain a presence in Europe. There was a widespread feeling throughout Western Europe that if the Americans abandoned Berlin, they would do the same to the rest of Europe if the Red Army decided to march westwards; the Soviet Union presumably felt the same way. If they thought the Americans would be an easy target, however, they had been proved wrong; right from the start of the Blockade the Americans and British had set up an airlift, initially to fly in supplies for their garrisons, but which had rapidly expanded into an operation whose objective was nothing less than to supply the entire population of West Berlin, the name now being given to the combined American, British and French sectors. Despite the fact that when the Airlift had started, there had been only thirty-six days of food stocks and forty-five days' worth of coal in West Berlin, somehow the assortment of USAF, RAF and British civilian aircraft, flying round the clock into Gatow, Tempelhof and (during the past few days) Tegel, had managed to keep two and a half million West Berliners supplied in the face of the Russians' impotent fury. Certainly there were still shortages - the Airlift was supplying just under half of West Berlin's normal daily requirements - but enough was coming into the city to keep people alive. Just. Cormack had seen the figures and knew how finely balanced the situation was, but, for the time being at least, they were holding on, although what things would be like over the winter was anybody's guess. The problem was that nobody really knew how the Soviets would react - would they just stand idly by and let the Western Allies off the hook? Or would they decide to act? An awful lot of people would dearly love to know the answer to those questions, and part of Cormack's job, he was sure, would be to try and find out what the Soviet intentions were.

He was suddenly aware that Galvin was turning the jeep into a large archway that led into a courtyard within an imposing building: this had to be their Headquarters. Cormack suppressed an ironic smile. The British Military Government was based at the Olympiastadion, where Hitler had held the 1936 Olympics and been upstaged by Jesse Owens, but Army Intelligence had their HQ almost half a mile away, off Heerstrasse; they were being kept well out of the way, very much the black sheep of the family... Galvin parked the jeep, then led the way to a large doorway, both men acknowledging the salutes of the MPs on guard duty. Inside was a spacious lobby, with a wide marble staircase and a glittering chandelier above, but the effect was ruined by the half dozen or so trestle tables scattered across the floor space, each one covered with documents and filing trays. Whatever the building might have been once, it was now a fully operational administration centre.

'We're through here, sir,' Galvin explained, pointing to an unobtrusive, unmarked door to the left. They passed through into an office, also furnished with the ubiquitous trestle tables, behind which were various uniformed clerks. Cormack was aware of the interested glances that were thrown in his direction and understood why; he was being sized up as their new Unit CO. He saw at least one pair of eyes widen momentarily as they saw the DSO ribbon on his chest, followed by a second penetrating look. Probably guessing my age, he thought sardonically - and perhaps wondering why a man in his middle thirties with a DSO was still only a Captain...

'Your office, sir.' Galvin held open yet another door to allow Cormack to enter a room that was about fifteen feet square, with a desk in front of a window that looked out onto the courtyard - except that the view was almost totally obscured by a damn great Bedford lorry at the moment... Talk about shoving me out of the way, he thought, smiling faintly to himself. He looked around, seeing the filing cabinet to the left of the window, the only other item of furniture, apart from the chair behind the desk, in the room. 'I'm afraid it's a bit Spartan, sir,' Galvin added nervously.

'It's alright - I'll manage.'

'Er - I'll leave you to get settled in, sir. Colonel Pallister would like to see you at eleven hundred. I'll take you up there, sir, then we'll see about your quarters-'

'Lieutenant,' Cormack said firmly, interrupting Galvin's nervous flow, 'I can manage. I'll give you a shout if I need anything, right?'

'Er - yes, sir.' Galvin saluted, then left, leaving Cormack alone in the office. Slowly, he walked around the desk and sat down, looking slowly around. *Right, Cormack, you're here. Your new job, and it's one that most Intelligence officers would give their eye teeth for, your big chance to gain promotion...*

Big deal.

***

Lieutenant-Colonel Pallister could not possibly have been anything other than an Army officer, Cormack decided: his back was ramrod-straight, his hair cropped almost to the skull, his moustache pencil-thin. The blue eyes were alert and penetrating, however, revealing a shrewd mind behind them and it would be as well to remember that he would not have been appointed the CO of Intelligence Corps in Berlin if he had not had a good deal of ability; it would not be a good idea to under-estimate him.

'Cormack,' Pallister said, in a clipped voice that Cormack was convinced was taught to all Sandhurst graduates. 'Do sit down.' A twitch of the arm indicated the chair in front of his desk; Cormack took his seat. Pallister sat down, his back still rigidly straight, then pushed a packet of cigarettes across the desk towards him. 'Smoke?'

'No, thank you, sir. I don't.'

An expression of surprise flickered briefly across Pallister's face, then he shrugged. 'Very wise,' he commented and pushed the packet aside. 'Right,' he said briskly. 'So you're Major Metcalfe's replacement.'

'Yes, sir.'

'Came as a bit of a surprise to us all, him being recalled back to the UK. Couldn't be helped, of course, but it left us in the lurch, somewhat. Damn good officer, though. You'll find that 'B' Unit is running very efficiently, Cormack. No troubles there. Bit of a tough act to follow, actually - Metcalfe.'

'So I gather, sir.' Cormack's voice was bland, noncommittal; Pallister shot him a sharp glance.

'Ye-es,' Pallister said doubtfully. 'I gather you were running a similar unit in Hamburg?'

'Yes, sir.'

'And your field of activities there?'

'There's been a good deal of Soviet infiltration there, especially in the docks, so we had to do a fair amount of surveillance work. Some black market investigations. Mostly, though, our work involved hunting through whatever records were left from the War to check up on stories being told by refugees. We spent something like half our time responding to requests from all over Germany to check birth certificates and so on.'

'Really?'

'It's one of the favourite towns for ex-Nazis to claim they came from,' Cormack explained. 'Hamburg or Dresden - they know damn well virtually all the records were destroyed there by the bombing, so all they have to do is claim to have been born there and it's just about impossible to disprove it.'

'I see,' Pallister said, staring thoughtfully at Cormack. He cleared his throat, then continued, 'I think you'll find that your field of responsibility will be largely the same as in Hamburg. There is, of course, quite an extensive black market operating in Berlin, as you might expect, given the present situation. However, there is evidence to suggest that the Russians are involved in at least part of it, as an element in their subversion tactics in West Berlin, so the situation becomes rather more complex.

'In any case, there is a high level of espionage and intelligence-gathering being carried out in Berlin by the Soviets. It's made easy for them because thousands of people travel to and from the Soviet Sector every day. They've set up checkpoints to search people, but they're not going to stop their own agents coming through, are they?'

'Hardly, sir.' Cormack agreed.

'To he honest, we don't know how many Soviet agents there are in our sector, but we do know that both the MGB and GRU are active in all three Western sectors. A large part of your duties will be to deal with such agents and networks.'

Cormack nodded. The MGB - the Soviet Ministry of State Security - was the successor to the NKVD, while the GRU was its military counterpart. Both were highly efficient - and ruthless if the situation demanded.

Pallister paused, staring appraisingly at Cormack, before he continued, 'I've always allowed 'B' Unit a fair amount of independence, Cormack, mainly because Major Metcalfe produced consistently good results. You've come to us with an impressive record, so if you keep up the good work, you won't find me interfering very much. Unless I think it's necessary.'

'Naturally, sir.'

'I'll expect regular reports, of course, but if you can deliver the goods, I'll have no complaints.'

'Understood, sir.' Which meant Pallister couldn't really be bothered with the counter-intelligence side of things, thought Cormack: he was probably more interested in 'A' Unit, the ones competing with MI6 in that they would be running networks in the Soviet Sector - the Glamour Boys, they'd called them back in Hamburg. That did not worry Cormack; he would far rather be left alone to run 'B' Unit his own way. In fact, it suited him down to the ground.

***

It was almost noon when Cormack returned to his office, deep in thought after his meeting with Pallister. He came to an abrupt halt in his office doorway as he saw someone standing in front of his desk, a woman dressed in a grey cardigan and skirt. She turned round, startled, and he could see that she was holding a bundle of documents; she had evidently been placing them in his 'In' tray. She was about thirty, slim, with auburn hair pulled back into a loose bun, and blue eyes in a face that was attractive without being stunningly beautiful - but which was registering a combination of surprise and trepidation.

She recovered fast, however. 'You must be Captain Cormack,' she said, in English.

'I am,' he replied levelly. 'So who are you?'

'Elise Langemann,' she said, glancing nervously away to the right for a moment. 'I am your personal typist.'

'You are, are you?' Cormack asked. 'First I've heard of it.'

'Well - not exactly yours, I suppose,' she continued, flustered. 'Major Metcalfe's. I used to type his lower classification material.' Her English was fluent, with only a trace of accent. 'I have a Grade Two security clearance.'

Cormack raised his eyebrows: that was high, for a civilian, especially a German, which meant she must have been checked very thoroughly. 'OK,' he said, shrugging. 'We'll keep that arrangement for the moment - see how it works out.' He caught a momentary flicker of relief on her face, then walked around the desk and sat down. 'So what do we have here?' He indicated the documents she was holding.

'Just some circulation documents, sir, plus other material that's been passed on to us - you. To be honest, all you need to do with most of the papers is to sign and return them.'

'Frau Langemann,' Cormack said, glancing at her left hand, 'I'll decide what I do with those documents - it's my job, after all. Understand?' He spoke in fluent, accentless German, as if to emphasise the point.

'Yes, sir,' she replied, her lips setting themselves in a grim line. There had been a momentary flash of anger in her eyes, instantly suppressed.

'Good. Send in Lieutenant Galvin, will you? Tell him to bring in the current operational files.'

'Yes, sir.' There were two spots of colour high on her cheeks as she turned on her heel and walked rapidly out. Cormack watched her go, his expression thoughtful, and the moment the door closed behind her, he went to the filing cabinet to see if it was locked.

Galvin came in, carrying a bulky folder but, before he could speak, Cormack said, 'Elise Langemann.'

Galvin smiled briefly, as if at some secret joke. 'Sir?'

'Why is she here?'

Galvin hesitated, then said, 'She's very efficient, sir - and very knowledgeable about ex-German military installations in the Russian sector. She worked for both the German War Ministry and their High Command during the war, so she has a good deal of detailed information at her fingertips. She's also fluent in English, a fast typist, and she has been security vetted... Major Metcalfe thought very highly of her, sir.' Again, there was that secret smile, gone almost before Cormack could be sure it was there, but he decided not to pursue it - yet.

'Right,' he said briskly, changing the subject. 'Let's take a look at the operational files. Is there anything that needs urgent action?' He gestured to Galvin to sit down.

'Well... There *is* one, sir.' Galvin put the folders on the desk and selected one, which he passed to Cormack. 'We were just about to make an arrest when Major Metcalfe was taken ill.'

Cormack nodded and was about to open the folder when he paused, looking thoughtfully at Galvin; now was as good a time as any to get to know the calibre of his assistant. 'Why don't you give me the bare essentials, Lieutenant?'

'Right, sir,' Galvin said promptly, apparently untroubled at the prospect. 'The suspect is a civilian pilot named Logan. We're virtually certain that he's part of a well-organised black market set up. We've established links between him and known black market operators here in Berlin, but the reason why we're particularly interested in him is that one of these contacts is a man named Fogelmann who we believe is working for the MGB in addition to his black market dealings. Major Metcalfe decided that it would be better to leave Fogelmann alone for the moment, but if we could nail Logan for smuggling in contraband then we might be able to get him to talk about Fogelmann. The thing is that we don't have any hard evidence on Logan at the moment. We've got details of meetings between Logan and black market contacts, phone calls, that sort of thing - but we've never actually seen any money changing hands. Nor have we managed to intercept any contraband material on the airfield itself.'

Cormack nodded thoughtfully. 'Has his plane been searched?'

'No, sir, but his shipments have been periodically checked once they've been unloaded. Nothing's been found. The trouble is that we can't spend too long on the search because the shipments have to be shifted off the airfield pretty damned quickly to prevent a bottleneck building up so we can't be as thorough as we'd like.'

Cormack nodded slowly. 'So what exactly do you want to do?'

'Search the plane itself, sir, the minute it lands. The Flight Controllers don't like us doing that because they want to get the planes turned round as quickly as possible, but there's a distinct possibility that some of the unloading personnel are involved. We think they might be diverting the contraband before it ever reaches the storage points where we carry out the searches. We'd like to get to the shipment before they get a chance to do that.'

'And if you find anything, we pull Logan in and find out just what he and Fogelmann were talking about?'

'Yes, sir. Then we turn him over to the civilian authorities so they can throw the book at him for smuggling contraband.'

Cormack nodded again. 'So you need my authority to go ahead?'

Galvin hesitated, then said, 'Actually, Major Metcalfe *had* authorised the search, sir, but I thought it would be improper to proceed without your say-so.'

Very neat, Lieutenant, Cormack thought, suppressing a smile. *Makes it virtually impossible for me to refuse, doesn't it?* He bowed to the inevitable: 'Very well, Lieutenant. Go ahead.'

Chapter 2

Gatow Airfield

Cormack looked round sharply as the door of the office opened and a moustachioed Group Captain came in. 'We've just picked him up on the radar,' the RAF officer said, almost regretfully. 'He'll be landing in five minutes or so.'

Cormack nodded and rose to his feet, glancing out of the window at the rain drizzling down outside. 'Thank you, sir - for everything.' He gestured vaguely around the borrowed office.

'Any time,' the Group Captain muttered, then turned to go. Before he went out, however, he hesitated and turned back to Cormack 'You're sure about this?' he asked. 'Bill Logan and I served together during the War, you see.'

'The evidence is pretty substantial, sir.'

'Yes,' the Group Captain said absently. 'But Bill Logan - he's the last one I would have expected...' His voice trailed away.

'That's generally the way, sir.'

'Ye-es,' the Group Captain said again. He seemed about to add to this, but then he turned away suddenly and left.

Cormack stared at the closed door for a moment then began to pull on his coat. He hoped the evidence *would* be substantial - but it was, he told himself as he buttoned up his coat and headed for the door. The evidence was overwhelming: Logan *had* to be involved up to his neck, DFC or no DFC. Briefly, he wondered how much Logan's medal would affect the sentence, then pushed the thought from his mind - it wasn't his concern.

There were two jeeps parked outside, with three MPs in each, one driving, the others in the back. Galvin was standing beside the leading jeep; he snapped Cormack a sharp salute, then pointed to the second vehicle. 'If you'd like to take that one, sir.'

Cormack nodded wordlessly and climbed into the passenger seat; moments later, they were following Galvin's jeep across the concrete apron towards Bay Fifteen. Once there, they took shelter in the lee of a seven-ton lorry, Cormack wondering morosely why the hell Logan couldn't have picked better weather for his flight in. Not that he'd had much choice, of course - the Airlift kept on running, rain or not; all that stopped it was ice on the runway or if the cloud cover was less than two hundred feet up, or visibility at ground level less than a hundred yards - and, often, planes still came in to land under those conditions.

Like now. A Dakota suddenly appeared out of the low cloud and came in to land as smoothly as if these were optimum conditions, turning at the end of the runway before taxi-ing towards the unloading area. It came to a halt, then the roar of the Pratt & Whitney engines died away as the ground crew moved the chocks into position. There was a pause, then the cargo hatch opened and the pilot emerged, a burly man of just above medium height, wearing the ubiquitous battered leather flying jacket. He seemed to see the line of waiting MPs for the first time and, for a moment, Cormack saw a fractional slump in Logan's shoulders that spoke volumes. *End of the line*, Cormack thought - *and he knows it*. Yet Logan recovered fast - his expression as he jumped down was one of puzzlement and anger. He went stalking up to Galvin; Cormack had remained seated in the second jeep.

'What the hell's going on?' Logan demanded. 'Why aren't you unloading? These are medical supplies, for God's sake!'

Galvin handed Logan a typed document. 'We're searching the aircraft, Mr Logan,' he said calmly. 'That's my warrant.'

'Like hell you are! This is a priority cargo-'

'Let's not waste time,' Galvin interrupted him brusquely. 'You and I both know this warrant entitles me to carry out a search, so shall we get on with it?' Galvin was poised, completely in control of the situation: Cormack was impressed by the confident display of authority.

Logan glared at him, then muttered sullenly, 'All right, get on with it.'

Galvin turned away to nod to the MPs and, for a few seconds, neither he nor the MPs were looking at Logan. The pilot looked rapidly around, evidently assessing his chances of making a run for it, but then his eyes met Cormack's unblinking gaze. Slowly, Cormack shook his head, a very faint, almost predatory, smile on his face, as if daring Logan to try it. The pilot let out his breath in a long sigh and, again, his shoulders slumped heavily in defeat.

The search was over in less than five minutes. Cormack heard the shout from inside the plane and, within moments, had climbed up into the cargo hold. One of the MPs was standing over a crate with 'Medical Provisions' stencilled on its side - but he was holding up a pack of two hundred Chesterfield cigarettes. 'The whole crate's full of 'em, sir - fifty packs or more.'

'And this one's hooky as well, sir,' said a second MP from the rear of the hold, a bottle of whisky in his hand. 'It's got bottles of whisky, brandy, bourbon and God knows what else in there.'

'Worth a damned fortune,' Galvin commented exultantly. 'We've got the bastard.'

Cormack nodded. 'Well done, Lieutenant,' he said, aware he was sounding pompous, but unable to avoid it.

'Thank you, sir.' Galvin jerked his thumb in the general direction of Logan outside. 'Do you want to do the honours, sir, or-?'

'It's your show, ' Cormack replied off-handedly. 'You should get the credit.'

'Thank you, sir,' Galvin said again. He took the pack of cigarettes and called to the second MP, 'Jarvis, give me one of those bottles, will you?'

'Sir.'

Galvin took a bottle of whisky in his other hand then went to the hatch and clambered down, Cormack following him. Slowly, Galvin walked up to Logan and held up the contraband items. 'Well?' he demanded starkly, then added, with heavy sarcasm, 'Or are you going to tell me you knew nothing about them?'

Logan licked his lips nervously, his eyes flickering from Galvin to Cormack and back again. 'Can you prove I *did* know anything about them?' he asked, but his voice lacked any conviction.

'Of course we can, Logan,' Galvin said impatiently. 'Did you think this was all pure luck on our part? We *knew*, Logan - we knew.'

Again, Logan looked quizzically at Cormack as if trying to figure out just what part he was playing, then said, 'OK, OK, so I knew - but the rest of the cargo is genuine, two and a half tons of medical supplies, like it says on the manifest. I've brought those in, and God knows how many more tons in the past ten weeks.' His jaw jutted forward defiantly. 'Doesn't that count for anything?'

Galvin stared at Logan in disbelief. 'Are you trying to tell me that entitles you to earn extra money on the side? Or - what's the other one they use? - oh yes, it doesn't make any difference to the payload, so why worry about it?' He shook his head slowly, disgustedly. 'Look, Logan, your two crates of goodies mean that two crates of medical supplies that should be here in Berlin have been left behind at Fuhlsbuttel, or, worse, they've been diverted into the black market. It all adds up, Logan - a couple of crates here, a couple there - when we need every last ounce of medicine we can lay our hands on here. To save lives, Logan,' Galvin said slowly, prodding the pilot in the chest to emphasise his words. 'People are dying here because we don't have enough medicine or painkillers or drugs to go round - and you're bringing in cigarettes and booze, for God's sake!' Galvin's eyes were boring into Logan's now. 'How many people have died, do you reckon, Logan, just to line your pockets, eh? Just tell me that!' He shook his head again, contemptuously. 'You make me sick, Logan. You all do.' Abruptly, he spun on his heel and walked rapidly back towards the Dakota.

Cormack watched him go, taken aback by his vehemence: Galvin really did feel strongly about all this. But then, why not?

He was right, after all...

***

Cormack stood in the doorway for a moment, looking around the cell, a slightly bored expression on his face giving the impression that such a place was by no means a new experience for him. Which it wasn't, of course... The cell, which was in the basement of Military Police Headquarters, was about ten feet square, with a solitary window set high up on one side; the walls were of painted bricks. There was a single bunk, a bucket in the corner and a strong smell of disinfectant that caused Cormack's nostrils to twitch momentarily as he looked at Logan, who had been sitting on his bunk and was now rising to his feet, his eyes full of a half-fearful hope. Cormack stared impassively at the man for several seconds, then nodded to the MP who had let him into the cell; the MP went out, pulling the heavy iron door shut behind him.

'You wanted to see me, Logan?' There was a tinge of impatience in Cormack's voice, a conviction that this would all be a complete waste of time.

'Yes, I did,' Logan replied, swallowing nervously. 'You're the senior officer around here, aren't you?'

'As senior as you're going to see before we hand you over to the authorities, yes.' Cormack pushed his hands deep into his trench coat pockets and stared quizzically at Logan. 'Well?' he said, bluntly.

Logan hesitated, licking his lips, unsure of where to start. 'Look - I didn't really want to get into this, you know. You've got to believe that.'

'Have I really?' Cormack asked drily.

'I needed the money - it was as simple as that,' Logan said hurriedly, desperation in his voice. 'It's damned expensive keeping a Dakota in the air and these one month contracts they give us only just keep us going-'

Cormack sighed. 'Look, if all you've got me down here for is to give me some sob story, then forget it. I've got far better things to do.' He spun on his heel and headed for the door.

'Wait!' Logan called out. 'Look - I want to do a deal.'

Slowly, Cormack turned back towards him. 'A deal?' he echoed quietly. 'I see,' he added noncommittally and nodded thoughtfully, his hands still in his pockets. 'Just what do you have to offer, Logan?' His tone left no doubt that Logan had absolutely nothing in which he would be remotely interested.

Logan stared helplessly at him, then looked away. 'Look, I knew the risks when I got involved in all this - as I said, I didn't have much choice, but that's by the by. I know I'm not going to get away with it, but if I give you some information, maybe you could see to it that they don't throw the book at me?'

Cormack pursed his lips in a brief grimace, his eyes gazing blankly down at the bunk. Slowly, he walked over to the wall, apparently deep in thought, and leaned against the brickwork, negligently crossing his legs. 'It'll be out of our jurisdiction by then,' he pointed out. 'It'll be up to the German authorities to decide whether any books are to be thrown. The only reason we became involved is because the arrest had to take place on the airfield.' He shrugged elaborately. 'I suppose I could testify that you'd been co-operative, which might make some difference,' he said, but without any great conviction. 'It would depend on what you have to tell me. It had better be good, though, because as far as I'm concerned, they can lock you up and throw away the key. Understand?'

'I can name names,' Logan said, with a pathetic eagerness. 'One in particular - the one who's organising the consignments at this end.'

'Oh yes?' Cormack asked, looking at his watch.

'Yes. Look, if I tell you, is it a deal?'

'Just say your piece - then we'll see.'

Logan hesitated, then said suddenly, 'Fairhurst.'

There was no discernible reaction on Cormack's face. 'Fairhurst,' he echoed. 'The Dispersal Controller at Gatow.' His voice was off-hand, almost disappointed, as if he'd known all along.

'Yes,' Logan said feebly, the wind taken out of his sails.

'So that's it, that's all you've got - a name?' Cormack said witheringly, pushing himself away from the wall. He strode across to Logan, and when he spoke, it was with sudden impatience. 'You're going to need a hell of a lot more than that, old son. I want *evidence*. Names, dates, places, times, the whole kit and caboodle and then I might think about it, but if you think just giving me one name is going to get you off the hook, then you've another think coming, my friend.' He paused, wondering if this was the time to bring Fogelmann into the conversation but instinct told him to hold back for the moment. Instead, he said, as if the thought had just struck him, 'I'll tell you what might make me sit up and take notice. Tell me how they smuggle the contraband in and out of the airfields.'

Logan shook his head despairingly. 'I don't know. All I do know is that Fairhurst tells me when the next shipment is coming through, so I don't check that shipment - I just load it aboard and take off. I don't know how it gets into Fuhlsbuttel or what happens to it after it's unloaded at Gatow.'

Cormack nodded impassively. Fairhurst's involvement made sense; as the officer responsible for the unloading operation at Gatow, it would be relatively easy for him to divert the relevant crates upon their arrival - especially as he would also be involved in the periodic checks of the shipments. 'You said Fairhurst told you when each shipment was due to come up?'

'Yes,' Logan replied, his face suddenly animated. 'Actually, there's a special one coming up in the next couple of weeks.'

'Special? Why?'

'I don't know, but Fairhurst said I'd get double the usual rate.'

'Why double?'

Logan shrugged. 'I don't know. That was all he told me.'

Cormack's lips turned down momentarily at the corners. 'Within the next couple of weeks?'

'Yes. He didn't say exactly when.'

Cormack nodded thoughtfully. 'I see.' He turned abruptly and went to the door, knocking briskly on it.

'Captain?'

'Yes?' Cormack looked back at him.

'Is it - is it a deal? Will you put in a good word for me?'

Cormack stared unblinkingly at the other man, his eyes totally opaque. 'I'll think about it,' he said, then walked out.

***

'Nice place you've got here,' Woodward commented, looking approvingly around the apartment overlooking Alt-Moabit.

'Not exactly mine, Tony,' Cormack replied, pouring Woodward a whisky at a large drinks cabinet next to the left-hand window. 'My predecessor's, actually - Major Metcalfe. A lot of the stuff belongs to him, to be honest - there hasn't been time to move it out yet.'

'Nor will there be if this Blockade goes on,' Woodward said gloomily, taking one of the glasses from Cormack. 'Thanks. It's still not bad, though,' he repeated. 'Looks as though it didn't suffer too much from the Ivans, anyway.'

Cormack nodded in agreement. True, there were lighter patches on the wallpaper where paintings had once hung, and there was a threadbare carpet surrounded by floorboards in the centre of the room instead of the expensive rug one expected to see there, but the apartment had evidently escaped the worst of the looting: very likely, it had originally been appropriated by a fairly senior Russian officer. The armchairs and sofa were comfortable, although the coverings were beginning to look frayed and faded, while the wooden furniture, bulky and obviously expensive when new, now had cracks in its veneer, chips and scratches in its surfaces. Nevertheless, compared to almost ninety nine per cent of living accommodation in Berlin, it was virtually unashamed luxury.

Woodward rested his elbow on the mantelpiece above a fire whose coals glowed sullenly; one learned not to stoke up a fire in Berlin these days until it was nearly out, in order to make the fuel ration last. There were no photographs or pictures on the ledge, no links with Cormack's past at all; this did not surprise Woodward, but he reflected that this fact told you a good deal about Cormack... Woodward held up his glass. 'Cheers.'

'Cheers,' Cormack echoed. 'To old times,' He paused, then added softly, 'And absent friends.'

'Amen to that.'

They drank the toast, then, as if an unspoken message had passed between them, they sat down, each to an armchair, facing each other. There was a moment's pause before Cormack said, 'OK. Long time no see, Tony. What have you been doing with yourself?'

'Flying a bloody plane into Berlin,' Woodward replied lugubriously. 'Seems like I've been doing it for ever.'

'How come you're in civvy street? I thought you were going to stay in the RAF.'

'So did I - but that was before I was exposed to the peacetime Officers' Messes. Suddenly it all got amazingly boring, with mountains of paperwork and bumf. Even the flying was bloody boring as well - I mean, when you've spent six years genuinely fighting and being shot at, simply pretending to do it seemed a bit tame somehow. I was a bit too much the maverick, anyway, I think.' He grinned suddenly, the expression lighting up his gaunt features. 'Must have got it from you, old boy.'

'As our American cousins would say, bullshit,' Cormack said, without heat. 'You always were a law unto yourself, from what I heard.'

'Yes, I suppose I was,' Woodward conceded. 'The thing was, there were hundreds of us highly trained and experienced pilots swanning about and too few planes to fly, so when they asked for volunteers to get out, I was first in the queue.'

'That's typical too,' Cormack grinned. 'You always were a sucker for volunteering, weren't you?'

'I know. So I left the RAF and went back to Huntsbrook.'

Cormack nodded. Huntsbrook was the family estate in Berkshire, that would, one day, belong to Woodward. Cormack had been there once as a weekend guest, back in late 1945; he could still remember the meaningful looks amongst the other guests when he had admitted that he had never ridden a horse and so would not be able to take part in the hunt - *Of course, what could one expect, with an accent like his? So vulgar...* The fact that he had then outscored all of them at clay pigeon shooting had not exactly helped either... He had never been back, although Woodward had invited him on several occasions. 'Did your father want you to start running the estate, then?' he asked.

Woodward grimaced. 'He decided it was time I began to take my family responsibilities seriously, yes. All this gadding about for King and Country was all very well, but it was time to get on with the important things in life.'

'Like hunting, shooting and fishing,' Cormack commented sardonically.

'And raising thoroughbreds,' Woodward added, wincing. 'Not to mention being treated like a prize stud by all the families in the district with unmarried daughters.' He rolled his eyes theatrically. 'So I rebelled. I told Dad that I was going to set up my own air charter business. He was dumbstruck - for all of half a minute, if I remember correctly - then he began questioning my intelligence, sanity, even cast doubts as to my parentage - then lent me the money to buy a war-surplus Dakota.' Woodward shrugged. 'I still don't know why he did it - maybe he wanted to give me enough rope to hang myself - but here I am, wondering if perhaps he was right after all. I must be mad.'

'I won't argue with that,' Cormack said drily. 'Is it working - running your own airline? Or are you going to have to go running back home with your tail between your legs?'

'I'm getting by, although I'm hardly rolling in filthy lucre. I could certainly do better running Huntsbrook, but I think I'd die of boredom inside a year.' He shrugged. 'Although I suppose I'll have to do it some day...' He sipped his drink, then gestured vaguely at Cormack. 'What about you? The last I heard, you were in civvy street as well, working as a translator for the FO or something, swearing blind you were never going back into uniform. Where did that go wrong?'

Cormack nodded. 'Same as you, I suppose - I got bored, plus I couldn't take any more civil servants telling me what a bloody awful war they'd had as well - did you know that they nearly ran out of paperclips in 1943?' Cormack shook his head in mock sympathy. 'Anyway, I got offered a job in Intelligence Corps - they said my wartime experience would be quote invaluable unquote, so here I am.' He shrugged. 'The military red tape still pisses me off, but so does the civilian sort - and this is the only job I know, when you come down to it. Working for MI6 and SOE doesn't really leave you very well qualified for much else, does it? I mean, there isn't really much demand for someone who knows a dozen ways to kill someone with his bare hands, or how to place an explosive charge to bring down a bridge, is there?'

'No, I suppose not,' Woodward agreed, nodding slowly. 'So what exactly are you up to these days?' he asked doubtfully.

Cormack grinned. 'I'm not up to those tricks any more, don't worry. I'm on the other side of the fence - counter-intelligence. It's my job to catch saboteurs and undercover agents, although mostly it involves taking on the black market these days. I think it's a case of setting a thief to catch a thief and so on. They think I know all the dodges.'

'Probably true,' Woodward said seriously. 'You were pretty good at it, after all.'

'Just lucky, Tony,' Cormack said quietly. 'Just lucky.'

Woodward hesitated, then said, 'So what else has been happening? What happened to Marianne, for example - or shouldn't I ask?'

Cormack grimaced wryly. 'It didn't work out, Tony. It couldn't have done, to be honest. To use the time honoured cliché, we were ships in the night and all that... A wartime romance. We just drifted apart, really. I still get the odd letter from her, but that's all.'

'So you're back on your own?'

'Afraid so. What about you, Tony? Still seeing Sarah, or whoever?'

'Good Lord, no. She had some idea about a reconciliation with her husband, so I got the old heave-ho. Didn't do her much good - he divorced her a year later. Anyway, it was hardly a grand passion, was it?'

'No, I suppose not.'

An awkward silence fell. *What do you talk about after nearly three years?* Cormack wondered. It was strange that you could trust somebody with your life in wartime - as he had done with Woodward more than once - then find you hardly know him when peace breaks out. It had been like this for most of the six months after the war had ended: they had stayed in touch, but what did they have in common? Woodward, with his father's hereditary knighthood and large estate, not to mention an annual income once he inherited the title that topped six figures, belonged in a different world to Cormack, who had grown up in the East End and whose father had worked as a fitter in an aircraft factory. The few social contacts they had made - the weekend at Huntsbrook, a visit to Cormack's local pub - had been strained, artificial affairs, with neither of them really enjoying them, yet - and this was still the same, Cormack realised suddenly - if there were anyone that he could rely on, could trust totally, it was Woodward.

Which didn't make what Cormack was going to ask him any easier... *Better get the sodding thing over with then...* 'Tony... look, I've got a confession to make.'

'Sounds ominous.'

'It is... I didn't invite you over tonight just to talk about old times. I need your help.'

'Of course, old boy,' Woodward replied without hesitation - as Cormack had known he would. Somehow, that didn't help at all...

'You might not like it,' Cormack said slowly. 'It involves digging into the seamier side of things here.'

'The Black Market, you mean?'

'Afraid so, yes.'

Woodward shrugged. 'Go on, fire away.'

Briefly, Cormack told him about Logan's arrest and Fairhurst's alleged involvement: Woodward seemed taken aback by this. 'I knew Fairhurst during the War,' he explained. 'I'd have thought he'd be the last man to become involved in anything like this.'

'People change, Tony,' Cormack said bleakly. 'Logan won a DFC during the War, remember.'

'I suppose so,' Woodward agreed gloomily. 'But where do I come into all this?'

'Logan said something about Fairhurst wanting him to fly an important shipment into Berlin sometime during the next ten days or fortnight - said he'd be getting double the normal rate for it. I'd like to know just what this shipment is going to be - and why it's so important.'

'Don't tell me,' Woodward interjected, a faint smile on his face. 'You want me to take Logan's place - is that it?'

Cormack grinned ruefully. 'Well, yes - if it's possible. But before you go into your knight on a white charger act, there are a few things you need to bear in mind. We're talking about the black market, after all. Things can get pretty nasty. There've been at least four murders related to the black market in the British Sector since the blockade started and those are only the ones we know about. I'm not saying that Fairhurst was involved in any of these - he probably wasn't, actually - but it could get rough if they realise what you're up to.'

Woodward shook his head, good-naturedly. 'Look, I'm not a complete imbecile, you know. I know what goes on here, probably better than you do.'

'Very likely,' Cormack conceded. 'I just don't want you to get into anything you couldn't handle.'

'Oh, come on,' Woodward protested. 'We made a pretty good undercover team during the War, didn't we?'

'We did, yes.'

'You trusted me then to look after myself, so what's changed?'

'*Touché.*' Cormack grinned wryly.

'Seriously, if I can do anything to help stop the black market, I'll do it.'

Cormack shook his head, smiling faintly. 'You know, you still sound like the wide-eyed romantic who volunteered for clandestine ops just because it was the patriotic thing to do.' There was grudging admiration in his voice. 'I thought I'd taught you better than that.'

'As you so graphically put it, bullshit. You're just as big an idealist as I am, only you keep it well hidden. No, I'm quite willing to give this a go - those bastards need to be caught.' He chuckled suddenly. 'It'll be just like old times, won't it?'

'Jesus wept, I hope not.' Cormack said feelingly.

'Why not?'

'Because, if you remember, those old times damn near got us killed more than once, didn't they?'

Chapter 3

It was almost nine thirty before Cormack wandered through the outer office the following morning, uttering monosyllabic responses to the various greetings on his way. Although he was well aware of the suppressed grins and knowing looks being exchanged by his subordinates at their desks, he ignored them. He could hardly blame them, after all; he knew he must look pretty awful, if the reflection in the shaving mirror that morning had been any guide. Gaunt, pale-eyed, looking at least ten years older - it had not been a pretty sight, made even worse by the headache that a couple of aspirins had done nothing to subdue. OK, so he and Woodward had rather hit the bottle the night before, but they hadn't drunk that much - had they? *Getting out of practice, Cormack old son, you used to be able to drink far more than that, couldn't you? Spent too long being a sober, respectable member of the community, that's your problem...* It hadn't been helped by the realisation that Woodward, when he had left for the airfield, had not shown the slightest sign of any after-effects at all.

He stuck his head around the door of the tiny cubby-hole that Elise Langemann used as an office and wished her good morning, his voice little more than a harsh croak. There was a momentary flicker of amusement on her face, instantly suppressed, before she said, her tone carefully neutral, 'Good morning, sir.'

'Any chance of a cup of coffee?' he asked.

'I'll see if I can rustle one up,' she said, rising to her feet, her face as expressionless as her voice. 'Lieutenant Galvin is waiting for you, sir.'

'I thought he might be,' Cormack said drily. 'Get me the coffee, then send him in, will you? Better get him a cup as well, I suppose.'

'Yes, sir.'

'Thanks.' He grinned sheepishly. 'I think you've just saved my life.'

She smiled uncertainly at him, then headed along the corridor towards the small kitchen. Cormack went into his own office, collapsed heavily into his chair and shook his head wearily, deciding an instant later that the sudden motion had not been a good idea. The back of his head felt as though it were about to drop off. For a moment, he wondered if Woodward had really been as unaffected as he had appeared that morning; he hoped so, because Woodward was due to fly out round about now.

Woodward. He hadn't changed much, really, in the past two and a half years or so - a little more tired-looking, perhaps, but still with those boyish features and hail-fellow-well-met approach that made it impossible to dislike him, even if people meeting him for the first time tended to dismiss him as a harmless, genial prankster. Yet Cormack had seen him wielding a machine gun with ruthless efficiency, had sat beside him as he had brought in a plane with one engine on fire for a night time landing along the East-West Axis, less than half a mile from here, with the Brandenburg Gate coming straight at him, without a flicker of emotion on his face. Woodward had saved his life more than once, knew how to look after himself - so why was he worrying about him?

Because he *was* worried, Cormack knew that, there were no two ways about it. OK, so Tony had known what he was getting into, but the fact remained that if Fairhurst or whoever was organising the black market operation found out what was going on, then it would be Tony Woodward who might well be found floating face down in the river, not Captain Alan Cormack...

There was a knock at the door. 'Come in,' Cormack said, pushing his fears to one side.

It was Galvin, but there was no sign of Elise - or the coffee. 'I've brought Fairhurst's file, sir,' he explained, holding up a manila folder. 'You said you wanted to see it - and to sort out what we do about him.'

'The second part's simple,' Cormack replied, taking the folder. 'We do nothing - yet. All we've got so far is Logan's unsubstantiated word that he's involved in all this, so I don't want him alerted until we've got something definite on him. If there *is* anything, that is.'

Galvin nodded, sitting down opposite Cormack. 'He would be in a very good position to run a black market operation, though, sir,' he pointed out.

'So would several others,' Cormack riposted. 'Logan might be deliberately covering for the real culprit.' He shrugged. 'The thing is, we'll have to set up a discreet investigation - and I mean discreet - and start going through his background with a fine tooth comb, but that's all at the moment. We're talking about a war hero here, don't forget.'

'Who's also a friend of Colonel Pallister's,' Galvin observed.

'Really?'

'Afraid so, sir. Related by marriage, or something. They're often at social functions together.'

'I see,' Cormack said. 'In that case, we'd better be very discreet, hadn't we?'

'Indeed, sir.'

Despite the headache, Cormack found himself smothering a grin: Galvin evidently thought that his CO did not want to upset Pallister, but he could think what he bloody well liked. The fewer people who knew that Fairhurst was under suspicion the better as far as Cormack was concerned; it made things that much safer for Woodward.

The door opened and Elise Langemann came in, carrying two mugs of coffee. She handed one to Cormack, with a hint of a smile as she said, 'Black, no sugar?' She gave the other mug to Galvin and went out.

Galvin watched her go, an appreciative look on his face. 'I know what I'd like to do to her,' he commented, then glanced half apologetically across at Cormack. 'Mind you, she won't look at anyone below the rank of Major, I don't think, sir.'

Cormack stared at him. 'You mean Major Metcalfe?' he said slowly.

'Well, no disrespect, sir...' Galvin began hesitantly. 'But we all reckoned he and Frau Langemann were... you know.'

'Yes, I think I get the picture,' Cormack said drily.

'He certainly gave the impression they were, anyway.'

Well, he would, whether he was or not, wouldn't he? Cormack nodded noncommittally. 'OK, get as much as you can on Fairhurst, but lay off any surveillance for now.'

Again, there was a knowing look from Galvin. 'Will do, sir.' He rose to his feet and went out.

Cormack stared at the closed door for a few seconds and rubbed his eyes. Immediately, he winced; that hadn't been such a good idea, either...

Gatow Airfield

Woodward flicked the switches that turned off the two Pratt & Whitney 1,200 h.p. engines, then leaned back in the bucket seat and stretched, trying to ease the pain in his lower back that was the inevitable legacy of two hours wrestling with the control stick of a plane carrying nearly fifteen hundred pounds more than its official safety limit. He yawned hugely in relief as much as anything else: another flight completed, down in one piece - although God knew how, this time. It was not so much the weather - the cloud was down to under five hundred feet and, with a heavy crosswind, landing had not been at all straightforward - it was, purely and simply, the exhaustion that was beginning to catch up with him. His eyes felt red-rimmed, gritty, and the headache that seemed to have taken up permanent residence just behind his eyes was worse than usual now. OK, he thought, heading aft to unclip the main hatch, he had been boozing the night before with Cormack, but he had, in fact, slept longer after the binge than he had done for weeks. How long was it now? Three months, with only the odd break when he had to put the Dakota in for servicing and checking. Even then, with only the three ground crew that BEA were prepared to lend him, he had to spend a fair amount of that time working himself. He was becoming increasingly aware of lapses in concentration while he was in the air, of 'gaps' when he had flown virtually all the way to or from Berlin without remembering anything of the flight. So far, he had not been as far gone as one pilot who had landed at Gatow, taxi-ed his plane to a halt at the unloading bay and had then been found fast asleep in the cockpit, but he was not too far off it; he had even begun to talk to himself during the flights in order to stay awake. Sooner or later, he thought grimly, he would make one mistake too many and that would be it, the Dakota a pile of wreckage at the end of the runway, and Tony Woodward nothing but a set of fading memories in the minds of people who had known him...

Jesus, you're feeling pretty damn morbid tonight, aren't you? With a sudden impatient movement, Woodward undogged the hatch and pushed it open.

The Bedford lorry had already backed into position at the landing door and Woodward nodded to the supervisor as he clambered up into the cargo hold. 'Flour, is it?' the supervisor asked.

'Right. Two and a half tons of it.'

'Good.' The supervisor nodded and turned away to watch the unloading. As always, Woodward was impressed by the speed of the six man team as they manhandled the bags of flour into the lorry; on average, it only took fifteen minutes to unload the entire cargo. They, as much as the pilots, were responsible for the amount of supplies coming into Berlin, because, without their speed on the ground, impassable bottlenecks would soon occur. Woodward watched them for a moment, then jumped down onto the concrete apron; he had to report in at the Administration Block.

Once he had completed the necessary forms, he went through into the canteen for a quick cup of coffee - and there was Fairhurst, standing over by the window, talking to an RAF Flying Officer. Woodward was aware of a sudden tension in the pit of his stomach, but he ignored it as he went over to Fairhurst.

'Hallo, Geoffrey. How are things?' he asked.

'Tony!' Fairhurst's face lit up in sudden recognition. 'Hello, Tony, good to see you. I'm fine, thanks - although a bit rushed, of course. And you?'

Woodward's face clouded momentarily. 'To be honest, I'd like to have a quick word with you if I may.'

'Of course! Er - you don't mind, do you, Greene?' Fairhurst asked the Flying Officer.

'Of course not, sir.' Greene nodded briefly to Woodward, then went over to a group of RAF flyers. Woodward smothered a momentary flash of resentment at the condescending look in Greene's eyes as he had looked at him; a civilian pilot, almost beneath contempt, an attitude shared mostly by the younger RAF officers, the ones who had joined since 1945, who tended to think they were God's gift to flying. *I was flying Pathfinder missions to the Ruhr while you were still at school, sonny...*

'You said you wanted a word, Tony?' Fairhurst prompted.

'Yes, I did,' Woodward said apologetically, aware that he had been momentarily distracted. He glanced around the busy canteen. 'Look, it's a bit awkward here. Is there anywhere more private?'

Fairhurst shot him an intent glance, then nodded. 'Come along to my office. It's just along the corridor.' He led the way to a small office with a window that looked out over the unloading area, where there were over a dozen aircraft of various shapes and sizes being turned round at the moment. Fairhurst glanced at his watch, a less than subtle reminder that his time was precious, then motioned Woodward into a chair in front of the desk. 'Right, Tony, what can I do for you?'

Woodward hesitated, looking nervously around the room in evident embarrassment. 'To be perfectly honest, Geoffrey, I'm not entirely sure there *is* anything you can do for me.'

'Let me be the judge of that.'

Woodward shrugged. 'OK... The thing is, things are not going too well. I'm up to my ears in debt on the Dak and the bank's been making all sorts of noises about calling in the loan.'

'I see,' Fairhurst said slowly. 'They know you're involved in the Airlift, surely? I know the rates aren't wonderful, but they're still better than you'll get anywhere else - and it's steady revenue, after all. Won't that make them think again?'

'It hasn't so far,' Woodward said gloomily. 'In any case, I've heard that all the civilian Dakotas are going to be withdrawn - they're not going to renew the contracts.' He looked significantly at Fairhurst, who grimaced and nodded slowly in confirmation.

'I'm afraid that rumour is true,' he admitted, spreading his hands in a helpless gesture. 'The idea is that only four-engined civilian aircraft should be retained. They're more economical than the Dakotas or Vikings, you see.'

'I know that,' Woodward said bitterly. 'But where does that leave me? My contract runs out in a fortnight, so what do I do then? It's a cut-throat business back in Blighty and all of us smaller operators are going to be squeezed out by the bigger concerns, I suspect.'

Fairhurst nodded sympathetically. 'I can see your predicament, Tony. If you could get hold of a Halton or a Lancastrian, you'd be alright, I should think.'

'What with?' Woodward demanded disgustedly. 'The bank's hardly likely to increase the loan to buy a bigger plane, is it? In any case, just about all the four-engined jobs have been bought up already, haven't they?'

'I imagine so, yes.' Fairhurst pursed his lips thoughtfully, then leaned back in his chair. He shrugged, as if at a loss. 'You could always try going for a job with one of the bigger airlines - BEA or BOAC, perhaps. With your record, I would think you would be well in contention.'

Woodward snorted impatiently. 'Come off it, Geoffrey. There are hundreds of ex-RAF types in the same boat as me - the big airlines are spoilt for choice.'

'True,' Fairhurst conceded. He stared shrewdly at Woodward, then said, 'Look, Tony, I don't think you came here just to tell me your troubles, did you? What exactly do you want?'

Woodward nodded slowly. 'Perhaps I'd better come to the point... only it's a little embarrassing. I could be barking up entirely the wrong tree.'

'Come on, Tony, spit it out.' There was an undeniable edge of impatience in Fairhurst's voice now.

Woodward sighed. 'OK. Look, stop me if I'm way out of line, but I've... heard that you know some people, er... some people who might be able to... to put a bit of extra business my way.' He shrugged and grinned apologetically.

There was no expression at all on Fairhurst's face. 'Who told you this?' he asked stonily.

Woodward shrugged again, nervously. 'Just something I heard. If it's wrong, then just forget I ever said anything - humblest apologies and all that. I - I wouldn't have asked if I wasn't in a bloody awful jam...' His voice trailed away ineffectually, but there was no mistaking the tension inside him; he was perched on the edge of his seat, leaning forward with his elbows on the desktop, hands clasped together.

Fairhurst stared impassively at Woodward for what seemed an age but was probably no more than ten seconds or so. Then, he leaned back in his chair, toying with a pencil. 'I might be able to help,' he said slowly. 'I can't guarantee anything, though. I'll ask around and get back to you within the next few days. But no promises, mind.'

'Understood,' Woodward replied, the relief on his face only too evident. He rose to his feet. 'Thanks, Geoffrey.'

'Don't thank me yet - it may be that nothing will come of this.'

'Fair enough - but thanks, anyway.'

'Any time. What else are old comrades for?'

Old comrades. The phrase came back to Woodward as he made his way out of the building and trudged heavily back to his aircraft. He had served with Fairhurst for nearly a year in a Pathfinder squadron back in '44: Fairhurst had flown over forty missions in that time, several times nursing crippled aircraft back home that, on one occasion at least, had no business still being in the air. DSO, DFC and bar, one of the best pilots Woodward had ever known - and now what was he doing? Running a sordid black market operation for all the money he could grab. All right, so he hadn't actually admitted being involved, not in so many words, but he hadn't denied it either. The Fairhurst Woodward had known would have been outraged at even the slightest suggestion of any involvement in the black market... *or maybe he wouldn't,* Woodward thought with a tinge of sadness, because how well did you ever really know anyone in wartime? How much of what you saw was simply a facade, a mask to keep the wearer sane? To be honest, apart from his flying abilities and the way he behaved in the Mess, Woodward had known next to nothing about Fairhurst - he might have been capable of anything. You didn't probe, not in wartime, all you asked was that a man be good at his job, and Fairhurst had been one of the best.

None of which mattered a damn in peacetime - was that why Fairhurst had become involved in all this? A desire for danger, the need to live on the edge that sitting behind a desk could never fulfil? Perhaps... More than once, Woodward had heard former colleagues complaining about how boring peacetime was - he'd even thought it himself.

Woodward nodded to the mechanic who had been checking the Dakota's interior, then climbed up into the plane, his lips set in a grim line. OK, so he'd found post-war life dull at times, lacking challenge - but he still hadn't stooped to making money out of other people's misfortunes, for God's sake...

Berlin

Cormack stared down at the sheet of paper in front of him, which was almost entirely covered with random pencilled swirls and squiggles; at the moment, he was shading in an enclosed area, with apparent concentration. He paused and looked again at the few lines of writing at the top of the page: *Shipment? Cigarettes/booze - why twice the money? Ditto drugs/medicines.* Then, on a separate line: *Worth it to somebody* with the last word heavily underscored. Slowly, he drew a large question mark in outline and began, absently, to shade that in as well.

His reverie was interrupted by a knock on the door. 'Come in,' he called out, belatedly realising just what a mess he had made of the sheet of paper with his doodling. He rolled it up and lobbed it into the wastebasket as Galvin came in, holding a message flimsy.

'This has just come in from Colonel Pallister, sir,' he said, handing the message over. 'He's approved Hamburg's request for Logan. We've to transfer him the day after tomorrow.'

'Oh great,' Cormack muttered, rapidly scanning the message's contents. The authorities at Hamburg had formally requested that Logan be transferred to their custody, so that they could interview him about his contacts at that end. This in itself was not a major problem as Cormack was virtually certain that Logan had revealed everything that might be of use to the Unit; the irony was that his conversation with Fogelmann - the incident that had triggered the sequence of events that led up to Logan's arrest - had proved to be nothing more than a simple arrangement of a cash deal for the shipment that had been intercepted. No, the difficulty was that the short notice of the transfer did not leave much time to process the necessary documents. *Gee thanks, Colonel,* Cormack thought sourly; *just what I needed, more sodding paper work...* 'OK,' he said resignedly. 'We'd better set the wheels in motion, I suppose. Tell Elise - Frau Langemann - to come in, will you? We'll have to get at least some of the bumf sorted out tonight.'

'Looks like it, sir,' Galvin agreed gloomily, glancing up at the clock on the wall.

'Yes, I know it's nearly five thirty, but we've got to get the preliminary notification of transfer documents sent off by tomorrow morning, so we'd better get our skates on, hadn't we?'

'Sir,' Galvin acknowledged, suddenly aware of the peevish edge to Cormack's voice; he was already learning not to cross his superior when he was in this sort of mood. Cormack might seem pretty easy-going most of the time, but catch him at a bad moment and you'd regret it...

He went out, leaving Cormack staring intently at the flimsy, but the disgruntled expression soon gave way to one of puzzlement. Why the rush, all of a sudden? OK, so Somers, his old CO in Hamburg, wanted to question Logan, but why did it have to be within forty-eight hours? What the hell was he playing at?

Cormack sighed - there was bugger all he could do about it - then looked up as Elise came in. Like Galvin, she looked surreptitiously up at the clock, probably realising that she was not going to get away on time this evening. 'Frau Langemann, we've got to process a prisoner transfer pretty damn quickly so we'll have to get at least some of the relevant documents done tonight. Can you get the preliminary notifications drawn up for signing?'

'Er - yes, sir. Of course.' Her reluctance was evident; again, her eyes flickered momentarily towards the clock.

'Is there some problem?' Cormack asked curtly - and then promptly wondered why he was being so brusque. Softening his tone almost apologetically, he went on, 'Look, I know you'll be a little later than usual, but the standard arrangement applies - you can leave earlier tomorrow night.'

'Yes, sir, I know that, but...' Her voice trailed away uncertainly.

'But what?'

She hesitated, then said, 'It - it's just that I help out at the local hospital on Tuesday nights. I'm an auxiliary nurse, you see.'

'Ah...' Cormack said doubtfully, nonplussed.

'They're very short staffed and by the time I get home and get changed...' Again, her voice died away.

Cormack nodded. 'Would it help if I gave you a lift home, then to the hospital? It's just that we need to get these damned forms done tonight.'

'That - that's very kind of you, sir,' she replied, her voice betraying her surprise. 'That'll be fine.'

'OK - let's get weaving, shall we?'

***

Cormack wandered idly around the cramped Wilmersdorf apartment, feeling a bleak helplessness at its Spartan condition; virtually everything here - the table, wooden chairs and threadbare carpet - was strictly functional, the only concessions to 'luxury' being a battered leather armchair with a six-inch rent in the back through which the horsehair stuffing was visible, and two framed photographs on the mantelpiece. One was of a family group, evidently taken some years before, with a teenage Elise standing between a middle-aged man and woman who were presumably her parents, the other, bordered in black, was of a Wehrmacht captain in full dress uniform, his face old before its time: her husband. Somehow, far from giving the apartment a homely effect, the photos only seemed to heighten its bleakness, perhaps because he knew that, apart from Elise herself, all the people in them were dead.

Yet the rooms were clean, he had to give her that, and without the musty, damp smell of boiled cabbage that pervaded most Berlin dwellings, but that had not unduly surprised him; Elise Langemann was far too conscientious and efficient to permit any lapses in her home. It could not have been what she had been used to, though, he thought absently, because, although Langemann had only been a captain when he was killed on the Russian Front in 1944, he had come from a well to do family and so she would have lived in far more comfortable quarters than these. On the other hand, given the destruction wreaked on Berlin by the Allied bombing and Soviet occupation, she'd been lucky to get any place to herself... *Had Metcalfe arranged it for her?* he wondered suddenly, remembering what Galvin had said about their relationship. Had Metcalfe been a regular visitor to the bedroom next door where she was changing into her nurse's uniform?

And if he had, then what business was it to anyone, apart from the security angle? OK, so there were rules about fraternisation, but they were observed more often in the breach and unless Metcalfe had been betraying classified material as part of his pillow talk, then what the hell did it matter?

He suppressed a shiver and pulled his coat more closely around his shoulders: as in almost every building in Berlin, the apartment was cold and draughty and, although there was some chopped wood in the fireplace - probably bought on the black market - there was obviously no point in squandering it for the few minutes that they would be there, He wandered over to the window to look down at the darkened street below. What do you do, Frau Langemann, when you're here? *Do you stare at the photos, re-living the past, do you spend the evening reading one of the half dozen or so tattered novels piled neatly next to the armchair - how do you exist?*

None of my business... So why am I thinking about it?

Well, if you don't know the answer to that, old son, then you're even thicker than I thought...

'Penny for them?' she said suddenly, in English, startling him so that he spun round, fast. She seemed momentarily taken aback by his almost reflexive response, but then said, 'That is the expression, isn't it? A penny for your thoughts?'

He nodded slowly, wondering at the sudden jolt of adrenalin that had surged through him a moment before. It had almost been like being behind enemy lines again: why was he so tense? Again, the answer wasn't difficult and, this time, he acknowledged it. He was very aware that he was alone with her, in her flat, and that even in the forbidding starched uniform, she still looked pretty damned attractive... 'Yes, it is,' he said, belatedly answering her question and wondering if she had noticed his preoccupation. 'They weren't worth that much. Are you ready?'

She pulled on her coat and picked up her handbag. 'Yes, thank you.'

'Then we'd better get going.'

She nodded awkwardly. 'This is very kind of you, sir.'

'Least I could do after forcing you to stay late. It's my pleasure.'

They went out, Elise taking care to lock the door, then descended the stairway to the lobby. Cormack noticed the *blockwart* in the cubby hole giving them a knowing look as they passed, but Elise did not seem to notice - was he remembering previous visits by Metcalfe?

None of your business...

It was raining slightly as they emerged onto the street, but Cormack had pulled up the hood on the jeep; they climbed in and drove off, neither of them saying anything.

The hospital was about ten minutes' drive away, on Viktoriastrasse, and was clearly in the process of being rebuilt, but, even so, almost half of it was still little more than a pile of rubble from which jagged girders and remnants of brickwork protruded at drunken angles. Impossible to know whether the damage had been caused by bombs or Russian shells, but the legacy was still there, three and a half years later. Cormack pulled up outside.

'Here we are,' he said awkwardly, aware of the banality of his words.

'Thank you, sir,' she said and began to swing her legs out of the jeep.

'I don't know how you do it,' he said suddenly. 'How can you do a - a four hour stint, isn't it? - after a day in the office? How do you manage it?'

She paused, and looked back at him, her expression suddenly thoughtful. After a few seconds, she said, 'Do you have a few minutes to spare?'

'I'm in no great rush.'

'Then come with me and I'll show you how I manage to do it.'

He stared at her for a moment, then shrugged and switched off the engine. 'OK,' he said and climbed out, falling into step beside her as she walked up the steps to the front entrance. He held the door open for her and followed her in.

And came to a halt in surprise.

All along one wall of the entrance lobby was a line of beds, ten or a dozen of them, each one occupied; at the third one along, an exhausted looking woman doctor was holding a stethoscope to her patient's chest. He was coughing feebly, his face pale, drawn.

'It's like this all over the hospital,' Elise said beside him. 'We put beds wherever there's space - in the corridors, on the landings, anywhere. And we still don't have enough room.' She headed across the lobby, towards the flight of stairs, Cormack following her.

'Why are there so many patients?' he asked.

'Why do you think?' she retorted. 'We've got malnutrition, hypothermia, TB, pneumonia, influenza - and that's on top of the usual ailments you'd have at this time of year. Look, most of these people are trying to survive on not much more than a thousand calories a day - that's about half of what they should be getting. That's why the black market is booming. Do you know how much a kilogram of butter costs on the market these days? Five hundred marks. As you can imagine, most people can't afford that, so they're having to get by on almost starvation rations. Then there's heating - the electricity is only on for four hours a day in most areas and coal isn't easy to come by, so people are beginning to freeze to death out there - and it's still only November. We've got the worst of the winter to come yet and God help us if it's as cold as usual. We'll have hundreds dying.' She gestured at the scene in the lobby. 'This will seem like nothing then.' They had reached the first floor now, and she pushed open a door that led into a large ward. 'This is where I work,' she explained. 'Mostly, anyway - it's a medical ward, but I also assist in surgery sometimes, when we're short-handed. Which is at least half the time, unfortunately...'

'Pretty grim?' he asked.

'Sometimes, yes. The other night, for example. We had to amputate a foot - but he came round halfway through the operation. We'd bought the drugs on the black market, because we'd run out of our normal stocks - they'd been diluted.'

'The bastards...' Cormack hissed involuntarily. Then, 'Sorry about that.'

'Don't apologise - those are my feelings exactly. OK, that's an extreme case, but... The problem is, a lot of the patients who need operations are already weak through lack of a proper diet, so they take longer to recover, so they need the bed longer, and we've got still more patients coming in every day - it's a vicious circle, and we don't have enough resources to do the job properly. We're coping, but only just.' She paused, then stared directly at him. 'Now do you see how I can do it?'

Cormack looked around the ward, trying to imagine what it would be like and wondering how the hell *anyone* could cope with it, then nodded grimly and said slowly, 'Yes, I think I do.'

Gatow Airfield

'Tony?' Fairhurst said quietly.

Woodward looked up, his pen still poised over the form he had been about to sign, then nodded slowly. 'Geoffrey,' he replied.

'Can you spare a moment?'

'Yes, just as soon as I've finished here.' Woodward scribbled his signature at the bottom of the sheet of paper, handed it back to the harassed-looking clerk, then turned to Fairhurst. 'OK, what can I do for you?'

'A word in private?'

Woodward was aware of a sudden dryness in his throat, of his pulse accelerating. 'Certainly,' he said. 'In your office?'

Fairhurst shook his head. 'No. Out there.' Fairhurst waved vaguely towards the door to the unloading area. 'I'll walk you back to your plane.' He led the way out, looking around him as they emerged into the open, presumably to see if anyone was within earshot - but Woodward noticed that, even now, four years after he had last flown a plane, Fairhurst still cast a professional eye up at the lowering clouds above. 'Glad I'm not flying in that,' he commented absently - yet there was a hint of wistfulness in his voice. 'Rather you than me, old boy.'

Woodward shrugged. 'Somebody has to do it.'

'Quite.' Fairhurst glanced quickly around again, then said briskly, 'About that matter you mentioned the other day.'

'Yes?' Woodward replied cautiously.

'I may be able to do something for you.'

Woodward flashed him an intent look. 'Go on.'

Fairhurst seemed to hesitate before he said, 'The thing is, it's not exactly legal.'

'The black market, you mean,' Woodward said resignedly.

'Something like that, yes. It would mean flying in a special consignment - one that would not be included on your manifest.'

'I see... How big would this - consignment - be?'

'No more than two hundred pounds in weight.'

Woodward nodded again, his eyes narrowing as he made rapid calculations. It wouldn't be that much of a problem, actually - out of a payload of almost seven and a half thousand pounds, an extra two hundred would barely be noticed, but what the hell was it? OK, so it amounted to less than two large sacks of flour, but it certainly wasn't cigarettes or stockings, not at that weight... 'When?' he asked briefly.

'Before I tell you any more, are you in?'

'Depends,' Woodward said reluctantly. 'How much are we talking about?'

'Five hundred pounds,' Fairhurst said without hesitation.

Woodward whistled softly, impressed. It was not a sum to be sneezed at, not in the austerity of the post-war era; you were halfway towards buying a semi-detached house with that, back in the UK. 'I'm in,' he said bluntly.

'Good,' Fairhurst said and seemed to relax slightly. 'Sometime between the twelfth and the sixteenth, a man calling himself Schmidt will approach you at Fuhlsbuttel with further details. He'll give you a hundred pounds as the first payment of your fee. Just do exactly as he tells you and everything will be fine. You'll be paid the balance when you complete the - ah - assignment.'

'I see,' Woodward said slowly, then looked suspiciously at Fairhurst. 'How do I know I'll get the other four hundred?'

'How do I know you won't just go to the MPs and betray me?' Fairhurst retorted. He shrugged. 'It's up to you, old boy. Take it or leave it.'

'I'll take it,' Woodward said, allowing an edge of bitterness to creep into his voice. 'I don't really have much choice, do I?'

'Probably not, old boy,' Fairhurst agreed affably. 'Beggars can't be choosers, can they?'

Chapter 4

Berlin

'It's getting colder these days, isn't it? Never mind, I can promise you a warm, bright Christmas when it comes - the Allies are airlifting it into the middle of July.'

There was a roar of laughter that swept around the smoky, dimly-lit nightclub, much louder than the joke warranted, but Cormack guessed that there was more than a hint of desperation in the forced mirth of the audience. They were going to have a good time come what may... the comedian standing in the spotlight on the tiny stage waited for the laughter to die down then looked exaggeratedly at his watch.

'Ah well, time to go,' he said regretfully. 'I'll leave you with this thought. Just remember, things could be a lot worse. Think what a mess we'd be in if the Americans were blockading us and the Russians were running the Airlift... Good night!' He bowed deeply, then disappeared into the wings of the stage, reappearing a few moments later to take a second bow.

Cormack joined in with the loud applause, glancing around at Galvin and the other officers around the table at which he was seated, no more than five yards away from the stage. They had evidently enjoyed the comedian's act, which, in all honesty, had been no more than a rehash of the various *Insulaner* jokes that were going the rounds these days: *Der Insulaners* - islanders - that was how Berliners were beginning to perceive themselves, marooned on an island surrounded by the Soviets. But the mere fact that they could laugh at the situation was an encouraging sign in itself...

'Have another one, sir?' asked Galvin, when the applause had died down, nodding towards the empty glass in front of Cormack.

'No thanks,' Cormack said, holding up his hand. 'I only intended to drop by for one drink. I'd better be going.' He stood up, gesturing to the others around the table to remain in their seats. 'Enjoy yourselves.'

'We'll try to,' Galvin said, a touch self-consciously. 'Thanks for dropping by, sir.'

'My pleasure. Cheerio.'

As he made his way through the restaurant tables towards the exit, Cormack was wondering if he had been imagining the sense of relief around the table as he had stood to go. True, Galvin *had* invited him to drop in on the celebration - it was his twenty-fifth birthday - but it had probably been no more than a polite gesture on the lieutenant's part; Cormack had been the oldest there, by several years, not to mention the difference in rank, and the atmosphere had been undeniably strained, embarrassed, during the fifteen minutes or so he had been there. It was understandable, because Galvin was with his friends and Cormack was an outsider, but it had brought home to Cormack the realisation that he was not getting any younger - even the prospect of going along later to Daisy's House, the high-class bordello off Kurfurstendamm, had failed to appeal.

Getting past it, old son...

Cormack's face was sombre as he emerged onto the street; he looked around him, seeing the stark, bombed-out silhouette of the Kaiser Wilhelm Memorial Church in Breitscheidplatz, about thirty yards away. He stared for a moment at the broken stump of the church's steeple before he began walking slowly back along Tauentzienstrasse to where he had left the jeep, fifty yards or so away. Back in the Twenties, he reflected idly, Tauentzienstrasse had been the nightclub centre of Berlin, featuring striptease and political satire, often on the same stage; even the satire had managed to survive into the Nazi era, but the Allied bombers had left the street little more than a pile of rubble. The Kabarett Club had only re-opened a year or so before, but there was precious little sign of any others being rebuilt at the moment...

The brief visit to the nightclub had depressed him, and not just because he had seen the spoils of the black market being flaunted openly: caviare and champagne when most of Berlin was only just fending off starvation. No, the malaise went far deeper than that: just where was he going with his life? Here he was, thirty-four years old, still only a captain and unlikely to rise any higher, not unless he did something about his reputation for insubordination; a damned good investigator and intelligence officer, superb war record, yes, but too much of a maverick, don't you see, not really suitable senior officer material... He knew damn well how he was regarded by his superiors and what he needed to do if he were going to move up the promotion ladder, but there was no way that he could bring himself to do it, not if he wanted to live with himself. Galvin wouldn't have any trouble, he thought suddenly: the young lieutenant was efficient, conscientious - and knew how to keep his nose clean. He also had the right accent, Cormack decided sourly, then grimaced tiredly at his own bitterness. If you really wanted to, you could mimic that accent to perfection, but you're too bloody-minded to do it, aren't you? *You're the one who's decided to play the game your own way, so stop bitching about the consequences, OK?*

Which still didn't answer the question: where was he going with his life? No real career prospects, no steady attachment or relationship, no close friends, except for one he had neglected for nearly three years... Just what was he doing? Where would he be, say, ten years from now?

No answer.

'Hallo, do you have a light?'

The voice came from about twenty yards away, one of the prostitutes who lined the pavement approaching a raincoated man who was hurrying along the street. She was young, no more than seventeen, at a guess, and thin, with a pinched, almost emaciated face that had dark hollows under the eyes. Her right hand was holding a cigarette to her lips as she stared enquiringly at the man. He seemed embarrassed more than anything, shaking his head nervously and pushing on past her; she shrugged and looked at Cormack, evidently sizing him up as a potential client. Before she could make any move, however, he turned away, feeling vaguely guilty at avoiding any involvement. What was she doing on the streets, for God's sake? But the answer to that was only too evident in her gaunt features, the look of desperation in her eyes. She needed to eat and to live in a city that was still largely in ruins, where children fought for scraps from dustbins. There would be dozens of other girls like her, hundreds, perhaps, around Berlin tonight - and there was damn all he could do about it, so why was he hanging about on the corner worrying?

The realisation that he had in fact come to a halt and was standing aimlessly at an intersection brought a rueful grimace to his face. He reached into his pocket for the jeep's key - it was parked only ten yards away now, in the side street - then, as he turned the corner, he glanced back towards the girl.

He saw it all; the girl motionless, still looking in his direction, the two figures silently emerging from the alleyway behind her, grabbing her, a hand over her mouth, pulling her back into the alley as she struggled frantically, trying to break free. As the three shadowy shapes disappeared from view, Cormack was already running full pelt along the street, skidding on the wet pavement as he reached the alley, but then he saw them, ten yards away, the girl pushed up against the wall, pinned there by the taller of the two attackers, the second one speaking, a woman's voice, hard with menace, '-warned you about being on my patch, you bitch,' and a glint of light on metal, the blade being driven into the girl as Cormack yelled 'Police!' and launched himself forward. The two assailants spun round in his direction, their faces frozen in stunned surprise, then, abruptly, the woman raised the knife and hurled it at Cormack. He twisted aside, but lost his balance and crashed heavily into the wall before he regained his footing, dimly aware of the two attackers turning and running away along the alley. Cormack took a single step after them, then checked the impulse: *How was the girl?*

She was slowly sliding down the wall, clutching at her ribs, her eyes wide in shocked incomprehension as she tried to stem the flow of blood, her knees buckling under her. Her mouth was open wide as if she wanted to scream, but no sound came out. Her eyes rolled up in her head and she slumped tiredly to one side, the hand at the wound falling limply away. Cormack sprang forward and let out his breath in relief as he felt a pulse at her wrist, rapid, irregular, but strong enough; it had probably been shock more than anything else that had made her pass out, although she'd still bleed to death if he didn't do something fast.

Galvin.

***

Galvin brought the jeep skidding to a halt outside the hospital entrance, then leaped out to help Cormack lift the girl carefully out of the back. The makeshift bandage - a towel taken from the nightclub's toilet - was sodden through with blood now, but she was still breathing stertorously. Cormack lifted her up, wincing at a low moan of pain from her - at least she could still feel it, he thought grimly - then went into the hospital reception area, Galvin holding the door open for him. A passing nurse took one look at him and his burden, then burst into action, calling loudly to a doctor at the desk. Within moments, the girl was being laid gently onto a bed in a cubicle, the doctor issuing rapid, crisp instructions as the nurse politely but firmly ushered Cormack away. Elise Langemann appeared, staring momentarily at him in surprise, before she pushed past to help the doctor - Cormack remembered her saying she often assisted in surgery. She pulled the curtain across, cutting off the view of the girl, lying on the bed, her face deathly pale now.

Cormack turned to Galvin, feeling the tension beginning to drain out of him. 'Thanks, John,' he said quietly. 'I appreciate your help. Made a bit of a mess of your party, though.'

Galvin shrugged. 'Think nothing of it, sir - only too glad to help.' He glanced across at the cubicle. 'What was it all about, anyway?'

'I think she was probably trespassing on somebody else's patch,' Cormack said tiredly.

'Playing a bit rough, weren't they?' Galvin asked. 'Did you get a good look at them, sir?'

Cormack shook his head. 'I didn't see their faces at all.'

'Pity.' Galvin looked genuinely disappointed, but only on a professional level, Cormack realised suddenly: the policeman's attitude. He wanted an arrest, whereas Cormack was not quite sure what he'd do if he were to get his hands on those attackers... His trouble was - and he knew it only too well - he got too involved in things. The girl was nothing to him, after all.

'Maybe she'll know who they were,' Galvin mused, cutting into Cormack's train of thought. He had to backtrack for a moment to figure out what Galvin was talking about, then he said absently:

'Perhaps. We'll have to ask her - if she pulls through.' He turned to Galvin. 'No point in you hanging on here, really. I'll take you back to your celebration, if you like.'

Galvin shook his head gently. 'Thank you, sir, but, to be honest, I don't feel much like celebrating any more. My quarters would do me fine.'

'Sorry about that - spoiling your birthday.'

'It's all right, sir,' Galvin insisted. He glanced at the cubicle again, then said, 'Will you be coming back here, sir, after you've dropped me off?'

'Yes. Why?'

'Let me know how she gets on, will you?'

Cormack stared at him thoughtfully, then nodded and turned towards the street door. Maybe Galvin wasn't as uncaring as he'd thought.

***

Cormack looked at his watch, then stood up from the uncomfortable wooden bench and wandered aimlessly around the lobby. It was nearly an hour since he had returned to the hospital after leaving Galvin at his quarters and there was still no news of the girl beyond the fact that she had been taken into the operating theatre just before he had come back. Yes, they'd let him know just as soon as there was any news - the receptionist had seemed surprised by his concern. After all, she was only one more prostitute who had landed herself in trouble, wasn't she?

But she was somebody's *daughter*, for Christ's sake...

A door opened and Elise came into the lobby. She saw Cormack and came over.

'How is she?' he asked.

'She's probably going to be all right,' she replied, a hint of relief in her voice.

He let out his breath in a long sigh and felt himself beginning to relax. 'You're sure?'

She nodded. 'There are no internal organs damaged - the knife missed anything vital, apparently. She lost a lot of blood, but they've given her transfusions - Doctor Ludwig gives her a seventy per sent chance of recovery.' She looked up at Cormack. 'Although it would probably have been a different matter if you hadn't brought her here so quickly. Or if she'd been stabbed a second time.' She hesitated, then added softly, 'You probably saved her life.'

'Least I could do,' he muttered awkwardly.

'There was one thing,' Elise said, watching him intently. 'She had over fifty marks in her purse - do you think they were trying to rob her?'

'Possibly,' he conceded, his tone neutral; he had, in fact, put the money in her purse while Galvin had been driving them to the hospital. Pure guilt, of course... Maybe if he had stopped to speak to her, even for a moment, she wouldn't have been attacked.

'I can imagine how she earned it,' she said, her eyes still on him. 'I expect she'll need it now, though.'

'I expect she will,' Cormack said, then added slowly, 'For the record, I was just a passer-by. I - er - wasn't one of her clients.'

There was a ghost of a smile on her face. 'I never said you were, sir.' She held his gaze a moment longer, her expression unfathomable, then shrugged. 'Anyway, that's me finished for tonight, so I'll be getting off home.'

'Can I give you a lift?'

Again, her eyes studied his face thoughtfully. 'That would be very kind of you, sir. Thank you.'

***

Neither of them had said much on the way back to her apartment; she had seemed tired, which was hardly surprising after a full day at work followed by four hours in the hospital, while he was still feeling a reaction from the knifing incident and its aftermath, a sense of anticlimax. He was dead beat, he knew that - and, again, perhaps that was only to be expected. Elise had filled in a few more details about the girl and her progress - her name was apparently Ulrika Neumann and she was only a few days over sixteen, for God's sake - but Elise seemed uncomfortable, somehow, on edge.

He brought the jeep to a halt outside her apartment block, trying, with only partial success, to stifle a yawn. 'Here we are,' he said, before he could stop himself. *Good old Alan Cormack, always one for the original line. Jesus, I must be more tired than I thought.*

'Yes,' she said absently, as if she had not heard him. 'It was very kind of you, sir.'

'Look, you don't have to keep on calling me 'sir', you know - you're not in the Army, after all.'

'I'll try to remember,' she said, her expression suddenly opaque. 'Thank you for the lift.'

'Any time.'

She leaned forward in the bucket seat as though to climb out, then she paused and stared intently at him. 'Can I ask you something?' she said quietly.

'Ask me what?'

'That girl - Ulrika Neumann. Why were you so concerned about her?'

'Why shouldn't I be? She'd been stabbed - what else could I do but bring her in?'

'I didn't mean that. You'd done all you could by then, so why did you come back to find out how she was? You could have telephoned in the morning.'

'It isn't as simple as that,' he said slowly, 'The Chinese have an old proverb - or maybe it's the Indians, I can't remember - but it says that if you save someone's life, you're responsible for them from then on. I'm beginning to think they were right.' He shrugged. 'I was worried about her, that's all.'

'I thought perhaps you knew her.'

'Never seen her in my life before.'

She was still giving him that intent, unwavering look, but then, suddenly, she shrugged. 'Anyway, she should be all right. She should pull through. '

'Yes, but for what?' Cormack asked gloomily. 'So she can go back on the streets again?'

She reached out her hand and placed it gently on his arm in a gesture that he was certain was unconscious. 'There's nothing you can do about it, you know. It's pointless worrying about it. You do what you can and be thankful that there is something you can do, even if it isn't always enough.' She smiled lopsidedly. 'The Nurse's Philosophy.'

'I suppose so,' he said reluctantly.

'Look at it this way. At least you did *something*. A lot of people would have just ignored what was going on. I... respect you for that.'

There was something in her voice, some undertone that made him look sharply at her, suddenly very aware of her hand on his arm, the closeness of her and the look in her eyes. Slowly, he leaned across towards her and kissed her gently on the lips, a part of him wondering what the hell he was playing at - *what if she slaps you around the face, what then, lover boy?* She did not pull away, however, but stared into his eyes until he pulled her towards him and kissed her again, more lingeringly this time. Her lips parted and he felt a surge of pure joy as her tongue began to move against his, thrillingly.

Abruptly, she pulled away, her eyes confused, twin spots of colour burning high on her cheeks. 'I - I'd better be going,' she stammered breathlessly. 'Thank you for the lift,' she blurted out, then swung her feet hurriedly to the pavement and climbed out of the jeep. She walked rapidly up the steps to the apartment block and opened the street door, but, before she went inside, she paused and looked back at him. Her mouth opened as if to say something, then she shook her head slowly, almost sadly, and disappeared inside.

Chapter 5

Cormack looked at his watch, his lips twisting briefly in an impatient grimace before he let out his breath slowly in a conscious attempt to relax. The escort party to take Logan to the airfield was only five minutes late, after all, nothing to get steamed up about - except that it meant he was stuck here, twiddling his thumbs, waiting. There was no alternative, however, because Logan remained his, Cormack's, responsibility until he and the Escorting Officer signed the transfer form that took Logan off his hands. *Bloody bureaucracy...* The regulations demanded that both he and the Escorting Officer be present when the document was signed, otherwise he would have been out of here long since, instead of hanging around the Detention Unit like some sort of ghost that hadn't faded at cock-crow - he *did* have better things to do, dammit...

Again, he checked his watch and looked up in time to see a young woman clerk look away hurriedly, guiltily, as if she had been staring at him. Certainly, she looked unusually intent on her typing all of a sudden... Cormack smothered a grin; probably she and the other clerical workers and MPs in the Unit's lobby area were only too aware of the Intelligence Corps captain obviously fretting and fuming over the delay and were, very likely, trying not to catch his eye in case it brought a torrent of abuse down on their heads. Deliberately, he looked away, idly surveying the room. The Unit had once been a police station, in fact, with half a dozen cells through the door at the rear of the lobby and a counter to the right of the main door behind which the Duty Military Police Sergeant, his assistants and various clerks and typists worked; two armed MPs were on sentry duty outside the double doors that led to the street, with a third beyond the door leading to the cells. Naturally, the Sergeant would also have a weapon available and there were other MPs upstairs if, say, a Red Army detachment tried an armed assault on the Unit and...

What the hell was he thinking about, for Christ's sake? An armed Soviet assault - the Unit was over two miles from the Russian Sector, so if a detachment had penetrated this far, defending the Unit would be the least of anybody's problems, because it would mean war had broken out, so why in God's name was he wondering about it?

Because he was getting thoroughly pissed off hanging about, that was why - where the hell were they? He turned abruptly and, once again, saw the young woman look away hurriedly. Cormack watched her as she resumed typing: she was small, mousey and not really his type at all, he decided regretfully, then stifled a wry grin - he was assuming she was eyeing him up, which was a trifle conceited to say the least. More likely, she was wondering who he was and why he was prowling around the lobby like a caged tiger, rather than regarding him as a prospective 'catch'. *Big-headed so and so, since when were you God's gift to women?* Anyway, she wasn't anywhere near as good looking as Elise Langemann.

This time, a rueful grimace did crease his lips and he turned away from the counter to hide it. There he went again, thinking about Elise - but there was no denying the fact that he was finding it increasingly difficult to push what had happened the night before out of his mind. When he had been talking to her earlier this morning in his office, he had caught himself staring at her slim figure like some love-struck teenager and, judging by the sudden flush that had coloured her cheeks, she had realised what had been on his mind.

However, she had not said or done anything beyond the bounds of formality, nor had she dropped the slightest hint that anything had taken place between them. *Not that one kiss means very much, of course...* Perhaps he had offended her, or maybe she had simply had second thoughts, because he had been given the Big Freeze, pure and simple.

Forget it...

It was almost with a sense of relief that he saw, through the window, a jeep pull up outside and three MPs jump out, one of them in a lieutenant's uniform. About bloody time, too... Nevertheless, Cormack waited until the MPs had come in before he turned to face them, acknowledging their salutes off-handedly.

'Captain Cormack?' asked the lieutenant.

'Yes.'

'I'm Lieutenant Etheridge. I'm sorry we're late, but we were delayed in the air.'

Cormack nodded. 'You've come for Logan?'

'Yes, sir.'

'OK. Let's get on with it, shall we?' He went over to the counter and said, 'Sergeant, get Logan, will you?'

'Sir.' The sergeant produced a bunch of keys from a drawer, then came round the end of the counter and headed for the door leading to the cells. Etheridge took an envelope from the inside pocket of his tunic, withdrew a sheaf of typed documents, unfolded them and placed them on the counter.

'We've both got to sign these, sir,' he explained apologetically.

'I know,' Cormack replied, trying, not very successfully, to keep the impatience out of his voice. He took a fountain pen out and signed each sheet rapidly, passing them to Etheridge to counter-sign, forbearing to point out that, strictly speaking, Etheridge should have waited until Logan was physically present and had been identified; he'd wasted enough time as it was. In any case, the matter was largely academic as Logan emerged into the lobby as Etheridge was scribbling his signature on the final sheet. Logan shot the two of them an anxious look as the sergeant brought him over.

'Sir, I formally assume responsibility for the prisoner William Logan,' Etheridge intoned to Cormack, saluting again.

'Carry on, lieutenant.'

'Sir.' Etheridge turned to the two MPs who had accompanied him. 'Corporal Fowler!'

'Sir!' The corporal snapped to attention.

'Secure the prisoner.'

'Sir!' Fowler stepped forward, holding a pair of handcuffs. Deftly, he fastened them to his left, and Logan's right, wrists, handing the key to Etheridge.

Etheridge turned back to Cormack. 'I think that's about it, sir. We'd better be getting back to Gatow.'

'Carry on, lieutenant,' Cormack said again.

Etheridge saluted once more, then turned and led his party out through the double doors. Cormack followed, impatient to get back and had just pushed the left hand door open when he saw Logan suddenly lurch backwards, pulling Fowler after him. It was only then that Cormack heard the shot, the bullet outpacing the sound, and he broke into a run towards Logan as the pilot jerked convulsively, a second bullet ripping into him. Only now did Fowler's face register shocked comprehension, but too late, *too bloody late...* Cormack slammed full-pelt into Logan and Fowler, sending them both sprawling, dimly aware of the sound of the second shot, then Fowler gave a muffled grunt of pain and clutched at his shoulder as the third shell scythed into him. Etheridge was shouting something, pointing to a building along the street, on the far side, but then he reeled backwards, clutching at his arm, face contorted in agony.

Cormack scrambled away, rolling to his feet, parachutist-style, and sprinted towards a low wall, hearing the MPs returning the fire, shooting at the brownstone building. Another shot and the other MP went down, *bloody hell, this guy is fucking good,* five shots, five hits, but what the hell was he playing at because he should be running for it now, not hanging around playing Cowboys and Indians... Cormack dived flat behind the wall as stone chips flew from it, the sixth shot and it had missed, but he'd fired at least three too many because Logan must have been the target and he'd gone down already... Cormack lay flat, hugging the ground, waiting for the next shot.

It never came. A stunned silence seemed to envelop the scene and Cormack suddenly realised why: it had been a six-shot magazine and he'd fired them all off, which meant he'd be running for it *now*... 'Come on!' he yelled to the two sentries, taking out his sidearm, a Browning High Power automatic pistol. He jumped to his feet and vaulted over the wall, gesturing towards the brownstone. 'Grab the bastard!'

He sprinted across the street, heading towards the building from where the shots must have come; it was about three hundred yards away. Say forty-five seconds to reach it - how far could the gunman get in that time? Four storey building, but he wouldn't have had to be on the top floor, the second would have given him a clear shot, so he'd just have to come down a single flight of stairs, then out the back, into a waiting car - twenty seconds, thirty at most? Forget that, just get your head down and run...

Up the steps from the pavement, slamming the street door back on its hinges, a quick scan round as he skidded to a halt, gun held in front of him in both hands, aimed at the staircase, but no sound of anyone coming down the stairs. Straight through then, shout at the following soldiers to check upstairs and yes, the back door was open, out into a small yard with washing pegged out, cursing as it whipped into his face but then he was at the wooden doorway out into a back alley, swinging the door open before he flattened himself against the wall next to it. Wait a moment, then duck through the opening, looking both ways.

There. A running man, still carrying a rifle, fifty yards along the alleyway, to the left. Cormack checked his gun, took a deep breath, then pivoted round, launching himself along the alley in a headlong sprint. The fleeing figure glanced behind him, then skidded to a halt, bringing up the rifle for a rapid snapshot. A momentary thought - *had he had time to reload?* - then Cormack threw himself to one side, hearing the sound of the shot as he hit the ground and rolled over, bringing up his own gun and loosing off a shot but there wasn't a hope of hitting him, not at this range... Cormack scrambled into cover behind a dustbin as the gunman fired again, then risked a quick view over the top, Browning pistol at the ready.

The marksman was running again; Cormack forced himself to his feet and went after him, aware of an increasing breathlessness, *getting too old for this lark* then the gunman disappeared from view to the right as he emerged into the street at the end of the alley - which was where the getaway car would be... *Move yourself, Cormack!* He sprinted the last forty yards, drawing in breaths in huge gasps, waiting to hear the sound of a car pulling away, the bastard escaping and almost certainly nothing he could do about it, not with just a handgun, not at any sort of range...

Then he was emerging into the street, looking to the right - and there was no car. The street was empty - except for the gunman, who was standing only twenty yards away in the middle of the road, looking frantically around, a disbelieving expression on his face. *There should have been a car here*, Cormack thought, bringing up his gun, *something's gone wrong...* 'Keep quite still!' he yelled in German.

The marksman's head snapped round, his eyes widening as he saw Cormack and the gun, then let out an incoherent cry and brought the barrel of the rifle whipping round to fire from the hip, but Cormack squeezed the Browning's trigger and the gunman reeled backwards as the bullet slammed into his chest. He went down on his knees, the rifle clattering to the ground, his hands clutching at his ribs as he tried to staunch the flow of blood that was already staining his shirt bright red. He looked up at Cormack, who was still holding the gun on him, then, slowly, the gunman's eyes dulled and he pitched heavily forward, to lie unmoving in the road.

Slowly, Cormack moved towards the gunman, still keeping the gun levelled at him, then kicked the rifle away. He bent over the marksman and felt at the neck for a pulse, knowing what he would find, however, because when someone is about to shoot at you with a high-powered rifle and all you have is a handgun, you don't mess around trying to wing the bastard, you aim for the heart, stop him in his tracks, *stop him dead.* That's what he'd been trained to do in the Commandos and that was what he'd done just now.

Stopped him dead.

There was no pulse, none at all, which was why the pool of blood under the body wasn't spreading more rapidly... Cormack settled back on his haunches, his chest heaving as he sucked in great gasps of air. 'Shit...' he murmured, shaking his head slowly. 'You made a right balls up of that, didn't you?'

***

Cormack paused in the doorway for a moment, eyeing up the man sitting behind the trestle table, before he walked into the interview room. He stood in front of the table, looking down at the man, aware of the assured, almost arrogant expression on the other's face, then nodded to the MP standing guard at the door. The MP went out, closing the door behind him, leaving Cormack alone with the seated man.

'Joachim Heynckes,' Cormack said quietly.

'Correct. And your name?' The voice was as arrogant as the facial expression. Yes, he had been given little choice about coming here, it seemed to say, but there had been some mistake and it would soon be cleared up - and his questioner would do well to remember that.

'Is irrelevant,' Cormack said, still studying Heynckes. Expensive suit, not too flashy like most of the other black marketeers, an air of sophistication, the thinning light brown hair immaculately groomed, brushed carefully back from his forehead, the blue eyes intelligent, relaxed; *an unfortunate mistake.* 'Klaus Mohrer,' Cormack said abruptly.

Heynckes frowned slightly. 'What about him?'

'You know him?'

'Of course I do.' An impatient gesture. 'I employ him.'

'What as?'

'A driver, mostly.'

'Mostly?'

Heynckes shrugged. 'He also carries out errands and odd jobs for me.' He stared insolently at Cormack. 'Would you mind telling me what all this is about, Captain?'

Cormack ignored the question. 'How long has he been working for you?'

Heynckes compressed his lips, a momentary gesture of impatience, before he shrugged again. 'Two years, approximately.'

'What do you know of his war record?'

'Not very much. He served in the Army, but that's about all I do know. He does his work well enough, which is all I ask. I prefer to forget the past,' he added pointedly.

'Very commendable of you,' Cormack said drily. 'So you are unaware of the fact that he was trained as a sniper and was an expert marksman?'

Heynckes stared suspiciously at Cormack, the first hint of unease in his expression. 'Of course I did not know that,' he asserted. 'Why?'

'Because this morning, he shot and killed a prisoner who was being taken to the airfield and put three MPs in hospital,' Cormack said, never once taking his eyes from Heynckes' face. 'He works for you, which is why you're here.'

The shock was evident on Heynckes' face, but there was also indignation... 'You're not suggesting I had anything to do with it?'

'Why not? You paid his wages, after all.'

'I know nothing about it! Is that what he is saying?'

'It doesn't matter what Mohrer said,' Cormack said flatly. 'I'm asking you, Heynckes. Did you order the shooting?'

'How dare you!' Heynckes protested. 'Order the shooting? What are you saying? Do you know who I am–'

'Of course I bloody do,' Cormack snapped. 'Look, let's stop pretending, shall we? You run the biggest black market operation in Berlin, along with a string of prostitutes and nightclubs whose entertainment is - well, let's just say it's exotic, shall we? We know about you and you know that we know. You also know damn well that the only reason we haven't arrested you is because of your contacts in the Soviet Sector - you supply us with information, so we turn a blind eye to your other activities. A very nice, cosy, arrangement, but it doesn't include taking potshots at British Military Policemen, understand? Am I getting through to you, Heynckes? You'd better get this clear - whatever 'understanding' you might have had with Major Metcalfe is dead and buried. I am not interested in your little snippets of probably outdated gossip from the Soviet Sector - I'd just as soon pull the plug on your operations, to be honest, and I can do it, so don't make the mistake of thinking I can't. Stop playing games with me, Heynckes, and start telling me what you know, because if you don't, you won't know what fucking hit you - and that is a promise.' Cormack leaned forward, resting his hands on the table so that he was glaring down at Heynckes. 'In case you're interested, Mohrer is dead,' he said silkily. 'And I'm the one who killed him. Single shot to the heart, that's all it took.'

Heynckes' eyes widened in dismay; perhaps he had suddenly realised that he was alone in the room with a man who had killed a trained marksman. 'I see,' he said slowly, no longer poised, assured; there was a hesitancy about him now. He drew in his breath, then said, 'Very well. I knew Mohrer's background,' he admitted heavily, 'But I did not give him any orders to carry out a shooting, especially not involving British MPs.' He gestured impatiently. 'Do you think I would be mad enough to do that? I know the rules - if I don't rock the boat, you won't. I'd have to be crazy to start shooting at British soldiers.'

'So what was Mohrer up to?'

'I don't know! I haven't actually seen him for - what? Five days? Yes, Sunday, it was.'

'So you're asking me to believe that he wasn't working for you this morning?' Cormack asked, his voice loaded with disbelief. 'Come off it - you'll have to do better than that.'

'I tell you, he was not working for me!'

'But he *has* carried out shootings for you in the past?'

Heynckes stared at Cormack, then shook his head. 'Of course he hasn't!'

Cormack nodded slowly, then, finally, sat down opposite Heynckes. He stared intently at the other man, then said casually, 'You see the problem I face, Heynckes? My superiors want some answers as to who was behind the incident this morning - as you can imagine, they're rather upset about it. Now, I could find it pretty easy to build up a case implicating you and they'd be pretty keen to let me because they really would like to catch *someone* for it. It'd do my promotion chances a lot of good if I were to serve up your head on a platter, you see - it'd solve the murder and smash a black market network all in one go, wouldn't it? I must admit I'm very tempted to go down that road.'

'You have no evidence!' Heynckes protested, but there was a shrill edge to his voice now.

'Evidence? In a British military court, when the victims were British? Do you really want to take that chance?'

'I've told you - I know nothing!'

Cormack sighed. 'To tell you the truth, I'm inclined to believe you - but I need to come up with someone I can point the finger at and I think I can fit you up for that very nicely.' He paused, giving Heynckes time to absorb that, then said off-handedly, 'Of course, if you were to come up with the true culprit, it would be a different matter, I suppose.'

Heynckes' eyes glinted in sudden hope. 'What are you saying?'

'You have an extensive information network, Heynckes. Use it to find out who employed Mohrer - somebody certainly put him up to it, so it's up to you to find out who. The minute you do, tell me.'

'Then I'm off the hook?'

'We'd rather prosecute the real culprit than a substitute - but the substitute will do if there's nobody else.'

Heynckes nodded eagerly. 'I'll see what I can find out.'

'You do that.'

***

'You're letting Heynckes go then, sir?' Galvin asked.

Cormack glanced sharply at him, wondering if there were a hint of criticism in his subordinate's voice. 'Why not?' he asked. 'We don't actually have any evidence against him, when it comes down to it. Despite what I said to Heynckes, we'd have a hard job making anything stick.' He shrugged. 'He'll figure that out for himself once he's had time to think about it, but he knows we can make life bloody awkward for him. I think he'll try and find out who *did* hire Mohrer - and tell us if he does.'

'So you think he didn't have anything to do with it?'

'I'd be very surprised if he did. Like he said, he'd have to be bloody stupid to jeopardise what he's got by taking us on in a shooting situation. He'd come off worst, and he knows it. In any case, if he *was* behind the shooting, he'd have made damn sure he'd covered his tracks. Why use Mohrer, his own driver, for God's sake? Bit of a give away, really, wasn't it?'

Galvin nodded glumly. 'I suppose it is, when you think about it. Unless that's what he wants us to think.'

'Maybe. But I can't help thinking that Mohrer was set up. He was never meant to escape. The poor bastard looked utterly bewildered when I caught up with him - I'm damn sure he'd been told there would be a car waiting there for him - and there wasn't.'

Galvin nodded again. 'So whoever it was wanted us to catch Mohrer, so we'd think it was Heynckes behind it all?'

'I reckon so. They made bloody certain Mohrer wouldn't get away.'

'Wasn't it a bit risky, though, from their point of view?' Galvin asked. 'Supposing we'd taken Mohrer alive? He might have talked, which would have blown the whole thing wide open.'

'I think they guessed he'd try to shoot his way out and probably get killed. Even if he didn't, he probably thought he was working for Heynckes, anyway. They'd have had a cut-out of some sort who'd have disappeared straight after giving him the instructions. There'd have been no way back to the real culprits. Either way, Heynckes is implicated - and we're left with no other leads to follow.'

'Unless we're giving Heynckes more credit for planning than he deserves. It could still be him.'

Cormack shook his head. 'I don't think so. He'd have made damn sure Mohrer got away afterwards, for one thing. No, my guess is that someone set both Mohrer and Heynckes up - and I would very much like to know who. With any luck, Heynckes himself might turn something up if we let him go.'

'But will he tell us?'

'I think so. He'll want us off his back and he knows this is the only way he'll manage that. We just keep on hounding him until he produces the goods - raid his clubs, arrest his distributors, whatever. He's had it easy for long enough, anyway.' He nodded to Galvin. 'That's the part I want you to start setting up. Put Heynckes and his organisation under surveillance and start squeezing, see what comes out. With any luck we'll be able to pull him in for something else when all this is over.'

Galvin nodded, then said hesitantly, 'What about Fairhurst, sir? Do you think he might be involved in this?'

Cormack leaned back in his chair and steepled his fingers in front of his face. 'He could be,' he said at length. 'But we've still only got Logan's word that he's involved in anything illegal. We'll leave him alone for the moment, until we see if Heynckes can come up with anything.'

'There's no guarantee he will,' Galvin pointed out gloomily.

Jesus Christ, are you always this optimistic? Cormack bit back the angry comment and said instead, 'He will, if only to get us off his back.' He wished he were as confident as he sounded.

Galvin made a noncommittal noise, then stood up. 'I'll get this Heynckes thing set up, then, sir.'

'Yes,' Cormack said absently, staring across the room with unfocused eyes: he barely noticed Galvin leave. He had to get in touch with Woodward - and fast.

***

Woodward was already waiting, leaning against the balustrade, when Cormack arrived, carefully scanning the surroundings as he approached. It seemed clear enough, he decided: beyond Woodward was only the moonlit water of the Havel, while the street was deserted in each direction, but it was as well to be sure - especially now.

Nevertheless, Cormack's nerves betrayed him to the extent that, as he came to a halt, and leaned forward on the balustrade next to Woodward, he asked, 'You're sure you weren't tailed?'

Woodward shot him a pained look. 'No, I've got half the Soviet Secret Police hiding behind that lamp-post. What do you think?'

'Sorry,' Cormack said heavily. 'Stupid question.'

'What's the flap, anyway?'

'Logan was shot dead this morning outside the Detention Centre,' Cormack said bluntly.

Woodward's head snapped around towards him, the surprise only too evident in his face. 'Bloody hell,' he murmured. 'Who by?'

'An ex-Wehrmacht sniper called Mohrer, but it's who he was probably working for that's the problem.'

Woodward stared at him, then nodded in sudden realisation. 'Fairhurst, you mean? That's what all this about, is that it?'

'We don't know that it is Fairhurst,' Cormack admitted. 'But he seems a pretty strong candidate. Or someone who's trying to protect him.'

Woodward nodded again, slowly. 'Won't the sniper say who paid him?'

'He can't. He's dead,' Cormack said flatly. 'I doubt very much if he knew anyway.'

'I see,' Woodward said heavily. 'So you don't know if it *is* Fairhurst?'

'Not definitely, as I said, but-'

'Look, I can figure things out for myself, you know,' Woodward said peevishly. 'I'm not a complete idiot.' He broke off suddenly, stared out over the water for a few seconds, then seemed to sigh. 'Sorry about that,' he said eventually. 'It's just that I'm dead beat at the moment - been flying since six this morning... The thing is, you think I could be next on the list, right?'

'It stands to reason, doesn't it? If Fairhurst or whoever else he's working with did order the shooting, then it could be because of this special consignment you're supposed to he flying in. If they're prepared to knock off one of their own to stop him talking, they won't think twice about an outsider, will they?'

'Probably not, no.'

'The thing is, Tony, if I'm right and Logan was killed because of that consignment, then this whole thing's beginning to get out of hand - they're playing rough. I felt that you ought to know.'

'What, so I can have the option of calling it all off if I want?'

Cormack nodded. 'Right. You're a civilian - you don't have to be taking these kinds of risks any more. Why the hell do you think I was so worried about the two of us being seen together? If they know you know me, they'll have you pushing up daisies before you can turn round.'

'You said it might be dangerous,' Woodward pointed out.

'Might be, I said - but I thought then that this was simply a black market operation.'

'And now you don't?'

Cormack shrugged. 'I don't know. It seems a bit too big for that, somehow. Black marketeers don't go round taking pot shots at MPs - but this bloke did.'

'The thing is that you don't actually know if Fairhurst is behind the shooting or not, do you?' Woodward said. 'If he isn't and I've pulled out of this special flight, then we'll have missed a golden opportunity to nail him, won't we?'

'Oh, bugger the special flight,' Cormack retorted, gesturing impatiently. 'If that's all it is - a black market delivery - then I'm not that bothered about it. If it isn't, if it's something more dangerous-'

'Then you'll want to know all about it, won't you?' Woodward interrupted, a slight smile of triumph on his face.

Cormack was brought up short; he simply stared at Woodward, his lips set in a grim line until he said, 'Look, Tony, this is no time for one of your death-or-glory stunts. You could be sticking your neck out an awfully long way if you go through with this.'

'It's my neck, isn't it?' Woodward observed mildly. 'The way I see it, either Fairhurst is totally uninvolved in Logan's death, in the which case, all I'm being asked to do is fly in a dodgy cargo, or he *is* involved. If that's the case, then I'm probably the only chance you've got of finding out why this shipment is so important - right?'

'Probably, yes,' Cormack agreed reluctantly. 'We might be able to intercept it-'

'Don't give me that. You know that your best bet by some distance is for me to fly the damned thing in, whatever it is, yes?'

'OK, yes, but-'

'But nothing. Look, I'm not a complete amateur at this sort of thing, am I? We got out of some pretty hairy scrapes during the War, and it wasn't all down to you, was it?'

'No, it wasn't,' Cormack admitted. 'The thing is, though-'

'Put it this way, Alan,' Woodward said slowly. 'If it were you instead of me at the sharp end, you wouldn't be thinking twice about it, would you? What you don't like is that you're having to stand by while I'm having all the fun, isn't that it?'

'I wouldn't exactly call it *fun*.'

'No, but you know what I mean. It's me who's going to be taking the risks and you feel responsible, don't you? You forget I'm a big boy nowadays - I can make my own decisions, you know.'

Cormack stared at him, then looked away across the lake. He let out a long sigh, as if in admission of defeat. 'So you're going through with it.'

Woodward nodded. 'Afraid so.'

'I had a horrible feeling you'd say that,' Cormack replied, still staring out over the water. He had known all along what the answer would be, but Woodward had to be given the opportunity to pull out if he'd wanted - *or am I simply salving my conscience, because I'm the one who got him into this?* Slowly, Cormack shook his head, then straightened up, turning to face Woodward. 'OK, you win, Tony. But if things do turn nasty, don't have any of your damn fool ideas about sorting it out by yourself - get to a phone and yell for help if you can, understand?'

Woodward smiled faintly. 'Don't worry. I *did* learn that much from you. No heroics - is that it?'

'Damn right it is, Tony,' Cormack said grimly. 'Damn right it is.'

Chapter 6

Fuhlsbuttel Airfield, Hamburg

'Visibility not too good tonight, Tony,' the Ground Controller said, handing Woodward the Flight Clearance form. 'Seven tenths cloud most of the way, down to a thousand feet.'

Woodward shrugged. 'So what's different?'

'True. We'd have welcomed seven tenths cloud over the Ruhr five or six years ago, wouldn't we?'

'Too bloody right we would,' Woodward chuckled, making his way to the door. 'See you later.'

'Not me - I'll be off duty by the time you get back.'

'All right for some.' Woodward pushed open the door and emerged onto the concrete loading apron. His Dakota was the third plane along to the right, lit up by the garish arc lights that enabled loading to take place twenty four hours a day. The lorry was already moving away from the Dakota; the loading must have been completed. Woodward checked his watch, nodding in approval as he realised he would be taking off on schedule. Sacks of flour again, two and a half tons of them, the Dakota's maximum payload. Hardly glamorous, he thought wryly, but vital, even if the inside of the Dakota did have to be hosed down after the cargo had been unloaded at the other end...

'Herr Woodward?' The quiet voice brought him abruptly out of his thoughts. He turned and saw a man in mechanic's overalls approaching him.

'Yes?'

'My name is Schmidt,' the mechanic said in fair English. 'I am to give you this.' He reached inside his overalls and produced a manila envelope, which he handed to Woodward. That in itself wasn't unusual - he had often been asked to deliver letters to

Berlin - but it was the name the mechanic had used that brought Woodward to full alertness: Schmidt.

Fairhurst's messenger.

'What's going on?' Woodward asked.

'There has been a change of plan,' Schmidt said succinctly. 'You're flying the consignment in tonight.'

Oh, great... 'What do you mean?'

'Please keep walking towards your aircraft, Herr Woodward. You don't want the Tower wondering about the delay, do you?'

Despite himself, Woodward flicked a nervous glance back at the Control Tower, then nodded and fell in step with Schmidt. 'What's going on?' he asked again. 'I was told the twelfth to the sixteenth.'

'Merely a precaution on our part,' Schmidt said smoothly. 'The envelope contains the first part of your fee, as agreed.'

'The cargo's already aboard, then?' Woodward asked, trying to keep his voice calm.

'Not yet, no. When you reach the end of the runway, wait a moment before you take off. The consignment will be waiting for you there. It will only take a few moments to load it, then you can take off as planned. Is this understood?'

'Er - yes. I've got it.'

'Good.' The mechanic nodded, then walked off abruptly to the right, leaving Woodward to walk the last few yards to his aircraft alone.

Good God Almighty, now what was he going to do? Mind you, he had to give them due credit, because they'd set it up beautifully so that there was no way that he could contact anyone to tip them off about the shipment... If he tried to transmit a message to Cormack by radio, Fairhurst would overhear it in Berlin. Very neat.

Oh, come on, stop getting cold feet, he told himself as he climbed up into the Dakota and pulled the hatch shut behind him. *You knew what you were getting into...*

He made his way to the cockpit, climbed into the pilot's seat and began the pre-flight checks, flicking on switches, checking instruments, the familiar routine helping to quieten his jangling nerves. *Hell, it can't be any worse than flying a bombing mission, can it?*

He started up the engines. 'Tower, this is Dakota Zulu Yankee. Requesting taxi clearance.'

'Dakota Zulu Yankee clear to taxi.'

'Dakota Zulu Yankee, Roger.'

Woodward released the brakes and opened the throttles; the Dakota moved ponderously forward, then headed towards the end of the runway. The plane ahead of him, a four-engined Halton, was already starting its take off run, but Woodward scarcely noticed; his eyes were still checking the dials in front of him, but his mind was racing, pondering this last-minute change of plan. Only it wasn't, he thought grimly, because they must have set it up like this from the start. It might not even be because they were using an outsider - perhaps even Logan would have been treated the same way; Woodward hoped so. If not, then they were going to great pains to ensure secrecy... *Just as they had with Logan?*

Where was the man who was supposed to give him the consignment, anyway? The Dakota had reached the end of the runway, time to turn, ready to take off - and there he was, a tall figure emerging from behind a distance marker only twenty yards away. Clearly, he had waited until the aircraft was hiding him from the Tower, but now the man began to run towards the Dakota.

'Tower to Dakota Zulu Yankee. Clear to take off.'

'One moment, Tower. I'm registering low oil pressure on one engine. It's probably the dial, but... can you just hang on for a moment?'

'Roger, Dakota Zulu Yankee.'

Woodward lifted himself out of the seat and scrambled back into the body of the plane, hurriedly undogging the hatch. It swung open and the tall man jumped up into the cargo hold, pulling the hatch closed again. He turned to face Woodward.

'You'd better take off immediately,' he said curtly.

Woodward stared at him. 'Where's the consignment?'

'I *am* the consignment.'

Berlin

The tall man had not said much during the flight, beyond monosyllabic responses that gave nothing away beyond the fact that he spoke adequate English, but with a definite German accent. Eventually, Woodward had given up and concentrated on flying the plane. All the same, he'd flashed the occasional quick glance sideways at the man in the copilot's seat, but when the only illumination in the cockpit was the light from the instrument dials, the passenger's face was little more than a pale blur in the darkness; Woodward was far from convinced he would recognise him again. Braun, he had said his name was, which was about as likely to be true as it was for the mechanic at Fuhlsbuttel to be called Schmidt. Tall, fair-haired, wearing a military-style trench coat - that was about all Woodward would be able to pass on in the way of a visual description, if he were honest about it, but there was one other detail that had stuck in his mind. Braun had an air of watchfulness, of coiled tension, rather like Cormack when he'd been behind enemy lines during the War, in fact, Woodward realised suddenly, stealing another brief look at his passenger.

Who the hell was he?

Woodward pushed the thought aside as the 'Rebecca' navigational equipment indicated that he was now approaching the Frohnau Beacon; twenty miles back, he had radioed Gatow Airways to give his call-sign, his ETA at Frohnau and the cargo he was carrying. Now, it was time to begin his approach to Gatow.

'Gatow Approach, Dakota Zulu Yankee over Frohnau at two point five.'

'Roger Zulu Yankee, change to one one five point nine megacycles, call Gatow Control.'

'Gatow Control, Dakota Zulu Yankee leaving Frohnau.'

'Roger Zulu Yankee, steer one eight zero degrees, descend to one point five. How do you read me?'

'Read you loud and clear. Roger.'

'Zulu Yankee, turn right, steer two six zero. Let down to one point two. Do your cockpit check for landing.'

'Roger.'

Rapidly, Woodward checked the instruments, then let down the undercarriage as he began his final approach - *always seems so damned morbid, that expression* - and brought the Dakota down in an almost textbook landing. Not bad for nearly midnight, after a full day's flying...

As the Dakota slowed, approaching the western end of the runway, Braun unstrapped his seat belt and said, 'Wait a moment at the end of the runway. I'll get out there. I'll close the hatch from the outside.' He reached inside his coat and took out an envelope. 'This contains your instructions for collecting the rest of your payment. I suggest you read them immediately. Goodbye, Herr Woodward.' He turned and made his way back into the cargo hold, leaving Woodward staring after him, bemused.

The Dakota rolled to a halt and Woodward twisted round in his seat in time to see Braun disappear through the hatch; a glance in the side mirror saw him closing and fastening the batch again. Then, he was running away from the plane and Woodward craned round in his seat so that he could see him through the perspex windows - and, for a second or so, as Braun looked back, his face was caught in the revolving light from one of the runway markers. A moment later, Braun had faded into the darkness, heading towards the perimeter fence. Woodward sighed and turned the Dakota towards the unloading apron.

It was only once he had completed the clearance forms in the Administration Block that he had an opportunity to open the envelope; he bought a cup of coffee in the canteen and went over to an empty table to read its contents. In the event, he never drank the coffee, because all that was on the sheet of paper inside was an address - 32, Kreutzwaldstrasse - and a time, 12.30. He looked hurriedly at his watch, then up at the canteen clock and swore under his breath.

He had less than thirty minutes to be there.

***

'What was the address again?' Cormack asked.

'32, Kreutzwaldstrasse. It's only about a mile from the airfield, so I can get there in time if I put my skates on.'

Cormack scribbled down the address, trying to blink the sleep out of his eyes - he had only just slipped over the edge when the phone had rung, three minutes before. 'You're at Gatow now?'

'Yes.'

'Is anyone watching you make this call?'

'I don't think so. In any case, I could be phoning anyone, couldn't I?'

Cormack stared down at the telephone cradle, trying to force his mind to function properly - he still was not fully awake, and knew it. 'I don't like the sound of this, Tony. It's looking rather like a trap.'

'You think I don't know that? But what choice do I have? If I don't go, they'll start getting suspicious, won't they? They'll start wondering why I didn't go and collect the money when there was no earthly reason for me not to. They'll do the same to me as they did to Logan - and, even if they don't, we won't have any leads to follow up, will we? Braun's disappeared, so the consignment's been delivered. If I go, then there might be some chance of finding out what the hell this is all about.'

'You could also get yourself killed. There is no way that I can get an arrest team there in that time - I'm not sure if I can get there myself, come to that.'

'Look, this is our only chance. If I don't go tonight, then we'll probably never find out what's going on. In any case, we don't have time to argue about it - if I don't get moving, there might not be anyone there, anyway.'

Cormack stifled an oath: Woodward was right, dammit, and if the situation were reversed, he, Cormack, would have no hesitation in going to the address. Well, hardly *no* hesitation, to be honest, a hell of a lot would be nearer the mark, but he'd still have gone... He looked at his watch, then said, 'OK, Tony, we'll do it your way. I'll try and get there in time.'

'Right. See you soon.'

'I bloody well hope so.' The line went dead. Cormack stared at the receiver for a moment, then slammed it down onto the cradle and leaped to his feet, reaching for his clothes. In less than three minutes, he was roaring away up the street in the jeep, his foot flat to the floor.

***

Woodward looked around as the taxi drew up outside 32, Kreutzwaldstrasse, then climbed out, handing over the money to the driver. 'Wait here,' he said, 'I'll only be a few minutes.' *I hope...* He stood on the pavement for several seconds, staring at the front of the house, then, taking a deep breath, he mounted the steps and knocked on the door.

There was a delay of about ten seconds, during which Woodward had to fight down an impulse to climb back into the taxi and just drive off, forget about the whole thing, then the door was opened by a bald, stocky man in an ill-fitting suit. 'Yes?' he asked.

'I'm Woodward.'

'Yes,' the man said again, then stepped back to let Woodward pass. 'Come in, please,' he said in heavily-accented English. Woodward did so, looking rapidly around him as he entered a narrow hallway. 'The door to your right,' the man said from behind him, closing the outside door. Woodward pushed the door open.

And found himself staring down the silenced barrel of an automatic pistol.

Shit...

'W-what is this?' he demanded fearfully, blinking nervously at the man holding the gun, a taller man than the other.

'Raise your hands,' the gunman said sharply in very precise English. Woodward did so, his eyes fixed on the other man; tall, a pencil-thin moustache, who held the gun with total confidence. A professional; he was standing about six feet away from Woodward, too far away to be reached with a foot or a fist, too close to miss with his first shot - and the gun was aimed unwaveringly at Woodward's heart. 'Search him,' the gunman said crisply.

The bald man frisked Woodward rapidly, expertly. 'He's not armed.'

'Good. Come in, please, Woodward.' He beckoned with his hand. Woodward obeyed, noticing that the gunman backed away from him as he did so, never allowing his target within striking distance. The gunman said something in German to the bald man that Woodward did not catch, but its import was soon made clear. The bald man went out through the street door and, a few moments later, Woodward heard the taxi drive away, the sound accentuating his sense of isolation.

'Look - what is all this?' he asked, his voice, strident, near panic - and it was not entirely feigned either, he realised, with a chill.

The gunman ignored the question, but his concentration seemed entirely focused on his victim - and Woodward was only too aware of the fact that the German had so much confidence in his own ability that the bald man had not produced a gun at all. The gunman knew he could handle the situation on his own... *Walked right into this, didn't you?*

Woodward looked rapidly around the room: it was a living room, with two battered armchairs and a sofa, a sideboard to his right, a vase that he might be able to reach and throw...

No. Not with this man. The German would put a bullet through his heart before he'd even grabbed the vase. There was nothing to be done: the gun said it all. 'Go back out into the hall,' the gunman ordered; Woodward hesitated for a moment, then obeyed.

There was the sound of a car pulling up outside and, for a moment, Woodward felt a sudden leap of hope - *Cormack* - but the gunman seemed unconcerned. A few seconds later, the outside door opened and the bald man appeared in the doorway. 'We're ready.'

The gunman nodded. 'Right.' He gestured with his left hand at Woodward. 'Turn round and go out to the car. Bring your arms down. I will be right behind you and if you try to escape, I will shoot you dead. Do you understand me?'

Woodward licked his lips, realising that his mouth was bone dry. 'Yes,' he said hoarsely, obeying the instructions.

As he emerged into the street, he looked rapidly each way along it, hoping to see, if not Cormack, then anyone, anyone at all. But the street was deserted and he felt a sudden leaden sensation in his limbs as a chill realisation struck him. These two men were going to take him away somewhere and kill him and there was nothing he could do about it. If he made a run for it now, the gunman would put a bullet into his spine before he'd gone three paces... *Come on, for Christ's sake, don't just go along with it, try something, anything...*

He came to an abrupt halt a yard from the car, hoping that the gunman would bump into him from behind, then he could pivot round, try and knock the gun aside, go for the groin or throat... but it was a forlorn hope. The gunman simply stepped back half a pace and said, 'Don't be foolish, Woodward. Get into the car.'

Fuck... Taking a deep breath, Woodward opened the rear door and climbed in. The gunman slid into the seat next to him, pressing the gun firmly into the base of Woodward's neck now, too high up to bring up his hand to knock away - the bastard knew what he was doing, all right. The bald man took his place at the wheel, slid the car into gear and drove off. Only now did the gunman relax, removing the barrel from Woodward's neck as he settled back more comfortably in the seat, the gun aimed once more at his victim's heart.

The car began to pick up speed.

***

Cormack pulled on the jeep's handbrake and checked his watch: 12.33. He'd probably broken every speed restriction in Berlin to get here - and it still might be too late; how long did it take to put a bullet through someone's skull, after all? Tony Woodward might already be dead...

Still no excuse for charging in like a bull at a gate, though.

Right. Which was why he'd resisted the impulse to bring the jeep screaming to a halt outside 32, Kreutzwaldstrasse and go in, guns blazing. Woodward was no fool; he'd known what he might be getting himself into and if he were still alive, the last thing he'd want would be to have someone bursting in, shooting from the hip. This was their lead to the people behind Fairhurst, and an incredibly fragile one at that, which Woodward was following. It was up to Cormack to wait in the wings, observing, not go blundering in and snapping the thread, which was why he had brought the jeep to a halt around the corner, coasting the last hundred yards or so with the engine turned off. Now, he climbed out and strode rapidly to the corner, peering around it towards Number 32.

There was a taxi parked outside, but, within seconds, someone came out and spoke to the driver. The taxi drove off and the man walked away down the street, towards a Mercedes fifty yards further along. He climbed into it, started the engine, then drove slowly along the street, bringing it to a halt outside Number 32. As Cormack watched, the man emerged from the car and went back inside.

Cormack looked rapidly around, checking the surroundings, then took a Browning automatic pistol from inside his tunic, checking it rapidly before he flicked off the safety catch. He looked around once more; dammit, he needed some back-up, but there had not been time to set it up, not if he were to be here himself on time. There was a telephone box about fifty yards behind him, though, in the side street: might it be worth calling for help?

Hold it. The bald man was emerging from Number 32 - and there was Woodward, followed by another man. Even at this distance, Cormack could see the gun that was levelled at Woodward's back. There was a momentary delay as Woodward seemed to hesitate, then he climbed into the back of the car, followed by the gunman. The bald man slid into the driver's seat.

So. It was all suddenly very simple; they were going to take Woodward somewhere and kill him and there would be no way that they would allow themselves to be followed without killing their prisoner anyway. Whatever Cormack was going to do had to be done here, now. Two men, that was all. *All,* for Christ's sake...

The Mercedes pulled away from the kerb, heading towards Cormack as he stepped out onto the pavement, lined the gun up on the pale blur of the driver's face and fired at a range of no more than five yards, holding the Browning in a two-handed grip. The windscreen exploded in a shower of glass as the driver reeled back, the Mercedes' engine racing as his foot jammed itself convulsively down on the accelerator. The car slewed round, the rear end slamming into the lamp-post on the corner, before it rebounded back into the road, the car skidding sideways across the junction before it smashed broadside on into the opposite lamp post.

The rear passenger door burst open and the gunman dived out, gun in hand. He hit the ground and rolled, loosing off a quick snapshot at Cormack, but then Cormack squeezed the trigger twice more, the Browning remorselessly tracking the gunman. The impact of the bullets threw the gunman backwards, arms outflung, the gun curling away in a high arc to land some feet away. The German landed on his side, clutching at his chest, trying to stem the sudden flow of blood there, then stared uncomprehendingly at Cormack. Somehow, he dragged himself up onto his hands and knees, his eyes fixed on his gun, but then he collapsed heavily forward to lie still, one hand stretched out towards the gun.

Slowly, Cormack headed towards the Mercedes, holding the Browning at the ready, letting his breath out in a sigh of relief as he saw Woodward force the other rear door open and climb shakily out. Cormack moved closer until he could see the driver, who was sprawled untidily across the passenger seat, his eyes wide and staring - and with half the side of his head blown away... Cormack averted his head, hurriedly, and looked instead at Woodward, feeling the adrenalin gradually draining away.

'You OK, Tony?'

Woodward shook his head groggily. 'I think so,' he said vaguely. Then, suddenly, his eyes came into focus and he stared intently at Cormack. 'Bloody hell...' he murmured as he saw the two dead men. His eyes came back to Cormack, then they seemed to roll up in his head as his knees buckled and he fell limply across the bonnet of the Mercedes.

***

Cormack rummaged morosely through the papers in the top drawer of the sideboard, then looked around the flat, only half-noticing the three men who were turning the place upside down as they searched it. Fairhurst had not done too badly here, he decided; the flat overlooked the Tiergarten and was comfortably furnished, but, despite the newspaper left carelessly on the coffee table, it had an indefinable air of vacancy now. Fairhurst was not coming back; ten minutes ago, Galvin had announced that there was no sign of Fairhurst's wallet, passport or identification papers, but Cormack had already known instinctively that the flat's tenant had gone to ground.

But how had Fairhurst found out about Kreutzwaldstrasse so quickly? It was barely two hours since Cormack had blown the Mercedes off the street, but in that time, Fairhurst had disappeared. Someone must have told him what had happened and he had made a run for it, knowing that Woodward could implicate him - but how had he been tipped off in time?

Who had told him?

And who the hell was Braun?

Woodward had only been able to give a sketchy description on his way to hospital, but there was no doubt that Braun was the key to this problem. By the looks of it, they - whoever 'they' were - had been prepared to kill Woodward in order to ensure that his presence in Berlin remained a secret.

The thing was, Cormack thought bitterly, if he'd acted sooner and pulled Fairhurst in for questioning, if he hadn't decided to involve Woodward, he might well now be a lot further on in this investigation. At least they'd have had Fairhurst in their hands...

And how much would he have told them? Sod all, probably - or given them a pack of lies... No, this had been the best way to find a lead into this situation; it had simply backfired, that was all.

Backfired? Two bodies in the morgue, each one with bullets from your gun in them - you call that backfiring?

Galvin came hesitantly over. 'There's nothing here, sir,' he said tiredly. 'No indication where he might have gone.'

'Well, there wouldn't be, would there?' Cormack asked mildly. 'We'd better get a full-scale search going for him. Have you notified the airfields?'

'Yes, sir. They're on the look out for him.'

'Right. Get his photo distributed around the MPs, get on to his friends and colleagues-' He broke off, seeing the careful lack of expression on Galvin's face. 'OK, OK, I get the message. I'm teaching my grandmother to suck eggs, aren't I?'

Galvin hesitated, then replied, 'Well, put it this way, sir, I think we've got that side of things well in hand.'

'Spoken like a true diplomat,' Cormack said, smiling faintly. 'The thing is, given the sort of contacts Fairhurst has, he might already be out of Berlin.'

'We've notified the airfields in the West as well, sir.'

Cormack nodded. 'Good. Which leaves us with the mysterious Herr Braun, doesn't it?'

'We don't have much to go on there, sir,' Galvin said doubtfully. 'Mister Woodward's description was a bit vague, wasn't it?'

So would yours be if you'd been in a car smash and seen two people gunned down right in front of you, Cormack thought sourly. 'I know that, but we need to start thinking who he might be. He's German, he's in his early thirties and he's flying secretly into Berlin - what does that suggest?'

'A wanted Nazi?' Galvin ventured. 'He can't come in openly because he'd be recognised and arrested?'

'Could be. Certainly, he doesn't want to be spotted, so I'd say the best bet is to dig out all the photos we've got in our files and show them to Woodward.'

'Will that do any good, sir? He said he only had one good look at his face and that was only for a second or so. Will he be able to recognise Braun again?'

You don't know Tony Woodward, old son - that'd be all he'd need. 'If he doesn't, we won't be any worse off than we are now, will we?'

'Very true, sir,' Galvin conceded. A thought seemed to strike him. 'It seems a bit odd, though, sir. Braun, I mean. If he *is* a wanted Nazi, then why is he coming *into* Berlin? I'd have thought he'd be wanting to be going the other way, if anything.'

'Exactly,' Cormack agreed emphatically. 'I wondered when you'd get around to that. Braun is here for a reason - and it's important enough for whoever's behind all this to kill any witnesses to his being here at all.'

Cormack paused for a moment, staring at Galvin, then added softly, 'So why *is* he here?'

Chapter 7

The time was exactly ten a.m. when Cormack knocked on Pallister's office door and opened it in response to a 'Come in' from inside. Pallister was seated behind his desk, but he rose to his feet as Cormack entered, closing the door behind him. If he was pleased to see Cormack, there was no trace of it in his expression, nor did he do more than nod in response as Cormack came to attention and saluted.

'Reporting as ordered, sir,' Cormack said formally.

Pallister walked slowly around the desk, coming to a halt a yard to Cormack's right. He stared at Cormack for several seconds as if he were a zoologist encountering some new species, then said abruptly, 'Cormack, what the devil has been going on?'

'Sir?'

'This Fairhurst business. Why wasn't I informed that he was under investigation? And what were you doing involving a civilian in your enquiries? I would expect, as your Senior Officer, to be kept appraised of matters like these, yet they only come to light following a full-scale gunfight in the street, the second in which you have been involved in less than four days, in fact.' He glared at Cormack. 'I think I am entitled to some sort of explanation, Captain. Why was I not told anything?'

Cormack swallowed. 'Sir, with respect, until all this happened, all I had was Logan's unsubstantiated word that Fairhurst was involved at all. As for the civilian participation, the individual concerned, who has had more undercover experience than anyone in my unit except myself, volunteered to act as an *agent provocateur*, but there was no way that anyone could have foreseen that what appeared to be a fairly routine black market investigation would escalate to this extent. Until last night, this was simply an intelligence gathering operation, which, as you are aware, is my area of responsibility, so there was no need to inform you, sir. Once I realised that this was more serious, I submitted a report to you immediately.'

Pallister continued to glower at him, his anger barely held in check, then let out an audible, exasperated, sigh and nodded slowly. 'Very well, Cormack,' he said with evident reluctance, 'I suppose you're right. Just. Very well, at ease.'

Cormack relaxed, letting out his breath slowly. *You only just got away with that, old son - especially as you were talking utter rubbish.*

Pallister went back behind his desk and sat down. 'All right, Cormack, sit down, sit down,' he said irritably. Once Cormack had done so, he continued, 'The point is, what the devil is going on? First Logan, then this business with Fairhurst - just what exactly is happening?'

'I wish I knew, sir,' Cormack said soberly. 'All I know is that someone was smuggled into Berlin last night and that whoever brought him in was so determined that we wouldn't get to hear about it that they were prepared to kill anyone who knew about it. In fact,' he said suddenly, the realisation only just striking him, 'we don't know for certain that Fairhurst *has* made a run for it. He might have met the same fate intended for Woodward.'

Pallister peered intently at him. 'Do you think so?'

Cormack shrugged. 'Again, I don't know, sir. It's possible. They - whoever 'they' are - are certainly ruthless enough. The point is that if they're prepared to go to such extreme measures, then Braun must be pretty important.'

'Quite.' Pallister continued to stare unblinkingly at Cormack, then said slowly, '*My* point, however, is that if this investigation is to continue, then I do *not* want any more pitched battles taking place on the streets in the British Sector.' He paused, then added icily, 'To be perfectly blunt, Cormack, I find it disquieting in the extreme that you personally have killed three men since arriving here. I am not sure I like that, or its implications.'

'I didn't exactly have much choice in the matter, sir,' Cormack pointed out. *But had he?* he wondered. This was peacetime, after all; had he let his training, which was intended for wartime situations, take over too much?

'That's as may be, but I still don't like it,' Pallister continued. 'It may be that someone whose methods are less - direct, shall we say? - might well be better suited to Berlin. Given the present delicate situation, the last thing we want is shooting incidents on the streets.'

'I'll try and bear that in mind, sir,' Cormack replied, with no expression at all in his voice.

Pallister glanced sharply at him, as if trying to detect any hint of irony in Cormack's tone, but then said, 'Be sure that you do.' He sighed, then leaned back in his chair. 'In the meantime, find out what you can.' He jabbed a forefinger towards Cormack. 'However, from now on, I want to be kept fully up to date with the situation. Is that clear?'

'Perfectly clear, sir.'

***

'Nope,' Woodward said, sighing, turning the last page of the bound volume of photographs. 'None of those.'

'You're sure?' Cormack asked.

Woodward shrugged. 'Not a hundred per cent, no,' he admitted. 'I only had a brief look at his face, but I'm pretty sure it wasn't among that lot.' He tapped the volume.

'OK,' Cormack said wearily. 'Try this lot.' He passed a folder over to Woodward, who opened it. This time, the photographs were not carefully pasted to the pages, but were loose, with annotations on the back of each. Woodward raised an interrogatory eyebrow at Cormack, who shrugged in turn. 'These are the ones we're not so sure about,' he confessed.

'In other words, we're getting desperate.'

'You could say that, yes.'

Woodward nodded resignedly and began working his way through the photographs, studying each one intently. He had been doing this for - Cormack checked his watch - nearly six hours now, ploughing patiently through the collection of photographs of wanted Nazis and criminals. The hospital had been reluctant to release him - he had a huge plaster on his right temple where his head had impacted with the car's door pillar and he was still suffering the lingering effects of concussion - but Woodward had insisted and had been sitting in Cormack's office ever since, trying to pick out Braun's face from the thousands of photographs on file. Even with a 'sifting' process - they had eliminated all photos of women, of course, as well as males over fifty - there were still far too many to examine and now that they were down to the 'unconfirmed' files, where the photos were generally grainy, ill-defined and quite possibly not even of the person whose name appeared on the back, Cormack could feel hope slipping away. It had to be done, however, because unless Fairhurst could be found, this was just about the only lead they had; not even Heynckes had managed to come up with anything so far. Cormack was not at all sanguine about finding Fairhurst: the speed with which he had disappeared implied that he had been given help to make his escape, which, in turn, meant that he was probably out of Berlin already.

While Braun could be anywhere at all, of course...

Elise Langemann came in, carrying half a dozen envelope folders that she deposited on the desk, nervously wiping away a layer of dust from them. 'Lieutenant Galvin asked me to bring these in, sir,' she explained, then turned to leave, carefully avoiding any eye contact with Cormack.

'Thanks, Elise,' Cormack replied; she flashed him a quick glance as if surprised at his use of her first name, then went out. Cormack caught sight of Woodward watching her with an only too easily read expression as she left. 'That's enough of that, Tony,' he said, trying to make his voice light-hearted. 'Keep your mind on those photos.'

'Easier said than done,' Woodward commented. 'She's an absolute cracker, Alan. Where did you find her?'

'She sort of went with the job, I suppose.'

'Lucky sod. She's as good a reason for working late as I've ever seen.' He looked questioningly at Cormack. 'Are you and she - er - you know?'

'Yes, I do know and no, we're not,' Cormack replied, hoping that his tone of voice would discourage further questions.

'Bit slow off the mark, aren't you?'

'You just concentrate on those photos,' Cormack said testily, then immediately regretted it: it wasn't Woodward's fault that Elise had been virtually ignoring him since that night outside her apartment, after all.

'Yes, sir!' Woodward's right arm shot up in a dazzling salute, then he grinned mischievously and slid out the next photograph. 'How many more of these are there, anyway?' he asked, exaggerated despair in his voice.

Cormack shrugged. 'Probably only another thousand or so,' he replied, an innocent smile on his face.

'Oh, terrific...'

***

'That's him,' Woodward said suddenly.

Cormack looked up from the file he had been unsuccessfully attempting to read for the past fifteen minutes and saw Woodward holding up a photograph. 'You're sure?'

'Pretty sure,' Woodward replied. 'If it wasn't him, then it's someone else who looks damned like him.' He pushed the photo across the desk top towards Cormack, who studied it. The face that stared back at him was of a fair-haired man in his middle or late twenties, with thin, almost fleshless, lips.

He turned it over and read the back. 'Dieter Kallmann,' he mused, then pressed the intercom button.

'Yes, sir?' said Elise's voice.

'Do we have anything on a Dieter Kallmann?' Cormack asked, then spelled out the name. 'If we have, could you bring it in?'

'I'll have a look, sir.'

Cormack stared at the intercom for a moment, then waved the photograph at Woodward. 'How sure are you about this, Tony?'

'Eighty or ninety per cent. I know I didn't have long, but I still had a good look at the time. Who is he, anyway?' he added, nodding at the photo.

'Haven't a clue,' Cormack confessed. 'He's wearing the uniform of an SS-Sturmbannfuehrer - that's a major to you - which means he can't have been anyone too important in the overall scheme of things - especially if all we have on him is a single, unconfirmed photo.'

'Yes, but if he *was* a major, he must have been good at something, especially if he was made one when he was as young as he looks in the photo.'

'A very good point,' Cormack conceded. 'The SS was not in the habit of promoting idiots to the rank of major. If it's the same man, of course,' he added dubiously.

Elise came in, carrying a single sheet of typed paper. 'This is all there is on him, sir,' she said, her manner still aloof, businesslike - but their fingers touched momentarily as she handed over the paper and it was like an electric shock running through Cormack. *Bloody hell, you've got it bad, old son...*

'Thanks, Elise,' Cormack replied; he did not look up as she went out. He studied the sheet, then compressed his lips as he saw the '*Tot*' stamped across the top of the document. He pointed it out to Woodward. 'See that?'

'I see it. He wouldn't be the first 'dead' Nazi to come crawling out of the woodwork, would he?' Woodward observed.

'Again, very true.' Cormack scanned rapidly through the typed commented. 'According to this, the only information we have on him was that he was in Skorzeny's Special Services Battalion, was awarded the Knight's Cross with Oak Leaves, although it doesn't say when, and that he was killed during the defence of Berlin. That's all there is, beyond his service number - no dates or details of previous service at all.'

'Skorzeny?' Woodward mused. 'Wasn't he the one who rescued Mussolini from a mountain top or something?'

Cormack nodded. 'The very same. He also organised the English-speaking soldiers who were parachuted behind the American lines during the Battle of the Bulge and, on top of that, he set up an operation to assassinate Tito in his headquarters. I've also heard rumours that he came up with a plan to kill Churchill, Roosevelt and Stalin at their Tehran Conference. A very capable customer - and his Special Services Battalion was a pretty elite unit. If Kallmann was in it, he'd have been highly trained in things like sabotage, espionage, assassination, undercover work - any or all of those things. Not only that, but he'd probably be good at whatever his speciality was.'

'Assuming he's still alive,' Woodward pointed out.

'You're the one who's claiming he saw him.' Cormack leaned back in his chair and steepled his fingers in front of his face. 'If it *is* Kallmann, then he's almost certainly a trained saboteur or killer... and he's right here in Berlin. That's all we bloody well need.'

Moabit Prison, Berlin

Cormack stood for a moment outside the steel door, nerving himself for the forthcoming meeting, before he nodded to the MP sergeant, who unfastened the door and opened it, standing aside to let Cormack enter. Inside was a room that had a solitary barred window up near the ceiling, and a table with two wooden chairs. There were two men in the room, a uniformed MP inside the door and a middle-aged, balding man sitting at the table, facing the door, dressed in prison garb. He rose to his feet the moment Cormack came in and stood eyeing his visitor impassively. Cormack nodded to the guard, who went out, closing the door as Cormack placed his briefcase on the table.

'Colonel Burgnich?' Cormack said flatly.

'Yes?'

'I've come to ask you a few questions.'

Burgnich nodded. 'Naturally. If I can be of any help, I will be.'

Cormack gestured to Burgnich to sit down, then did so himself. He stared at Burgnich for several seconds, collecting his thoughts, trying to overcome his initial feeling of surprise. Somehow, he had expected a convicted war criminal who was serving a twenty year sentence to have looked more... well, *sinister*. Instead, Burgnich looked more like an ineffectual, harassed clerk than someone who had been in the higher echelons of SS Headquarters; but then, so had Himmler, if truth be told... Although primarily an administrator, he had been involved in the transportation of Jews to concentration camps, as well as in running research programmes developing various 'sharpened' interrogation techniques for the Gestapo. Quite a number of observers at the Nuremberg Trials had expected him to receive a death sentence, but he had succeeded in escaping the hangman's noose by the simple expedient of memorising, and subsequently destroying, dozens of top-level SS files to which he had access before the fall of Berlin and then offering his knowledge as a bargaining counter to the Allies. He had kept his side of the agreement as well; Cormack had heard it said that his evidence had helped to convict at least ten other war criminals, from Kaltenbrunner downwards.

Cormack opened his briefcase and took out Kallmann's photograph. 'Do you recognise this man?' he asked bluntly.

Burgnich put on a pair of wire-rimmed spectacles and studied the photo intently before he turned it over: Cormack had stuck masking tape across the name. Burgnich thought for a moment, then said firmly, 'Kallmann. First name... Dieter, I think. But definitely Kallmann.' He handed the photo back to Cormack.

'Do you remember his file?'

Burgnich's eyes went momentarily unfocused, as if he were assembling the material in his mind, then he said, 'Part of it, at any rate. Born Dusseldorf, nineteen sixteen, recruited into the SS in nineteen thirty-six, trained as a marksman. Used in the Spanish Civil War for at least two assassinations of Republican guerrilla leaders and was later used for similar purposes in Yugoslavia, Greece and Crete. Transferred to the Special Services Battalion in nineteen forty-three.'

'An assassin?' Cormack repeated, his voice carefully without inflexion. *Jesus Christ...*

'Yes - and a very good one, by all accounts. He apparently used to boast that he only needed one shot at any range.'

'He used a rifle?'

'Always.'

Cormack stared intently at Burgnich. 'What happened to him?'

There was a momentary hesitation before Burgnich replied, 'I don't know. I do know that he was to be assigned to the Werewolves.' He glanced inquisitively at Cormack. 'You've heard of them?'

'Of course.' The Werewolves had been just about Goebbels' last propaganda ploy, a group of SS fanatics who were supposed to carry on a ruthless guerilla campaign against the Allies even after the rest of Germany had been over-run, but, in the event, the threat had never materialised. Either there never had been any Werewolves, or they had decided that discretion was the better part of valour. 'Go on,' Cormack prompted Burgnich.

'He was supposed to be based at the Alpine Redoubt and, according to the schedule, he should have been flown out there in early April, nineteen forty-five. I don't know if he did or not - the records for those flights were sketchy, to say the least.'

'I can imagine... So if he was supposed to fly out during early April, how is it that his file says that he was killed fighting Russian troops on the twenty-first of April - to the east of Berlin?'

Burgnich hesitated again, then shrugged. 'Perhaps there was a change of plan, but it could also have been a deliberate disinformation measure. Some of the leading Werewolf officers were issued with false papers and identities, while being officially dead.'

'What rank was Kallmann by this time?'

'I don't know. In the Special Services Battalion, rank was not taken as seriously as elsewhere - rather like your own Special Forces, I believe. In any case, they tended to keep information about their personnel confidential.'

Cormack nodded thoughtfully. He had thought Burgnich's hesitations had been preludes to giving out false information, but it looked now as if they were nothing more than a reluctance to admit he didn't know all the answers: he knew as well as anyone that his only chance of reducing his sentence was to be as co-operative as possible. 'So Kallmann could still be alive?' Cormack asked.

'From what I can recall of his dossier, I would not be at all surprised. It described him as being - let me see.' He paused for a moment, closing his eyes as he tried to remember the exact words. 'Resourceful and intelligent. Certainly, he escaped from some very narrow scrapes in Crete and Yugoslavia, for example.'

'I see,' Cormack said slowly. 'Was Kallmann part of a team, or did he work alone?'

'There were two others - they formed a virtually permanent team. Klaus Schell and Monika Huber.'

Cormack made a note of their names. 'Can you tell me anything more about either of them?'

'Very little. Schell seems to have been working with Kallmann throughout the War - both were transferred to Special Services at the same time - while Huber arrived on the scene in early nineteen forty-three. As far as I recall, Huber lived in Berlin, but I don't remember the address.'

***

'-So, if we've got an accurate identification on this Kallmann, then we've got an experienced assassin on the loose in Berlin at this very moment,' Cormack said, staring out of his office window at the courtyard.

Behind him, Galvin shifted anxiously in his seat. 'I see what you mean, sir. Only-' He hesitated.

Cormack turned to face him. 'Yes?' he prompted.

'If we're right and Kallmann *did* fly in secretly the other night, why is he needed? If we assume that Fairhurst is involved in all this, then presumably he wants Kallmann to assassinate someone, yes?'

'Seems logical.'

'But they already had a marksman - Mohrer. Now I know Kallmann didn't arrive until after Mohrer was - er - eliminated,' Galvin said, nodding apologetically at Cormack. 'But, by the looks of it, they'd arranged for Kallmann to come in some time before that. So why did they need *two* marksmen?'

'They didn't,' Cormack said succinctly. 'They only needed one. Kallmann is an experienced, proven assassin, while Mohrer was no more than a sniper. He was good enough for knocking Logan off, but he didn't even have his escape route properly organised. I know he was almost certainly left in the lurch for us to take, but Kallmann would have organised his get-out personally - he wouldn't have relied on someone else. Kallmann's a professional - and that was what they wanted.'

'If that's the case-'

Cormack nodded. 'Then they're after somebody pretty big. I would guess that they - whoever 'they' are - are either paying

Kallmann a hell of a lot of money to come back to Berlin - he's on the Wanted List, after all - or the intended victim is someone he'd like to kill anyway.'

'Yes, but who?'

'That's the big question. I don't think we'll find an answer to that until we sort out who's sent Kallmann in. Who's behind Fairhurst, in other words. I don't think we can go on treating this is just another black market operation.'

Galvin nodded soberly. 'Agreed, sir.'

'I'll tell you what else worries me,' Cormack continued, leaning back in his chair and clasping his hands behind his neck. 'Kallmann, a skilled ex-Nazi assassin - or maybe not so 'ex', I suppose - flew in from the west on a covert flight arranged by an Englishman and involving British pilots and aircraft.'

'Good Lord, sir, I see what you mean,' Galvin said, appalled. 'We really are moving in deep waters, aren't we? What the devil is going on?'

'I wish to hell I knew. Maybe Fairhurst could tell us - if he's still in Berlin, which I doubt. We'll still have to step up the search for him, though. Get in touch with the French and Americans and notify them about Kallmann, Schell and the Huber woman - if we can get a lead on any of them, we'll at least have something to go on.'

Galvin nodded. 'Do we know anything about Schell and Huber?'

'A bit. Schell ended up with the rank of Hauptsturmfuehrer - Captain - but like Kallmann, the rank was largely in recognition of services rendered. He was Kallmann's organisation man, apparently, the one who set up the logistics of any operation they took part in. Communications, safehouses, that sort of thing. The 'Can-do' man.

'Monika Huber was in the Strength Through Joy programme.' He paused, raising an eyebrow archly at Galvin who nodded, smiling faintly. The Strength Through Joy programme had been basically an official prostitution institution, where 'Aryan' women - tall, blonde and blue-eyed - were provided in various 'rest camps' for the benefit of SS members, all of whom had to be a hundred per cent Aryan themselves. The programme was intended to produce an Aryan super race, and, indeed, several hundred children had been born as a result of it, but the entire project was generally regarded as no more than a perk of being an SS member by those who found themselves being sent to one of the camps. 'There are references in the records to Huber having two children, one in forty-one, the other a year later, but there's no evidence that she showed any interest in what happened to them,' Cormack continued. 'She probably met Kallmann in forty-three at one of the rest camps, and was recruited by him. They seem to have been lovers, but they sound a bit of a rum pair, because he used her as a seductress in various operations, apparently. They went their separate ways at the end of the War, though, so there's no guarantee that they're working together this time. It's just that if Kallmann is going to look up his old colleagues, Schell and Huber would be the most likely candidates.'

Galvin nodded briskly, 'In that case, we'll see what we can turn up.' He rose to his feet but then paused as Cormack continued:

'One more thing. Get hold of all details of all VIPs visiting Berlin in the next three months, let's say, just to be on the safe side. For all sectors - including the Soviet Sector.'

'That last one will be a bit tricky, sir.'

'I *did* realise that,' Cormack retorted ironically. 'But Kallmann's here for a reason - for someone, rather. We've got to try and figure out who.' He paused, then added quietly:

'And why.'

Chapter 8

Cormack tried, unsuccessfully, to smother a yawn, then looked at his watch; it was almost six and time he went back to his apartment. He had been reading through the dossiers on Klaus Schell and Monika Huber, but they had not told him anything that might have any particular relevance to the investigation: in any case, there was no guarantee that Kallmann was working with them this time. They could be in South America for all anyone knew...

Admit it, old son, we're getting nowhere fast with all this. Kallmann's had days now to go to ground, while Fairhurst is probably safely back in the UK by now. Heynckes hasn't come up with a bloody thing - and neither has anyone else. Cormack grimaced, a tacit acknowledgment of the truth of the argument: they were spending a hell of a lot of time and effort chasing shadows at the moment and whatever trails there had been were growing cold. He knew that Pallister was beginning to show signs of impatience at the progress - or, rather, the lack of it - being made and had sent a couple of memos to the effect that there were several other current investigations that needed pursuing. Perhaps it was time to scale it down...

Cormack sighed and was about to rise to his feet when there was a knock at the door and Elise came in, carrying some documents. For a moment, Cormack was taken by surprise - he had assumed everyone else had gone home - then realised that it was her half day tomorrow: she always stayed behind the evening before in order to clear her desk. 'Some documents for you to sign, sir,' she said. 'I was hoping I'd catch you before you left.'

'You only just did - I was just about to go.'

'Sorry if I'm holding you up, sir,' she said awkwardly. 'It's just-'

'No problem, Elise. Just hand them over and I'll do the necessary.'

'Thank you, sir.' She smiled briefly at him and he felt a sudden tingling sensation in the pit of his stomach. *Dammit, she still has that effect on me.* He took the documents from her and began to scribble his signature on the bottom of each sheet, trying to concentrate on what he was doing but all the while, he was acutely aware of her proximity, of her perfume, of the fact that the red dress she was wearing seemed to cling to her body, accentuating her breasts - and then the vivid, erotic dream that had awoken him during the night came back to him: Elise, naked, lying back on a huge bed, holding out her arms to him, drawing him down into her...

Come on, for Christ's sake, cut that out!

He finished signing the papers, then passed them back to her. 'There you are,' he muttered, more to prevent himself dwelling on the memory of the dream than anything else, but, just for a moment, their eyes met and there was something in her expression that startled him - warmth? maybe even a hint of invitation? - before she looked away.

'Thank you, sir.'

'It's all right,' he said, aware of the inanity of their conversation. 'I'll see you tomorrow afternoon, then.' *Jesus, you really are a smooth-tongued Casanova, aren't you? That line of patter is bound to sweep her off her feet, isn't it?*

'Yes, sir,' she replied, her expression neutral. She made as if to turn away, then hesitated. 'Oh, by the way, I don't know if you had heard, but that girl you helped the other night has discharged herself from the hospital.'

'Really?' Cormack asked, taken by surprise, not only by the news, but by the sudden change of subject. 'Was she well enough to leave? She seemed quite badly injured.'

'The doctors advised her against it, but she insisted,' Elise said. It was only now that he realised that she had been staring intently at him, her eyes completely opaque, as if studying his reactions to the information she had given him. 'I just thought you might like to know, sir.'

'Er - yes. Thanks.'

Elise's eyes held his for a moment longer, then she said abruptly, 'Good night, sir.'

'Good night.' Trying not to make it look too obvious, Cormack watched her as she went out. She really had got to him, he realised; just being in the same room as her was enough to start him behaving like a lovesick adolescent. What was it about her? OK, so she was attractive and intelligent and...

And she gave every impression of enjoying that kiss in the car, the way she had responded... There had been no need for her to do that unless she'd wanted to...

Abruptly, Cormack rose to his feet, taking his cap from the hat stand, walked rapidly out through the main office and emerged into the courtyard. He jumped into his jeep and drove out into the street, turning left. Elise had already walked past the tram stop; although public transport was supposed to operate up to six o'clock, she had evidently decided that there was no chance of catching a tram now. Cormack pulled up alongside her. 'Can I offer you another lift?' he asked.

She stared at him, the surprise on her face giving way to confusion. She looked away along the street, as if hoping to see a tram approaching, then, slowly, brought her eyes back to him. *Jesus Christ, she's going to say no*, he thought and his stomach seemed to turn over.

'All right,' she said quietly. 'That's very kind of you.' She climbed into the jeep and sat down next to him as he tried to stop a huge smile from spreading across his face.

He let out the clutch and drove off, sneaking occasional sideways glances at her, wondering again how he could have taken so long to realise how attractive she was... She caught him looking at her and smiled briefly, noncommittally. 'I'm not taking you out of your way, am I?' she asked.

'Not really,' he replied. He hesitated for a moment, then mentally shrugged and took the plunge. 'I wanted to talk to you.'

She nodded slowly, as if she had been expecting this. 'About what happened in the car last week,' she said, her voice totally without inflexion.

'Yes.'

'I thought you might.'

'I just wanted to say... Look, if I offended you, I apologise.'

'You didn't offend me.' A momentary smile, instantly switched off. 'It was rather flattering, actually.'

No more than that? he wanted to ask, but did not: perhaps what he had interpreted as a genuine response on her part had been nothing more than compliance, a feeling that she could not afford to offend her boss.

'Look... You've probably realised that I find you very attractive, but if you don't want to know because of... well, because of what's happened since, just say so. Don't feel you have to put up with me pestering you just because you're my secretary - I'm not that sort of bloke.'

'I know you're not,' she said quietly. 'I never thought you were.'

'Oh. Right.' He glanced across at her again, but she was staring straight ahead through the windshield giving no indication of her thoughts. He carried on driving, trying to think of how could rephrase the question without appearing too persistent: *never my strong suit, talking to women,* he thought sardonically. It was only when he brought the jeep to a halt outside her apartment block that he twisted round in his seat to face her and said gently, 'You didn't answer my question.'

'What, about you pestering me?'

'Yes.'

She stared appraisingly at him for several seconds. 'You're not exactly pestering me, are you? You're only giving me a lift home, after all.'

'Am I?'

She looked away, then shook her head slowly. 'No, you're right. You're not just giving me a lift,' she said quietly.

'Like I said, if you want me to leave you alone, just say so.' He could feel himself tensing, appalled at the way he had left himself wide open, sensing that this was it, the moment when he would know for certain.

She stared through the windscreen, then shook her head again. 'No,' she said softly. 'I don't want you to do that.' She turned her face towards him. 'I don't want you to leave me alone at all.'

***

It was beginning now. Cormack felt her first internal movement, heard the low moan that escaped from her slightly parted lips and began to thrust into her more rapidly, more urgently. She gasped and coiled her slim legs around him, her hips arching convulsively as she clung on to him, sobbing loudly, her body writhing frantically under his until he could stand it no longer and seemed to explode inside her in a long, draining orgasm.

Gradually, their movements slowed and he looked down into her shining eyes. 'OK?' he murmured hoarsely.

'Mmm,' she purred languorously. 'You could say that... You?'

He chuckled and kissed her softly, on her lips. 'Can't complain.'

'I should hope not,' she grinned. Her eyes searched his face, then, softly, she said, 'Thank you.'

'My pleasure - and how.'

'No, listen. Thank you - for being so marvellous.' She touched his cheek, gently. 'It was wonderful.'

He stared down at her, feeling suddenly awkward - *what the hell do you say to something like that?* 'So were you,' he said quietly, then kissed her again, feeling a sudden wave of tenderness. It hadn't just been sex, he realised: there had been warmth and affection there as well. They had made love, not just had it off...

Carefully, he withdrew from her, then twisted round onto his back in the narrow confines of the single bed. She snuggled in against him, in the crook of his arm, her head resting on his shoulder. Neither said anything for a while, but, eventually, she murmured, 'I don't suppose you expected this to happen tonight.'

'No, I didn't,' he admitted. 'I didn't even know if you liked me, let alone anything else.'

'Oh, I liked you all right - that was the trouble.'

'What do you mean?'

'I mean that I knew that if I let anything start with you, then this would happen.'

'And you didn't want to become involved with someone like me, is that it?' he said gently. 'Someone who was a bit too handy with a gun?'

She hesitated, then nodded. 'That did come into it, yes, even though I don't think there was anything else you could have done on either count. It did make you a little... frightening, I suppose. But I was still attracted to you, although I tried to convince myself I wasn't. In any case, that wasn't the reason I wasn't sure about whether I wanted anything to happen between us.'

'So what *was* the problem?'

'It would cause complications. You're British, I'm German, you're my boss, to begin with, I didn't even know if you're married - all sorts of things.'

'I see,' he said, stroking her hair. 'Just for the record, I'm *not* married.'

'I'm glad about that,' she chuckled. Then, more seriously, 'But you know what I mean. This could cause trouble for both of us.'

'Only if we let it. I don't mind if you don't.'

She raised her head to look at him. 'I don't mind now. It's too late for that, anyway, isn't it?' She shrugged. 'I suppose this had to happen.'

Cormack stared at her, hearing an undertone of melancholy in her voice. 'You sound as if you're regretting it.'

She shook her head. 'No, I'm not. Really.' She smiled, her eyes soft, glowing. 'I wanted you. I have done for a while now, to be honest. I'm not going to fight it any more. I don't think I could now, anyway.'

'I'm flattered,' he grinned.

She grinned impishly. 'So you ought to be. It's not every man who has me behaving like a wanton harlot. You never even got your coffee,' she reminded him, her eyes twinkling.

Cormack chuckled. 'No, I didn't, did I?' That had been the pretext for his coming into the apartment, an offer of a cup of coffee - 'only *ersatz*, I'm afraid,' but, somehow, they had been in each other's arms almost as soon as the apartment door had closed: within minutes, they had been naked, in bed, exploring each other hungrily. 'I was looking forward to it, as well,' he grinned.

'Do you want me to get you a cup now?' she asked, smiling, but made no move to get up.

'No thanks. I think I can manage without.'

'Good.' She lowered her head onto his shoulder again and began running her hand lightly across his chest. 'Do you know something?' she said dreamily. 'I don't even know what to call you.' She giggled. 'Or do I still call you sir?'

'Hardly,' he chuckled. 'Alan's the name.'

'I know.'

'Really?'

'Really. We have our little ways of finding things out, we secretaries. Apart from that, I saw the original order transferring you to us. Captain Alan Cormack. But that's about all I do know about you, I'm afraid. Well, apart from the fact that you're a pretty fantastic lover.'

'You're not so bad yourself,' he grinned, squeezing her shoulder affectionately.

'It's not fair,' she said in mock petulance. 'I expect you've read my file and know everything there is to know about me.'

'Not exactly everything,' he protested mildly.

'But how much *do* you know?' she asked quietly, and Cormack sensed the importance of the question, at least to her. 'I've never seen my dossier,' she added, almost wistfully.

'No, I don't suppose you have.' He shrugged. 'I know when and where you were born, where you went to school, when you were married - all that sort of thing.'

'Just about everything, you mean.'

He shook his head. 'I know the historical facts, Elise. That's all. I still don't know the real Elise Langemann.'

'Are you sure you want to?'

'Yes, I am,' he said softly.

She was silent for a while, then, suddenly, she lifted her head from his shoulder again and positioned it on the pillow so that she could see his face. 'All right,' she said briskly. 'What sort of things would you like to know?'

He grimaced ruefully. 'Whatever you want to tell me.'

'Like what?'

He thought for a moment. 'Like - where did you learn to speak English so well?'

'Flatterer - it's nowhere near as good as your German. You'd pass for a native, you know.'

Just as well - it got me out of trouble more than once during the War. 'Now who's being flattering?'

'It's true. You've even got a Berliner accent.'

He grinned. 'Look, I thought we were supposed to be talking about you.'

'I'd rather talk about you,' she said seriously. 'You've got a head start on me. I don't even know how old you are, where you come from - nothing.' She paused, then added, 'Actually, there's one question that's been bothering me ever since you took over as my boss.'

'What's that?'

She hesitated. 'I'm not sure how to put this... How did you become an officer in the British Army? I mean, I'm not trying to be rude, but... well, you don't fit the image of a British Army officer at all. You don't talk like them, for one thing-' She broke off at his sudden giggle. 'What's so funny?'

'Of course I don't talk like them - I'd shoot myself if I did. I didn't go to public school, you see. The local grammar school, that was me - and lucky to get in there as well.'

'You come from a poor family?'

'Yes,' he said quietly. 'They were all killed during the Blitz.'

She reached out and touched his cheek. 'I'm sorry.'

'It's OK. It was a while ago now. I'm afraid you get used to it - not having them around. It's not that I don't miss them, but...' His voice trailed away.

'But you'd rather not talk about it?' she suggested softly.

'But I'd rather not talk about it,' he agreed heavily.

'All right,' she said thoughtfully. 'So, to get back to my original point - how did you become an officer?'

'I volunteered on the day war was declared,' he said simply. 'My patriotic duty and all that. The Army found out I was fluent in French and German and sent me out with the BEF as a liaison officer with the French. They had to give me a commission because the French were a bit touchy about dealing with someone who wasn't an officer. I sort of sneaked in by the back door, really.'

She nodded slowly. 'I wondered... It isn't just the way you talk, it's your whole attitude. You're not so bothered about military etiquette, for example. It doesn't seem to bother you if subordinates don't call you 'sir' or don't stand to attention. You also don't keep going on about what you did in the War, unlike most of them - in fact, you don't really ever say much about yourself at all, do you?'

'Occupational hazard, I suppose. Comes from working in Intelligence.'

'Maybe...' she said sceptically. 'So - you were, let me see, twenty-five, when the War started? What were you doing before that?'

'Working for an import/export firm in London.'

'Because you were trilingual?'

'Well, it did come in handy, I suppose.'

'Where did you learn French and German?'

'At school - I just seemed to have an ear for them, somehow.'

'So you were in the Army - how did you get into Intelligence work?'

'A very good question, that... Again, it was because of the languages. SOE collared me when it was set up and, like an idiot, I volunteered for overseas duty.'

'Working with the Resistance, you mean.'

'Right,' he said gravely. 'They sent me for an assessment course with the Royal Marines and they - the Marines, that is - kept me on for advanced Commando training.'

'You must have done very well.'

'I'm not sure the skills I learned are anything to be proud of... Anyway, I worked for SOE, went into Occupied Europe on various undercover ops, then got out when the War ended.' *Various undercover ops... Jesus Christ, why don't you tell her the truth, that you were shit-scared just about all the way through them, that your idealistic notions of Duty to King and Country lasted about six hours into your first operation behind enemy lines...* The only reason he had carried on with the bloody things was because he was too damn good at them - he kept on coming back with the goods and didn't have the nerve to say no when they asked him to go out again... Didn't want to admit he was afraid. 'I was in civvy street for a while,' he said, rushing on in an attempt to push the brooding thoughts out of his mind, 'but then they roped me back in - the Army, that is - for this lark.'

She stared at him thoughtfully. 'I have the feeling that you've left an awful lot unsaid.'

'I suppose I have, yes.'

'And it's going to remain unsaid?'

'If you don't mind.'

'Of course not. It's just that I... I really would like to get to know you now that...' She shrugged awkwardly. 'Well, you know.'

'Now that you've succumbed to my evil charms, you mean?'

'Something like that, yes. Or am I reading too much into this?' she asked anxiously.

'What do you mean?'

'Well... for all I know, this might be all you wanted. A quick roll in bed, then thank you and goodnight.'

He stared at her. 'Do you think that's all I want?'

She hesitated, then said, 'I don't think so, no, but...' Her voice trailed away uncertainly.

'But you don't know me well enough to say for sure, right?' he grinned.

She smiled in response. 'Something like that, yes. Why do you think I've been trying to find out about you?'

'Well, let me put it this way. If we were to call it a day after only one night, as it were, I'd be disappointed, to put it mildly.' He stared into her eyes, then kissed her gently on the lips. 'I'm not really one for one night stands, you see.'

'Neither am I,' she replied, her eyes sparkling. 'Although, come to think of it, you're probably thinking I am, the way I behaved earlier on.'

'I'm not complaining.'

'Believe it or not, I'm not usually that... eager. Although that sounds terrible, doesn't it? Anyone'd think I was bringing men back here all the time - and I don't.'

For a moment, Cormack thought of Metcalfe - *had he been here, like this?* - then pushed the thought aside. 'It's none of my business,' he said, gently.

'But I don't want you thinking I'm... you know... easy. To be honest, you're the first lover I've had for - well, a long time. It's just that...' She hesitated and looked away for several seconds before she fixed her eyes on his. 'It's just that, as I said, I wanted you so much. You're special, Alan - I want you to believe that. That's why I was so-' she grimaced wryly, '-so... welcoming... tonight.'

He grinned, then touched her cheek gently. 'I'm very flattered - and pleased. Tonight's been pretty special for me as well.'

'I'm glad.' Her eyes held his, then, slowly she brought her face closer to his and kissed him, her tongue probing deeply, erotically, into his mouth. As their lips clung together, she rolled over on top of him. She looked down at him, planting little kisses on his face and mouth, feather light touches of her lips. 'Tonight has been special,' she murmured throatily, reaching down with her hand into his groin, touching his growing erection, caressing him gently. 'But it isn't over yet,' she said, grinning mischievously at him. She drew up her knees, kneeling astride him, then, positioning him with her hand, guided him into her, lowering herself slowly, exquisitely down onto him; he closed his eyes momentarily as he savoured her moist, enclosing warmth. 'How does that feel?' she asked, smiling down at him, her head tilted interrogatively to one side.

'Beautiful,' he murmured. 'And so are you.'

'You say the nicest things,' she chuckled. She leaned forward, her hair brushing his face as her mouth searched hungrily for his, then, slowly, langourously, she began to move to and fro.

Chapter 9

Cormack was aware of a distinct sense of well-being when he reached his office the following morning; he had even found himself whistling as he'd stepped out of the jeep. The sun was shining, pale and wintry in the sky, and everything seemed brighter, clearer somehow this morning... And he was still behaving like a lovesick adolescent, he realised, stifling a grin as he pushed open his office door. *One night with a woman and you're walking around with a silly grin on your face...* Only it hadn't just been with a 'woman'; it had been Elise, and he knew that something special had come into his life.

Or are you fooling yourself, sunshine? Isn't this just the rosy glow you feel at the beginning of any relationship? How long is it going to be before it begins to fade?

He pushed the niggling doubts aside - he'd cross that bridge when he came to it, if he ever did - and sat down, still aware of a smile that was trying to escape across his face. *Like the cat that got the cream...*

Come on, old son, get a grip on yourself - you're supposed to be working... Sighing, he picked up the top document in his In tray, but, before he could begin reading it, there was a knock at his door and Galvin came striding in.

'We might have located Monika Huber,' he said, a barely suppressed grin of triumph on his face. 'There's someone calling herself Marta Haller living in Taubertstrasse in Wilmersdorf. Apparently, that was one of the operational names she used during the War.'

'Hardly conclusive,' Cormack pointed out. 'I don't suppose it's an uncommon name.'

'It isn't,' Galvin agreed. 'But there's a resemblance between the photo in Marta Haller's file and the one we've got of Huber. Not conclusive, maybe, but I reckon it's worth following it up. We're checking the background now.'

'Checking her background?' Cormack said sharply. 'What exactly do you mean by that?'

Galvin stared at him, nonplussed, then said, 'We see what else we can come up with in the Records and at the *Kommandantura*, maybe have a discreet word with her neighbours-'

'Forget that last part. A hunt through the files, yes, but I want her handled with kid gloves. If she is Monika Huber, the last thing we want is to alarm her by talking to the neighbours. If she gets to know about it, we could lose our only lead to Kallmann.' He paused, then shrugged. 'That's always assuming she's the one we're looking for - and also assuming she's working with Kallmann anyway.'

'Well, if she *is* Monika Huber, then why's she using a false identity? To hide something?'

'*If*,' Cormack said firmly. 'Let's get a positive identification before we start going off half-cock.'

Galvin stared at him dubiously. 'Does that mean we don't put her under surveillance at all?'

Cormack thought for a moment, then said, 'It'll have to be discreet. If it is Huber, then she'll have had training in detecting surveillance, so I don't want some clodhopping novice whose idea of disguise is a false moustache tipping her off that she's being watched. Put Watson and his team onto it - but make damn sure they know they're not to be spotted.'

Galvin nodded soberly, his earlier enthusiasm rapidly evaporating now he realised that they were still a long way from finding Kallmann. 'I'll get it set up, sir.'

***

'Sit down, Cormack,' Pallister said, nodding briefly towards the chair in front of his desk. Cormack did so, eyeing the folder that lay on the desktop. It had no title, but it was not difficult to guess what it contained: the reports he had been sending Pallister on the investigation into Fairhurst and Kallmann. It was also not difficult to guess why he had been summoned here, either...

'This Kallmann business,' Pallister began without preamble. 'I'm a little concerned about the amount of time and effort that is being devoted to it by your Unit. In particular, I'm worried about how much time you're spending trying to locate Kallmann. Shouldn't you be concentrating on Fairhurst?'

'We are doing all we can to find Fairhurst,' Cormack replied levelly. 'But I'm convinced that Kallmann is the more important of the two. Everything that's happened so far - killing Logan, setting up the flight into Berlin - has been because of the need to get Kallmann sent here under conditions of absolute secrecy. He's the key to all this.'

'If it *is* Kallmann we're looking for,' Pallister retorted. He held up his hand to forestall Cormack's protest. 'I know, I know. Your friend Woodward claims he is ninety per cent certain it was Kallmann on his plane, but how certain are *you*, Cormack? Firstly, Woodward admits he only caught a clear glimpse of his passenger's face for a few seconds at a distance of thirty feet or so - at night. Secondly, Woodward suffered some concussion later on the same evening, so how reliable is his recollection of that night's events? There is a very real possibility that it was not Kallmann at all - you know that as well as I do.'

'Woodward would not have picked him out at all unless he was certain it was Kallmann,' Cormack replied.

'So you say - I'm less easily convinced, I'm afraid. Supposing you and Woodward are wrong? You could be expending a good deal of effort and energy on a wild goose chase. For all we know, Kallmann could have been dead for the past three and a half years, or be living under an assumed name in South America. You're following an extremely tenuous lead in the first place - and now I understand you've put Watson onto watching an apartment that might - I repeat *might* - belong to an ex-colleague of Kallmann's? Don't you think you might be taking this a bit too far?'

'Perhaps I am,' Cormack acknowledged, suddenly realising how stilted and artificial his voice sounded. Was he deliberately suppressing his East End accent for once, refining his voice so that it would carry more weight with Pallister? Very probably... 'The point is, sir, that if Braun *is* Kallmann, then we have a major problem on our hands, because we're talking about a top-line marksman on the loose. He could be after anybody - or anything. We can't afford to ignore the very real possibility that he's here in Berlin.'

'Humph,' Pallister grunted irritably. 'On the other hand, all this could simply be a black market operation, in the which case, it's a matter for the Military Police, not us.'

'I don't think it's simply a black market thing,' Cormack said firmly, shaking his head. 'They've killed one British pilot, tried to kill a second and taken pot shots at British MPs - that isn't the black marketeers' style. In any case, if it was Kallmann on the plane, he's not going to be involved in some tin pot black market set-up.'

'If it *was* Kallmann,' Pallister repeated. 'It could have been anyone, yet, on the basis of a two or three second look at someone's face at night, you've got the entire Unit engaged on a hunt for just one man. Rather putting all your eggs in one basket, aren't you, Cormack? It would probably be a better idea simply to turn it over to the MPs and let them handle it while you focus on Fairhurst. Better still, turn that over as well - this is really a police matter now, rather than intelligence, isn't it?'

'With respect, sir, Mohrer shot at *our* personnel, and Logan was *our* prisoner. We're involved in it, like it or not.' Cormack stared levelly at Pallister for a moment, then said firmly, 'I would also like to remind you that this is *my* investigation and, unless you formally take me - and my Unit - off it, I'll continue to carry it out. Sir,' he added, as a calculated afterthought.

Pallister gazed back at him with no trace of expression. 'I see,' he said blandly. 'On your own head be it. As you say, it is your investigation - but I still have the final say as regards policy decisions.' He paused, then leaned forward in his seat, clasping his hands together on the desk in front of him. 'You have one week, Cormack. One week. If, by the end of that time, you have still not made what I would consider to be worthwhile progress, I will indeed take you off the investigation - officially. I will also request your immediate transfer away from Berlin, because I'm beginning to have serious doubts as to whether we can work together effectively - if at all. Is all this clear to you, Cormack?'

'Perfectly, sir.'

'It had better be. One week, Cormack. That's all you have. You'd better come up with something, for your own sake.'

'Yes, sir.'

Havel Lake, Berlin

'Watch this,' Cormack said to Elise, then bent down to pick up a flat pebble from amongst those at his feet. He grinned boyishly at her. 'Let's see if the old throwing arm still has its magic.' He walked to the edge of the lake, positioning the stone in his hand as he drew back his right arm, crouching slightly before he brought the arm whipping forward to skim the stone across the water. The pebble threw up five splashes before it finally disappeared from view.

'Very good,' Elise said, grinning.

'Just one of my many skills,' he said lightly, coming back to her.

'Learned on holiday at the seaside, I take it?' she asked. 'Did your family go on holiday much before the War?'

'A few times,' he answered, wondering if she would notice he was being evasive. There'd been the odd day trip or weekend away at Southend or Clacton, but nothing more than that; he'd really learned to skim stones on the banks of the Thames at Stepney, in amongst the piles of the wharves...

'We did too,' she said, linking his arm in his. Cormack took the opportunity to give her a long look. She was wearing a belted grey coat that had obviously been expensive when new but which was, inevitably, beginning to show signs of age - its colour slightly faded, a moth-hole on the right shoulder; for all that, she still looked damned attractive... They began to walk along the shore again, looking out over the lake. 'We went to the Baltic Coast just about every year,' she continued. 'Warnemunde, Stralsund, Zinnowitz, but I think my favourite was Sassnitz. It's on the island of Rugen,' she explained; Cormack nodded. 'They had a huge beach there - you could swim or sail or just lie in the sun.' There was a wistful note in her voice. 'I'd like to go back there some day - but that's impossible at the moment, of course.'

Cormack nodded again. Apart from a short stretch between Lubeck and the Danish border, all of pre-war Germany's Baltic coast was in the Soviet Zone now.

The sound of an aircraft distracted them and they turned to watch the plane as it came in low over the lake to land at Gatow on the opposite shore. It was a four-engined job, possibly one of the Haltons Woodward had been complaining about; they were steadily taking over from the Dakotas on the civilian flights these days. Momentarily, Cormack wondered what Woodward was doing now; he had been released from hospital and had flown back to Hamburg a few days before with instructions to take it easy for a couple of weeks. Cormack had hoped that it would also keep Woodward out of the way of any possible further attempts to kill him, but, in all honesty, he was probably safe enough now that he had passed his information on. Killing him would accomplish nothing except stir things up again, but there was still an outside chance they would try again. Not that that would be enough to make Woodward go into hiding; knowing him, he would still he flying into Berlin two or three times a day... Cormack and Elise watched the plane until it had disappeared from view, then continued walking along the shore, hand in hand now, neither of them saying anything for a while.

Cormack grinned wryly to himself as he remembered his momentary disappointment when she had suggested going for a walk this afternoon - if truth be told, he had been looking forward to another passionate session in bed: they had already spent a second night together, the evening before last, and he had been delighted anew at her uninhibited lovemaking. He did not really mind this turn of events, however, because he felt pleasantly relaxed just being with her, enjoying her company, getting away from the investigation if only for an afternoon. And he needed to forget about it for a while, he thought gloomily, because the week's deadline Pallister had imposed on him had only forty-eight hours to run and, unless the surveillance on the flat in Taubertstrasse came up with something, that would be it...

Come on, old son, you promised yourself you wouldn't think about any of that this afternoon, so stick to it... He squeezed her hand affectionately and smiled to himself as he saw her pleased response. They had left the jeep about half an hour before and had just walked along the shore, talking and occasionally kissing: for the moment, it was more than enough. It was almost like being an eighteen year old again, that lost innocence when holding hands was a thrill, and a French kiss meant things were really serious...

He liked being with her, that was all there was to it. He didn't feel the need to try and impress her, he could just be himself for once... And yet he couldn't, he realised with a tinge of regret. Not completely; otherwise he would not be evading questions about his family and childhood the way he was. Was he ashamed of it, because Elise had obviously come from a middle-class family that could afford annual holidays? Worried that she'd look down on him, even though he was her boss?

Very probably...

'Sassnitz was where I lost my virginity,' she said suddenly, startling him out of his reverie. She laughed at his reaction. 'You should see your face, Alan,' she said, her eyes glinting mischievously.

'Well, it *was* a bit of a conversation stopper,' he said, grinning wryly.

'I thought it would get you out of your brown study,' she said, still smiling impishly.

'Too right it did.'

'It's true, though,' she said, looking out over the lake. 'Hans, his name was. He was a local boy - tall and very good looking. He seduced me in the sand dunes one hot afternoon.' She turned back to face him. 'In case you're wondering, no, I didn't enjoy it. The sand got everywhere, if you see what I mean?'

'Er - yes, I think I do,' he stammered, taken aback once more.

'You're looking embarrassed again,' she said, chuckling, watching his face. 'Do I offend you? Would you rather I was more - ah - discreet? After what we've done in bed?'

'No,' he said, forcing a grin. 'I like you just the way you are.' Except that what she had said was true; she was capable of surprising, even shocking, him by her direct approach about matters sexual. He found it both disturbing - and exciting; certainly he had not met anyone like her before.

'Good,' she said, then turned towards him, clasping her hands around his neck. Gently, she kissed him, pressing herself against him, as if reminding him that they were lovers, that what she had been talking about was a long time ago. She looked up into his face, that impish glint in her eyes again. 'So what about you?' she asked.

'What do you mean?' he retorted, knowing exactly what she meant.

'Your first time. When was it, or would you rather not say?'

'I can't remember. I was probably drunk at the time, so I doubt if I enjoyed it much either.' The last part was true at any rate, he thought bleakly. His first had been Maggie Chandler in the back alley behind the local pub, the same as virtually every boy in the street, over in a couple of minutes without even getting his trousers off...

Elise stared at him, her expression opaque, yet Cormack had the sudden conviction she knew he was lying - but this was not the time for Maggie Chandler: he'd been lucky not to catch a dose from her, for Christ's sake... Elise shrugged, as if dismissing the matter, then smiled provocatively. 'I hope you enjoyed your last time, anyway,' she said archly.

He frowned and scratched his head. 'Well... I'm not sure if I can remember that far back.' He checked his watch with exaggerated care. 'It *was* thirty-six hours ago, you know.'

She pulled a face and punched him playfully on the arm. 'You're impossible.'

'I know,' he agreed cheerfully. 'Hadn't you realised?'

'I'm beginning to, yes.' She shrugged. 'But I don't mind.'

'Just as well.' They kissed again, then pulled apart and carried on walking. A few yards further along, they rounded a small headland and saw a restaurant ahead, on the lakeside. Cormack looked at her. 'Coffee?' he asked.

She seemed to hesitate for a moment, then smiled and nodded. 'I'd love one.'

***

'Two coffees, please.'

'Two coffees,' the waitress repeated. 'Will that be all?'

'Yes, thanks.'

The waitress nodded and clicked away on her high heels. Cormack grinned at Elise. 'I don't think she knows whether to be disgusted because we only ordered coffee or relieved because we might have wanted something they didn't have.'

'Very true,' she agreed, smiling faintly. She looked around the restaurant, which, apart from themselves, only had half a dozen customers scattered around the tables. 'You know, this place used to be one of the busiest in Berlin. No matter what time of day it was, it'd be packed. They say Goebbels used to come here regularly - but every restaurant used to claim that. Now they try to say that they would have barred all Nazis if it hadn't meant being arrested by the Gestapo.'

'Of course,' Cormack agreed drily.

'You could hardly move in here sometimes,' she said wistfully. 'Now look at it.'

'It's the same in most places,' Cormack observed. 'Hardly surprising, really, is it? I don't suppose they can get hold of their *filet mignons* or Mouton Rothschild these days.'

'More likely they're not prepared to pay black market prices,' she said scornfully. 'Some cafes and restaurants don't seem to have much trouble serving luxuries, do they?' There was an undertone of bitterness in her voice that made Cormack look intently at her. 'They've got to be buying them from the black market, but nobody ever does anything about it, do they?'

'That's probably because the powers that be like going to these same places and eating their caviar or whatever. They're hardly going to close them down, are they?' he asked lightly.

'No, I suppose not,' she said, grimacing. 'But how do these supplies get through when we're going short of things like milk and eggs, let alone caviar?'

Cormack nodded soberly. 'I know what you mean, Elise. The thing is, the authorities have got other things on their mind. They're tending to turn a blind eye to pilots who bring in a few extra pounds of contraband because what they want is the rest of the payload. And the pilots involved see it as a legitimate bonus that doesn't do anybody any harm...' He broke off and grinned sheepishly. 'Anyway, what are we doing talking about this? Do we really want to talk shop?'

'Not really,' she chuckled, then reached out and covered her hand with his. 'Thank you for taking me out this afternoon.'

'Any time.' He returned her smile.

The waitress brought a tray over and Elise took a preliminary sip from her cup. She grinned. 'At least it's not *Blumenkaffee*.'

Cormack smiled as he lifted his own cup to his lips: *Blumenkaffee* - literally 'flower coffee', so called because, according to *Insulaner* humour, it was so weak that you could see the flower pattern in the bottom of the cup through it. 'It isn't,' he agreed.

Elise set her cup down and looked around the restaurant. 'Actually, I used to come here quite often in the early days of the War. I suppose that's why I noticed the change so much.'

'Would you rather go somewhere else?' he asked, mentally kicking himself: trust him to bring her to a place that might bring back unpleasant memories.

'No, this is fine.' But she was staring down at her cup, stirring the coffee abstractedly with her spoon. An awkward silence fell and Cormack decided to drink his coffee down rapidly so that they could move on and recapture the relaxed, carefree atmosphere they had generated beside the lake.

'I used to come here with Heinrich,' she said quietly, as if talking to herself, but Cormack sensed that she had been deciding whether to confide in him; another barrier between them was about to be demolished. 'While he was stationed in Berlin. Actually, we met not far from here.' She broke off, then smiled shyly at him. 'I expect you know all this anyway from my dossier.'

'I haven't read it - not the complete file, anyway,' he said quietly. 'I've only seen the digest, so I only know the bare outlines.'

'Such as?'

'Born 1920 in Hannover, maiden name Weber, about to start a university degree to study English and French when war broke out so you were drafted into the War Ministry as a secretary-typist. A bit of a waste of a future graduate, but I expect you were told it was your duty to the Fatherland, right?' He arched his eyebrows interrogatively.

'Something like that,' she agreed, grimacing. 'Not that I had any choice in the matter, anyway.' She folded her arms and rested her elbows on the table, leaning towards him. 'Go on.'

'You worked as a translator there, originally on newspapers and magazines, then you were given a low-level security classification that enabled you to work on intercepted signals. You met your future husband around Christmas, thirty-nine - the digest didn't say how, but-'

'It was at a dance,' she said, her eyes far away now as she remembered. 'A Christmas dance at the Ministry.' She shrugged. 'I was nineteen, he was a dashing Captain six years older than me. He swept me off my feet, I suppose.' She saw Cormack's expression and shook her head. 'Don't get me wrong - I don't regret marrying him or anything like that. It's just that I don't think I ever really stood a chance, if you see what I mean. I'd hardly had a real boyfriend before Heinrich, really.' She smiled quickly, nervously. 'That time with Hans in the dunes was more curiosity than anything else - it wasn't anything serious - so Heinrich was the first man I'd ever been seriously involved with...' Her voice died away as she stared across the restaurant, her eyes unfocused, then she shook her head as if recollecting herself. 'Anyway,' she continued briskly, 'we were married the following year - as I'm sure you know.'

He nodded. 'August. I forget the exact date.'

'The fifth.'

Cormack nodded again. 'You carried on working, but you were transferred to OKH headquarters at Zossen, along with your husband. He was posted to the Russian Front in 1941 as part of Guderian's staff.'

Elise inclined her head briefly. 'Yes. I remember Heinrich wondering if they had made a huge mistake invading Russia. He thought they'd bitten off more than they could chew.'

'He was right, too,' Cormack agreed gravely.

She seemed not to hear him. 'I remember we talked about having a child,' she went on and now Cormack had the impression that she was not talking to him so much as replaying her memories. 'We decided against it. We didn't want to bring a child into a world at war... At first, everything was fine. Operation Barbarossa was a huge success, the Army was advancing towards Moscow and the first time he came home on leave, he thought he'd been wrong after all, that it was all going to work. But then he was transferred to a front-line unit and the next time he came back, he seemed more distant, somehow... harder, I think,' she said quietly. 'He talked about wiping out tanks or divisions in a kind of casual, off-hand way, as if all those deaths didn't matter. I mean, yes, he was talking about the enemy, but he seemed to be turning into just another military automaton, like all the others - and he hadn't been when I'd met him.' She paused, then sighed and shrugged. 'Or maybe he *had* been - I don't know. He was an Army officer, I suppose... It's just that he seemed to be changing, growing more callous... like I said, harder. It wasn't just the way he talked, either - his love-making changed as well...' She broke off again, smiling nervously across at Cormack. 'At first I put it down to him having to go months without a woman, then I thought he was being selfish for wanting it so often, even if I didn't. It was only later, when it was too late, that I realised that he was just the same as all the others who fought on the Russian Front - he was terrified of going back there and wanted to make the most of every leave he had in case it was the last one he'd ever have.'

I know exactly how the poor sod felt, thought Cormack, then pushed the thought aside as he held up his hand. 'Look, Elise, you don't have to tell me all this, you know.'

'I know,' she said quietly, putting her hand on his again and squeezing gently. 'But I want to... if you don't mind listening?' She tilted her head to one side interrogatively. 'You fought in the War, Alan - don't you understand how he must have felt?'

He nodded slowly. 'Yes, I think I do.' *Only too bloody well...* When you knew you were going back out to fight, the only ways you could forget it for a while were sex or booze - or both. Yes, he could understand Heinrich Langemann's desire to make every second count with Elise, only it would have to be sex because there was no way that he could have talked to her about his fear because you just never admitted to it, not even to yourself, and even if you did, what the hell difference would it have made? He'd only have upset Elise - as well as talking about the very thing he wanted to forget - and he'd still have had to go back to the Front anyway, back to the hideous slaughter. So he'd have taken Elise to bed and he'd have wanted it two, three, four times a night because it might be one of the last chances he'd ever have to do it and because, if only for a few minutes, he could forget what was waiting for him...

Poor bastard...

'He wasn't so bad until after Stalingrad,' she said suddenly, her eyes unfocused, far away now. 'That was when he came back looking gaunt, with a haunted look in his eyes. That's when he said he'd been right all along, that Germany was going to lose the War. The next time he came back, he drank just about all the while he was home, all night binges sometimes. Or if he did go to sleep, he'd wake up in the night screaming and shaking. I tried to get him to apply for a transfer back to Berlin.' She gestured bitterly. 'Of course, I didn't know then that the only ones who managed that had influential friends in high places, so he would have been wasting his time anyway. He wouldn't do it, in any case - he said it would be deserting his men and he couldn't do that. I think he was more afraid of being thought a coward than anything else.'

Jesus, I do know exactly how he felt, thought Cormack. All of those missions behind enemy lines, wondering what the hell I was doing there, and the simple answer was that I didn't have the guts to say no... Or was it simply stubborn pride?

'He was killed outside Minsk in July, 1944,' Elise said bluntly, her voice very quiet now. 'I think he knew it would happen eventually - he'd stopped talking about what we'd do after the War a long time before that. I was upset when I received the telegram, but not as much as I'd thought I would be. It took me a while to realise that I'd actually lost Heinrich some time before...' Her voice tailed away and she stared blankly down at the table, apparently oblivious to the fact that she was holding his hand in a vice-like grip. Suddenly, she seemed to realise where and when she was and looked up into his eyes, her expression confused. She released his hand and shrugged awkwardly. 'Sorry about that, Alan. I'm sure you didn't really want to hear any of that.'

'Don't apologise. I suspect you probably needed to tell somebody.'

She blinked in surprise. 'Perhaps you're right... But I have rather spoiled the mood of the afternoon, haven't I?'

It was his turn to shrug. 'Don't worry about it. I'm actually quite flattered that you felt you could talk to me.'

She nodded slowly. 'I've always felt that. You're a very good listener, you know.' She forced a smile. 'Even if you don't give away very much about yourself.'

'There's not much to tell.'

'I doubt that, somehow,' she said thoughtfully, her eyes fixed intently on his face. 'Anyway, thank you for listening - and I apologise again for spoiling things.'

'You haven't,' he assured her.

'A liar... and a gentleman.' She reached out and touched his cheek, very gently, her eyes holding his. She added, very softly, 'And someone very special.'

Chapter 10

Cormack stood in the centre of the small room, looking silently around, trying not to let his despair show. It was a dingy room; there was no other word to describe it, with its faded wallpaper that was beginning to peel away in long strips, the patched armchair and sofa that did not match, the threadbare carpet and curtains. Even the view from the front window did nothing to dispel the general air of decay, looking out, as it did, on a pot-holed street that still had buildings in ruins from the Allied bombing raids. The rear view was even worse, if anything, reminding him of the industrial north of England, with tiny, grimy backyards that had lines of washing strung across them.

Yet this was where someone calling herself Marta Haller had apparently lived for two years, in a two room apartment on the third floor of what would be described as a tenement block back in the UK. The living-room also served as a dining-room, with a small scullery at the back, while the bedroom was off to one side; she would have had to use the shared bathroom and WC at the end of the landing. Pretty squalid, but, looked at another way, she could be said to have been damned lucky to find it, because there were still apartments in Berlin where five or six people were sharing a single room. But if Marta Haller was indeed Monika Huber, then it was a bit of a come down for her; according to the files, she and Kallmann had shared a fairly expensive flat during the War. She couldn't have liked living here much, Cormack reflected gloomily.

Couldn't have liked. Past tense. There was no way of being certain at the moment, of course, but Cormack had sensed an air of abandonment about the flat, a feeling of vacancy, almost from the moment he had entered it. Marta Haller no longer lived here: she would not be coming back. He was strangely convinced of that, although it was difficult to say why. There were still clothes in the wardrobe, a few tins of food in the larder, a couple of dozen candles that would have cost sixty or seventy pfennigs each on the black market, two packs of cigarettes that would be worth a small fortune for barter, even a small jar of genuine coffee, but...

But what? Why was he so certain that she had left, never to return?

It could be a part of the increasing pessimism he was beginning to feel about this entire investigation, of course. His deadline had exactly fourteen hours to run, if he was to take midnight tonight as being the end of the week Pallister had granted him; that was why he had decided to take action here. Watson's team had been observing the apartment for eight days now without a solitary sighting of Marta Haller and so Cormack's hand had been forced. Like it or not, he had to move in and find out where she was - and if she was, indeed, the woman they were looking for. The assistant *blockwart* had been only too willing to let Cormack and his team in once they had brandished their ID passes, but, ominously, he had not been able to identify Marta Haller from Monika Huber's photograph. On the other hand, he had only been working there for a month or so and had only seen Haller once or twice in all - and not for at least a week, as far as he could recall...

Cormack sighed, then started slightly at the sound of a muffled curse from one of Watson's men in the bedroom; the flat was being minutely searched, but, so far, had revealed nothing remotely suspicious: not from their point of view, at any rate, although it was a safe bet that the coffee and the nylon stockings in the wardrobe had come via the black market.

Not really what they were looking for, though...

He heard footsteps along the landing outside and turned around as Galvin came in with a thin, almost completely bald man in his fifties or thereabouts, whose eyes seemed to be flickering everywhere as he watched what was going on. 'Herr Dorfmann,' Galvin said. 'The *blockwart*,' he added.

Cormack nodded and took out the photograph of Monika Huber. He passed it to Dorfmann. 'Do you recognise her?' he asked, without preamble.

Dorfmann gave it the merest glance, then nodded. 'That is *Fraulein* Haller,' he said without hesitation.

Bullseye. Cormack glanced momentarily at Galvin and saw the same suppressed excitement he felt himself. 'You're sure?' Cormack asked.

'Absolutely.'

'Right,' said Cormack. 'When was the last time you saw her?'

Dorfmann frowned in puzzlement. 'I don't know for certain - last week some time. Why? What has she done?' he asked, looking from Cormack to Galvin, then back again.

Cormack ignored the question. 'Last week? Can you be more exact? Which day was it?'

Dorfmann frowned. 'I'm not sure... let me see. It must have been Monday or Tuesday last week - nine or ten days ago.'

'You don't know which?'

'Monday. '

Cormack's lips compressed themselves. Was that the truth or was Dorfmann simply plumping for that day so as not to be thought unco-operative? 'What were the circumstances? Can you remember?'

'I beg your pardon?' There was a timorous air about Dorfmann and Cormack thought he knew why: as a wartime *blockwart*, he would have been expected to furnish the Gestapo with detailed, accurate information about the tenants in his block - and God help him if he didn't. *Probably thinks I'm like them - he's terrified because he didn't understand the question...*

'When and where did you last see her?'

Dorfmann thought for a moment, then said, 'She was leaving the block with a man. They got into a taxi. It was about ten thirty in the morning.'

'Could you describe the man?'

'He was tall, wearing a grey raincoat and a hat. A fedora. Blue eyes.'

'His hair?'

'I couldn't see. He wore the hat all the while I saw him.'

'Did he go up to the flat?'

'No. He waited by the taxi. She came down as soon as it arrived.'

'She was expecting it, you mean?'

'Yes. The driver didn't sound the horn or anything.'

'Was she carrying any luggage?'

'No, just a handbag.'

'What was she wearing?'

'A navy blue coat.'

Cormack nodded thoughtfully: Dorfmann had not missed much, that was evident. 'So the taxi arrived, she came down the stairs, went out and climbed in, yes?'

'The man pushed her bell when he arrived.'

'Right. Did they say anything, either of them?'

'Not that I heard.'

'The taxi - did you get its number?'

'No.' The defensive air again.

Cormack sighed; that would have been too much to hope for, although if they could trace the cab driver, they'd be able to find out where he'd taken them... He reached into his coat pocket and took out a sheaf of photographs, which he spread out on the dining table. 'Take a look at these, please,' he said to Dorfmann.

The *blockwart* nodded and came over to the table. 'You want to know if any of these is the man who collected her, yes?'

'Yes.'

'Very well.' Dorfmann studied each one in turn, then picked up Kallmann's photo, frowning at it in concentration before he shook his head and replaced it. Cormack let out his breath slowly, only then realising that he had been holding it. Of the dozen photos, ten had been taken at random from the files, while the other two were of Kallmann and Schell. Obviously, he could just have shown those two to Dorfmann, but he couldn't take the chance of the *blockwart* picking one of them out simply because he was too scared to do otherwise. But by the look of it, this was going to be a dead end because he hadn't chosen any of them yet...

Suddenly, Dorfmann tensed, then picked up another photograph. He peered intently at it, then nodded slowly and turned to Cormack. 'I think this is the man I saw with *Fraulein* Haller.' He held it out to Cormack.

'You think? You're not sure?'

'Fairly sure. If it wasn't him, it was someone very like him.'

Cormack nodded, trying not to let his exultation show, because the photo Dorfmann had picked out was that of Klaus Schell - Kallmann's second in command.

They were back in business...

***

'Well, this is it,' Cormack said hesitantly, standing aside in the doorway to let Elise in. '*Chez* Cormack.'

She smiled as she went past him. 'Thank you, kind sir.' She walked into the living room and looked around. 'Very nice,' she said approvingly.

'I'm afraid I can't take all the credit,' he admitted, closing the door and going over to her to take her coat, the same grey one she had worn by the Havel. Underneath, she was wearing a navy blue dress that had obviously come from a high-class couturier's - but several years before; it had been some time since anyone had been able to buy Paris gowns in Berlin... 'I inherited the apartment from Major Metcalfe.'

She nodded again. 'He didn't do badly for himself, then, did he?' she commented, a faintly sardonic grin on her face.

'Privileges of rank, I suppose,' he replied, hanging her coat on a peg in the door. 'Help yourself to a seat,' he added, removing his own coat. It was then that it dawned on him that she was behaving very much as though this were the first time she had been here. The realisation brought a smile of pleasure to his face as he put his own coat on a hook.

'Can I get you a drink?' he asked, going over to the tray of bottles on the sideboard. 'Not a lot of choice, I'm afraid. Whisky, gin or schnapps - that's about it.'

'Is it real whisky?'

'Well, it's in a Johnny Walker bottle, but that doesn't necessarily prove anything these days.'

'Well, we might as well see if it is the real thing, I suppose.'

'Coming up.' He poured two drinks, then came over to her, handing her one of the glasses. '*Prosit.*'

'Cheers,' she said in English, touching her glass to his before she sipped the drink, watching him thoughtfully. 'Penny for them, Alan?' she asked.

'Pardon?' he said, perplexed, then grinned apologetically in realisation. 'Sorry. I was miles away.'

'I know. You have been all evening.' She shrugged. 'Don't worry about it. I haven't felt ignored or anything, but it's pretty obvious you've got something on your mind.'

'Well... yes, I suppose I have.'

'Is it the Kallmann investigation?' she probed gently.

'Doesn't really need too much figuring out, does it?' he asked, grimacing ruefully.

'Not really, no.' She hesitated, then asked, 'Is it Colonel Pallister again?'

He glanced sharply at her, then grinned wryly. 'No, not this time. Well, not especially, anyway. Ever since we got those identifications of Schell and Huber, he's not really said very much.' For a moment, the thought crossed his mind that he really ought not to be discussing his superior officer with her, but what the hell... 'No, it's not Pallister,' he continued. 'It's just that...' He looked away, marshalling his thoughts, then said, 'I suppose I was beginning to wonder if maybe Tony Woodward had been mistaken, that it hadn't been Kallmann after all, but getting those identifications confirmed that we've probably been right all along.'

'Shouldn't that please you?'

'It did - for a while. The trouble is, we're still no closer to finding Kallmann than we were before. If anything, we've gone a step backwards, because if Schell came to collect Monika Huber, it must have been to take her to Kallmann, which means she won't be back - assuming she comes back at all - until he's carried out whatever he's come here to do. We were too late getting on to her.'

'You would have been anyway,' she pointed out. 'Schell came for her the day before Kallmann flew into Berlin.'

'Exactly,' Cormack said grimly, staring down at his drink, absently swirling it around in the glass. 'According to Burgnich, Schell was - is - Kallmann's organiser, the logistics man. He sets everything up, safehouses, contacts, communications, rendezvous, the lot, so that Kallmann can just go in and carry out the job. Kallmann's involved in the planning, but it's still Schell who does the donkey work, clearing the way for him. Schell's been in Berlin at least a fortnight now, so how far along are they in their plans? That's what worries me. We know that Kallmann is almost certainly somewhere in Berlin, with his back-up team, ready to carry out an assassination, but we don't have a clue where he is or who he's after, but they wouldn't have brought someone like him in unless the target was somebody pretty important.' He shook his head. 'We've got a delicate enough situation here as it is - the last thing we want is a VIP getting himself shot dead by an ex-SS marksman.'

She nodded soberly. 'I think I see what you mean,' she said quietly. 'It's more than just an abstract piece of detective work, isn't it?'

'You can say that again. We've got to find him - but I don't have a single clue where to start looking, even.'

Elise stared intently at him for several seconds, then set her glass down on the sideboard. Wordlessly, she took his drink from his unresisting fingers, placed it next to hers, then put both arms around his neck and pressed herself against him. 'Worrying about it isn't going to find him any quicker, is it?' she asked, her eyebrows arched interrogatively.

'No,' he conceded slowly, slipping his arms around her waist. He twisted his mouth in a wry grimace. 'And I'm being a lousy host as well, aren't I?'

'Indeed you are,' she said lightly, her eyes twinkling. 'I thought you'd brought me back here to have your evil way with me, not talk shop.'

Reluctantly, he smiled. 'Believe it or not, that was the general idea.'

'Well, your idea of sweet nothings isn't very impressive.' Her teasing expression faded abruptly. 'Seriously, Alan, there isn't anything we can do about it tonight, is there?'

'No, there isn't.'

'So...' she said huskily, seductively, 'why don't we just relax and forget about Kallmann and Schell for a while, hey?' She began to unbutton his tunic, pressing her lips gently against his neck. 'How does that sound?' she murmured.

'Sounds pretty good to me,' he chuckled, trying to prevent himself from grinning hugely as he realised once again how wonderfully lucky he was to be here with her like this. What the hell had he been thinking about babbling on about Kallmann when here she was, ready and willing to make love? Gently, he put his hand under her chin and lifted her face to his, pressing his lips eagerly to hers. He could feel her slim body tight against him as they embraced, the kiss seeming to go on and on, her tongue flickering and darting against his, arousing him. Almost of its own volition, his right hand found its way between them and cupped her breast, gently kneading it. She moaned softly, deep in her throat and clung on even more tightly to him...

***

It was almost eight o'clock when Cormack returned home the following night; he had been working late, ploughing through the files that had been sent over from the British Commission archives on Schell and Monika Huber. They had not really revealed anything new, but you had to try everything... He closed the door behind him and took off his coat, hanging it on the peg in the door, remembering how he had done exactly the same thing for Elise the night before... His face creased into a smile of fond recollection, as he pictured her astride him, her hips moving urgently to and fro, her head tilted back as she climaxed, calling out his name in a frantic sob...

Now cut that out! He chuckled, deep in his throat, aware of a swelling in his groin as he went over to the sideboard and poured himself a drink, as much to take his mind off the powerful, erotic images as much as anything else. Pity she's working at the hospital tonight...

The telephone rang, and he stared at it for a moment, the thought crossing his mind that it might be Elise, phoning to tell him that she wasn't working after all and would he like to come over? *Fat chance...* He picked up the phone, stifling a yawn. 'Cormack here.'

A voice spoke rapidly in English. 'This is Fairhurst.'

Bloody hell...

Cormack was suddenly wide awake as the voice continued, 'Meet me at the warehouse at the southern end of Sternfelderstrasse in half an hour. Come alone.' There was a click and the line went dead, leaving Cormack staring disbelievingly at the receiver. *Jesus Christ...*

Fairhurst wanted to do a deal.

Sternfelderstrasse: where the hell was that? Cormack pulled open a drawer of his bureau and took out a street map of Berlin, which he folded, running his finger down the index until he found it: K10. He located the area on the map; it was in Siemensstadt, in the industrial district on the north bank of the Spree. It was an excellent place for a rendezvous, in that there would be nobody around at this time of night. *It's also an ideal place for an ambush... Wouldn't it be an idea to lay on some back-up?*

He hesitated a moment, then went back to the telephone and dialled Galvin's number, drumming his fingers impatiently on the sideboard as it rang; there was no reply. *Where the hell is he when I need him?* He slammed the receiver down, thinking rapidly. No time to ask for an arrest squad from the MPs - it would take too long by the time it had been authorised through channels...

And he was wasting time anyway - he'd be hard pressed to get there himself...

***

Cormack wrenched at the wheel, sending the jeep into a skidding turn at an intersection, and swore as the rear end swung outwards; he whipped the wheel back the other way to straighten up, then pressed his foot flat to the floor on the accelerator again. He flicked a glance at his watch and saw by its luminous hands that there were only ten minutes left before the rendezvous: there was no way of knowing whether Fairhurst - if it *was* Fairhurst - would wait beyond that time, but Cormack doubted it. There had been an urgency in the voice that had indicated haste and, in any case, there could only have been one reason for the thirty minute deadline: Fairhurst was giving him no chance at all to call up any support and so he would not hang around after that time in case Cormack arrived with half the MP force in tow.

So what the hell's Fairhurst playing at? What does he want?

To do a deal. Why else would he make contact?

In that case, why has he taken so long? He's been missing almost a fortnight now...

Which was a bloody good question, Cormack thought, changing down and braking hard before taking another corner. Perhaps he'd been ditched by his bosses - he knew too much, after all - and had gone into hiding while trying to use his black market contacts to get out of Berlin. They'd let him down and so he was using this last card, the offer of a deal, to get himself off the hook. He'd either want a way out of Berlin, or he'd be giving himself up in exchange for protection, but, either way, he would have to tell Cormack everything he knew - or no deal.

He was crossing the Rohrdamm Bridge now, the moonlit waters of the Spree stretching out on either side. Cormack kept his foot down along Rohrdamm, before spinning the wheel to take the jeep through a sliding left turn into Motardstrasse. Now, at last, he eased off on the throttle, slowing down gradually before he took another left turn into Sternfelderstrasse itself. The jeep's speed was down to less than ten miles an hour now, and he turned into a narrow side street about two hundred yards along, coming to a halt in the shadows. He turned off the engine, looked around slowly, then took out his Browning automatic, which he checked carefully before replacing it in its holster. He reached into the back of the jeep and took out a torch, then, removing the key from the ignition, he climbed out and walked silently back to Sternfelderstrasse, pausing at the corner to check the surroundings again.

This was an industrial area; the street consisted of old, high-walled factories and warehouses, but it was the building at the end of the street that Cormack was interested in, about a hundred yards away. There was an arched entrance in front of it that led into what was presumably a yard, but there were no gates; in all probability, they had been melted down during the War for munitions and never replaced. But it was not the gates that caught, and held, Cormack's attention - it was the large warehouse beyond, its silhouette ominous, sinister in the moonlight. Pure imagination, he told himself, and knew it, but the fact remained that now he was here, he did not want to go into that *bloody* place but he was going to have to, like it or not and he was wishing to Christ that he had called in some back-up after all, but it was too fucking late now, he'd wanted to be the big hero, hadn't he?

He took a long, deep breath, looked around once more, then began walking towards the warehouse, keeping to the shadows, his eyes constantly darting to and fro as he approached the arched entrance. Dammit, the bloody building *did* look sinister, towering like a black slab in the darkness above him, something out of a Gothic nightmare - he pushed the thought aside and concentrated on his surroundings. Of course, there could be twenty or thirty men concealed in the shadows, or behind the piles of rubble of the bombed-out factory on the right, but he might just catch a glimmer of movement that could give him some sort of indication of what he was walking into...

Nothing. No motion, no sound.

Slowly, Cormack passed through the entrance. There was a large yard to be right of the warehouse, which was too exposed for his liking, the only cover being three rusting lorries whose tyres had been removed, and a construction shack of some sort whose windows had long since been broken: Cormack didn't need to see the holes in the warehouse roof to know that it had been disused for some time.

He made his way down the left side of the building, still looking cautiously around, until he found a wooden door, halfway along, which was very slightly ajar. Cormack stepped up to it and placed his ear against it. There was no sound from inside, so, taking his gun from its holster, he carefully eased the door open.

Inside, it was almost completely dark, although areas of the floor were illuminated by moonlight shining in through holes in the roof. He flicked the torch on, holding it a foot or so away from his body, half expecting the deafening crash of a shot - but there was nothing. Letting his breath out in an unconscious sigh, Cormack looked around. The lower level was littered with dusty packing crates, cardboard boxes and scraps of paper, but there were several sets of scuffed footprints criss-crossing the floor indicating that the warehouse was not quite as disused as it first appeared. Suddenly, Cormack tensed as he half-glimpsed a movement on the fringes of the torch's beam and was in the act of lining up his gun when he realised it was only a rat.

He shook his head slowly, once again releasing a long breath in a conscious attempt to relax; he was too keyed-up by half...

The torch beam picked out a rickety wooden staircase leading up to the upper level overlooking the ground floor - and there were signs that it had been used recently, scuff marks on the planked steps. Cormack ignored the stairs for the moment and swung the torch through a three hundred and sixty degree arc to make sure there was nobody on the ground level. Then, he started moving towards the steps.

He had just reached them when there was a muffled sound from above - *what the hell was that?* - gone before he could even be sure he had heard anything. Cormack stood stock still, straining his ears but it did not come again. Playing the sound back in his mind did not help; it could have been anything - and he certainly would not find any answers down here... Carefully, gingerly, Cormack mounted the stairs, his gun at the ready as he came up through a hatchway onto the upper level. The holes in the roof cast patches of moonlight, so Cormack turned off the torch and pocketed it, waiting until his eyes had adjusted the gloom before he moved away from the hatch. He could even feel the hairs rising on the back of his neck as some primeval instinct activated his adrenal glands.

He froze momentarily as he discerned an open door ten yards away. Slowly, he moved forward, his eyes flickering constantly from side to side. Through the door was a small office, its desk covered in cobwebs and there, sitting on the floor, with his back propped against the desk, was Fairhurst, his face transfixed by a shaft of moonlight, almost as if someone had shone a spotlight on it. It was Fairhurst; Cormack had seen too many photographs of him in the files for there to be any doubt...

Fairhurst's throat had been cut, a long, scarlet gash that went almost from ear to ear and which was still oozing blood; his eyes were staring sightlessly towards the moonlight. In that moment, Cormack realised that the muffled sound he had heard had been Fairhurst trying to cry out, the scream cut off as the knife blade had sliced through his windpipe.

Afterwards, Cormack could never remember if he heard the merest whisper of sound behind him, or if it was simply his keyed-up survival instincts, but the next second, he spun on his heel in time to see a figure lunging at him from the shadows. Cormack saw the glint of metal in the moonlight from a knife blade, then reached out almost reflexively with his left hand to parry the thrust while he tried to bring up his gun with his right. Too late; as Cormack's hand clasped itself around his attacker's wrist, he felt a jarring impact against his right forearm and the Browning fell from his grasp to go skidding across the floor.

For an instant, the two men were locked in a frozen tableau as the killer tried to force the knife in towards Cormack's ribs, but then Cormack pivoted suddenly to his left, pulling back with his left hand. The other man was thrown off balance and crashed heavily into the wall as Cormack looked rapidly around for his gun. It was over by the stairway, but there was no time to reach it because the attacker had launched himself from the wall, his knife arm scything forwards and upwards towards Cormack's ribs. *Shit, he's fast*, Cormack thought, and twisted aside, avoiding the thrust, but the knifeman cannoned into him, sending the two of them sprawling to the floor, the other man's weight pressing down on Cormack. Desperately, Cormack grabbed hold of the killer's right wrist again, holding the blade away from him, then pressed his other hand against his opponent's chin and pushed upwards, teeth clenched as he tried to force the other man's head back. Slowly, he forced the knifeman over towards the left and, with a lunging twist, threw him to one side. In an instant, Cormack was scrambling across the floor towards his gun, but the other man was coming at him again so Cormack twisted onto his back, drew his knees up to his chest and then straightened his legs convulsively. His feet slammed into the attacker's head and shoulder and he fell back, letting out a cry of pain, the first sound either of them had made. Almost of their own volition, the fingers of Cormack's right hand closed around the gun and, as the other man brought himself up on one knee, his arm pulled back to hurl the knife, Cormack aimed the gun, two-handed, and loosed off two rapid shots, the noise deafening in the confined space. The first bullet slammed into the knifeman's shoulder, the second took him in the chest, their impact throwing him backwards, arms outflung, over the edge of the upper level to fall to the floor below.

Slowly, Cormack climbed to his feet, drawing in great gulps of air, then moved unsteadily to the edge of the upper floor and looked down. The knifeman was sprawled on the concrete floor below him, arms and legs at impossible angles, but, as he watched, the man gave a low moan and moved his head feebly. Cormack made for the stairway in a shambling run and scrambled down the steps, heading towards the injured man. The bloodstained knife was lying four or five feet from the killer; Cormack kicked it away, then crouched over the other man, who was breathing stertorously, wheezing gasps that made Cormack think that a lung had been punctured. Blood was pouring from the wound in his chest and the lower part of his trunk was at a grotesque angle to the rest of his torso; Cormack suspected that the fall had broken the other man's back. He probably had only seconds to live...

'Who sent you?' Cormack asked, almost despairingly. *The man's dying, for Christ's sake - leave the poor bastard alone!*

'Who sent you?' he said again, fighting down a wave of self-disgust. 'Who sent you?' he shouted, seizing the man by his collar, about to shake him, for God's sake, when the knifeman's eyes filmed over and his head lolled lifelessly to one side.

Shit.

Slowly, Cormack sat back on his haunches, closed his eyes wearily and shook his head. Another dead end - it had all been for nothing. Sodding nothing... Vaguely, he wondered if he ought to go back up to the office and check that Fairhurst really was dead, but, even as the thought formed, he knew he was clutching at straws. There was no way Fairhurst could still be alive after having his throat slit like that and...

And what the hell was that sound?

He froze, eyes staring blankly into the darkness as he focused his entire attention on the sound that was steadily increasing in volume, then, a moment later, he was moving silently to the door he had come in by, as he recognised the noise: it was a car engine, approaching rapidly. Cormack waited at the door, listening intently as the car came to a halt in the yard outside - but there was a second vehicle as well now, slowing to a halt...

Carefully, Cormack eased the door open and peered out cautiously before he darted through, flattening himself against the wall outside. A quick look each way, then he was running along the side of the warehouse, crouching low, until he came to the front corner. There, he came to a halt, back to the wall as he peered round the corner.

A Mercedes was just coming to a halt no more than thirty yards away but there was no sign of the other vehicle; presumably, that was round the far side of the warehouse, in the main yard. As Cormack watched, three men climbed out and stood looking up at the warehouse for a moment. One of them said something, his tone that of a man issuing orders, then he began heading towards Cormack, while a second man headed off in the opposite direction. The third man, the driver, remained by the car; all three of them carried handguns.

Cormack looked around, trying to see if there was any way out of the yard that would not expose him to the fire from those three guns, but the wall was a good twelve feet high behind him, while heading back along the side of the warehouse would be taking him away from the jeep - although the chances of his ever reaching it seemed to be receding by the second... On top of that, the approaching man would be around the corner long before he could reach the far end of the warehouse; he'd be bound to spot him in the moonlight if he made the slightest movement - and if he stayed where he was, then the torch beam would pick him out anyway... Cormack glanced up at the sky, looking for clouds, but it was a bright, starry night, with the moon three-quarters full; it damn well would be, wouldn't it?

Right, think, for Christ's sake - this is supposed to be the kind of situation you excel at, according to your file...

Cormack flicked a glance behind him, back the way he had come, then felt his stomach lurch as someone came out of the door and looked his way, so there was no more time left, none at all. He launched himself into a full tilt run towards the approaching gunman, who was barely beginning to raise his weapon when the edge of Cormack's left hand scythed into his throat, sending him reeling backwards, clutching at his neck. The driver was still staring in astonishment, still trying to grasp what was happening, as Cormack brought his gun up and fired. The driver doubled up, clutching at his midriff, but Cormack was already sprinting towards the car, dimly aware of the second man shouting something as he raised a gun and fired. Cormack dodged instinctively to one side, then threw himself forward, rolling into cover by the Mercedes. He scrambled up and loosed off a shot over the bonnet, but the second man was already diving behind a pile of crates. Cormack wrenched open the car door, letting out a grateful sob of relief as he saw the key in the ignition, and slid behind the wheel, reaching out for the starter.

The engine caught first time and Cormack rammed the car into gear, jamming his foot flat to the floor as he let out the clutch, the tyres spinning before they gained traction and a figure was standing at the corner of the warehouse, his arm raised as if lining up his gun... Cormack ducked reflexively and the windscreen shattered into a thousand fragments, but then he was wrenching at the wheel, sending the car into a skidding turn, spitting gravel before he straightened up and headed towards the gate, crouching low over the wheel as a second shot rang out from behind; there was a metallic clunk as it slammed into the back of the Mercedes.

Another shot and this time from in front and Cormack saw the second man standing next to the pile of crates, holding his gun two-handed as he aimed it. Cormack yanked at the wheel, aiming the car straight at the gunman, leaning right over to one side as the gunman fired, the expression on his face in the headlights changing abruptly the instant before he leaped out of the way. Too late: the car's wing slammed into him, hurling him to one side, pirouetting around as Cormack spun the wheel back again, but too hard... The rear end slewed outwards, catching the brick pillar of the gate a glancing blow that jarred Cormack's teeth, but which straightened the car up as it roared through the entrance and away up the street.

Chapter 11

'Not very satisfactory reading, is it, Cormack?' Pallister demanded, tapping the typed report in front of him angrily.

'No, sir,' Cormack replied, standing rigidly at attention in front of the desk.

'No, sir,' Pallister echoed mockingly. 'Three dead at the warehouse - three, Cormack - and absolutely nothing to show for it. We couldn't even talk to their casualties - by the time we got there, they'd been taken away by their companions.'

Only to be expected, wasn't it? Cormack thought, but said nothing.

'How many dead is that now, Cormack?' Pallister demanded. 'Logan, Mohrer, the two men in the car, Fairhurst and two more last night - seven, isn't it? Of which you personally have killed five... Are you some kind of psychopath, Cormack? This isn't a game of Cowboys and Indians, you know - or should I say Commandos and Nazis?' He shook his head angrily. 'In any case, just what the devil were you thinking of, going to meet Fairhurst on your own, with no support whatsoever?'

'There was no time to contact anyone, sir,' Cormack pointed out. 'Fairhurst made sure of that.'

'More likely a case of you going off half-cocked - again,' Pallister countered. 'You're a law unto yourself. You decided to act independently, without informing anyone and where did it get you? Nowhere. You are no further forward in your investigation than you were before - but that's only to be expected, given your record to date, isn't it? You're still no closer to finding Kallmann than you were two weeks ago - but there have been three shooting incidents in that time, all of them involving you. All because you tried to do it your way, isn't that the truth? You're a maverick, Cormack - and a dangerous, unsuccessful one at that. I will not tolerate Chicago-style gunfights. As of now, I am taking you off this investigation before anybody else gets killed. I am also suspending you from duty and requesting that you be transferred out of Berlin immediately. I don't think it will be too difficult for you to determine what kind of fitness report will be accompanying you.' He glared at Cormack, then snapped, 'That's all, Cormack. Dismiss.'

***

It was a few minutes after eleven when Cormack returned to his apartment, carelessly throwing his wet raincoat over the back of a chair as he made his way over to the sideboard - and the tray of drinks. It had been raining ever since he had left Headquarters, but he had made no attempt to run to or from the jeep; he simply could not be bothered. He had been like this from the moment he had left Pallister's office, numbed by a sense of lethargy and despair. For all he knew, he no longer had any right to take the jeep - probably hadn't, if he had been suspended from duty - but he couldn't give a damn. Taking the jeep without authorisation was hardly likely to make his situation any worse, he thought bleakly - and what if it did? They could all go shag themselves... He poured a generous measure of whisky and drank most of it down before he walked moodily over to an armchair, taking his drink - and the bottle - with him.

'Bastard,' he muttered, sitting down heavily in the armchair. He stared unseeingly across the room, then shook his head slowly, his lips set in a grim line. He could not, in all honesty, blame Pallister, because, when you came right down to it, everything he had said was perfectly correct. Were he not personally involved, Cormack knew he would probably have sympathised with Pallister's desire to rid himself of such a troublesome subordinate.

The trouble was, he *was* involved. In fact, he was probably looking at the end of whatever career he might have had in

Army Intelligence, because he could imagine, only too well, the kind of report Pallister would be submitting. Cormack suspected that his next posting, if there was one, would probably be as a Mailing Officer in the Outer Hebrides, or something of that ilk. The worst of it was that he could not really argue with Pallister's assessment - but what the hell did he do now?

And Elise? What the hell am I going to say to her?

'Shit,' he muttered and took another sip from his drink, noticing distantly that the glass was almost empty. Drinking was not going to solve his problems, he thought vaguely - but, just at that moment, he could not have cared less. Drinking himself into oblivion seemed as good a way as any of handling the present situation... Everything was finished - Elise, the investigation, his career, so why not indulge in a little self-pity, why not wallow in maudlin misery?

Maudlin misery. He liked that phrase: he repeated it aloud before he realised that the whisky was having an effect. *Good. About bloody time...*

The worst of it was that he had been *that* close, regardless of what Pallister had said; Cormack knew he had come within minutes of finding out what the hell was going on. Fairhurst had still been alive when he'd reached the warehouse - the killer could only just have arrived himself, maybe a minute or so ahead of him. If only he'd been a bit bloody quicker getting there...

And how had they known where to find him?

Cormack sat up suddenly in his chair - now why the hell hadn't he thought about that question before? Too tired, a reaction to last night's events - but that was no excuse, because those bastards had known where to find Fairhurst. True, they'd only had time to get one man there before himself, but that had been all they'd needed - and the reinforcements had been on the scene only minutes later - *So how had they known?*

Almost of their own volition, his eyes focused on the telephone on the sideboard. *Jesus, was that what they'd done?*

That had to be it, he realised numbly; nothing else made any sense. They'd been one step ahead of him all the way...

'Bastards.' He shook his head wearily, then poured out another glass, raising it in an ironic toast towards the telephone. 'Cheers,' he muttered.

As if in response, the telephone rang making him jump involuntarily; he spilled some of the whisky over himself and swore loudly - that was all he damn well needed... It was only then that the coincidence struck him and he stared suspiciously at the telephone; why had it chosen that very moment to ring? *Talk about bloody paranoia...* He picked up the earpiece. 'Cormack.' *Were they listening in right now?*

'Alan, is that you?' said a man's voice. 'This is Frank. Frank Gordon. Hamburg, nine months ago, remember?'

'Hallo, Frank, good to hear from you,' Cormack replied, his voice registering pleased surprise. 'How are you?'

'Fine, never better. Look, I'm in Berlin at the moment. Can you manage lunch?'

Cormack smothered an ironic grin; that was hardly likely to be a problem now... 'Certainly.'

'Great. Fancy a beer or two, talk about old times?'

'Why not?'

'Name a place, old boy - I'm new here.'

Cormack thought for a moment. 'There's a good bar on the corner of Bismarckstrasse and Leibnitzstrasse - can you find it?'

'Can a duck swim? I'll be there. Say an hour from now?'

'Will do. Looking forward to it. See you at twelve thirty. Bye.' Cormack replaced the receiver, then stared at it, rubbing his cheeks thoughtfully. He was suddenly stone cold sober, because he had never met any Frank Gordon nine months ago in Hamburg - or anywhere else, for that matter.

***

The bar was almost deserted, with only a bored looking barman and a solitary waitress on duty; there were a mere four customers, sitting together around a table, and none of them paid any attention to him. Cormack checked his watch, then went up to the bar.

'Excuse me, I was meant to meet a friend of mine here. His name is Frank Gordon. He hasn't been in, has he?'

'He left a message by telephone.' The barman reached under the counter and took out a slip of paper, which he handed to Cormack. 'He said to apologise. He can be contacted at that number.'

'Thanks,' Cormack murmured, looking at the number.

'There is a telephone at the back you can use.'

'It's OK - I'll phone him later.' Cormack pocketed the slip of paper and walked back to the jeep, which he had left outside. He jumped in and drove off along Liebnitzstrasse at a brisk pace, checking the rearview mirror at irregular intervals.

He spent fifteen minutes zig-zagging through side streets in a random pattern before he finally convinced himself that nobody was following him. Only then did he go into a public phone box and dial the number. It rang once, then the same voice said:

'Gordon.'

'Cormack.'

'Go to a hundred and fifteen, Dusseldorferstrasse. Flat Five,' the voice said crisply. 'Got that?'

'Got it.'

The line went dead.

***

115, Dusseldorferstrasse was an anonymous three storey terraced house that had obviously been converted into individual apartments - what in London would have been called 'bed-sitters'. Cormack left the jeep parked just around the corner, partly to avoid drawing attention to the building, but also to give himself an opportunity to study the situation as he approached.

Because, once again, this could be a trap. The same arguments against this still applied as they had last night, however; they did not need to go to such elaborate lengths, especially now that he'd been taken off the investigation anyway. But they probably would not know that, of course...

Oh, come on, get on with it. We've been through all this once already... Taking one last look along the street, Cormack went up the steps and pushed open the outside door. Flat 5 was on the first floor, at the front of the building; he hesitated a moment in front of the door, then knocked firmly on it. Five or six seconds passed, then the door was opened.

By Tony Woodward.

Cormack stared at him, then said, 'Tony, what the hell-'

'You'd better come in, Alan,' Woodward said quietly, stepping aside.

Cormack stared stupidly at him, then raised his eyebrows in a bewildered grimace before he shrugged and went in, only then realising that there was another man in the room within, standing by the window. He was tall, with a ramrod-straight back that bespoke a military background, despite the civilian suit he was wearing. His hair was almost entirely grey, although he was only in his early forties at the most; Cormack recognised him at once.

'Guthrie,' he said tautly. 'Major Guthrie.'

'*Colonel* Guthrie, nowadays, actually,' the other man corrected him mildly. 'Good to see you again, Cormack.' He came over, holding out his hand.

Cormack hesitated, then shook it, staring appraisingly at Guthrie. The last time he had seen the other man had been nearly six years before, after the Dutch operation... He had been with SIS then: who the hell was he now? 'I was told you went back to your regiment,' he said suspiciously.

'Had it been left up to me, I would have done,' Guthrie admitted, a wistful note in his voice. 'But they never really let you go at SIS, do they?'

Not if you're any good, thought Cormack - and Guthrie had been one of the best planning and organisation men he had ever worked with; it hadn't been his fault that the operation had turned out the way it had... 'So what are you doing in Berlin?' he asked, glancing at Woodward, who was still standing with his back to the closed door. Woodward shrugged elaborately in reply to the implied question; he didn't have a clue, either. Cormack looked back at Guthrie. 'What do you want from us?'

'Dieter Kallmann,' Guthrie said simply. 'I want you to find him.'

Cormack stared at him, then shook his head incredulously. 'What the hell do you think I've been trying to do for the past two weeks? Without any noticeable success, I might add.'

'I know,' Guthrie said calmly. 'But, you see, I might be in a position to make your search a little easier.'

'How?'

'I know who Kallmann has been sent to kill. And why.'

Chapter 12

Cormack stared at Guthrie, then blew out his cheeks, exchanging another look with Woodward, whose face mirrored the astonishment that Cormack himself felt. He turned back to Guthrie. 'You certainly know how to grab someone's attention, Colonel.'

'I was hoping it might,' Guthrie said drily. He gestured vaguely at a pair of battered armchairs. 'You might like to sit down - what I have to say will take a little while.'

Cormack hesitated, then shrugged and went over to the dining table, pulling out one of the wooden chairs. He twisted it round, then sat the wrong way round on it, his legs splayed out on either side and his forearms resting on the chair back. Woodward also took one of the table chairs, but sat on it the right way round; it was as if neither of them wanted to feel too comfortable, too much at home. As if accepting the inevitable, Guthrie took a seat at the table as well.

'Right,' he said quietly. 'I'd like to be able to tell this in my own way, if I may.'

Cormack shrugged again. 'Be our guest.'

Guthrie paused for a moment, as if marshalling his thoughts, then began, 'Firstly, have you come across any reference to the Patton Group in your investigation?'

'Pattern?' Cormack asked, frowning, glancing at Woodward, who shook his head mutely. 'As in willow?'

'No. P-A-T-T-O-N, as in the American general.'

'Still doesn't ring a bell.'

'Right. As I'm sure you know, General George Patton was one of the most successful American generals during the War. He was killed in a road accident only a few months after the German surrender. Do either of you know what his attitude was towards the Soviet Union?'

Again, Woodward shook his head, but Cormack said, 'If I remember rightly, he wasn't too keen on the Russians. Eisenhower had to slap him down because of his opinions, which he voiced at every opportunity, didn't he?'

'He did indeed. Patton was something of an embarrassment to Eisenhower, but he was only saying publicly what a lot of politicians and military leaders were privately thinking.'

'Didn't he reckon that the Western Allies should just have kept on advancing at the end of the War, and taken on the Red Army because we were going to have to, sooner or later?'

Guthrie nodded. 'Exactly - and he said this to Soviet generals at conferences. The point is that the Patton Group consists of a number of military officers, politicians and senior officials in both London and Washington who share Patton's views - that, eventually, we are going to have to fight the Soviet Union, and that as this war is seen to be inevitable, then it should be at a time of our choosing. The West's, that is. It is this group that has sent Kallmann into Berlin to carry out the assassination of a leading Soviet military figure.'

'Look, get to the point, will you?' demanded Cormack impatiently. 'Which military figure?'

'Marshal Giorgi Zhukov,' Guthrie said quietly, a faint smile on his face as if he were relishing the moment. 'Their most able - and famous - general, the commander of their armies during World War Two. He is due to visit Berlin sometime during the next two weeks and while he is here, Kallmann is going to assassinate him.'

'Je-sus,' Cormack breathed. 'But why, for God's sake? Don't they know...' He nodded slowly in sudden understanding.

'Yes?' Guthrie prompted him, like a teacher encouraging a bright pupil.

'They know damn well we're on the brink of an armed confrontation here as it is,' said Cormack slowly. 'Shooting Zhukov will have the Red Army marching into the Allied Sectors as sure as eggs are eggs.'

'Which is exactly what the Patton Group wants,' Guthrie said grimly. 'They want a shooting war to begin right here in Berlin.' He paused, then added slowly, 'They want to start World War Three.'

There was a long, heavy silence, before Woodward said, 'But why, for God's sake? The Soviets have got far more tanks and manpower in Berlin than we have - we'd be swept aside in a matter of days.'

'It's the same story in Europe as a whole,' Guthrie agreed. 'Given the reduced level of manpower on the part of the Western Allies, the Red Army has a substantial advantage should war break out. Some estimates say that they could reach the channel ports in under six weeks - and there would be little we could do to stop them.'

'So why does this Patton Group want to start a war we're going to lose?' Woodward persisted.

'The atom bomb,' Cormack said starkly, staring across the room, a haunted look on his face.

'Precisely,' Guthrie said heavily. He gestured vaguely at Woodward. 'Ask yourself this. Why hasn't the Red Army done exactly that - driven us out of Europe? Because the United States has the atomic bomb - and the Soviets haven't. Although they would almost certainly win the opening battles, the Russians know that the Americans can, if they wish, obliterate Moscow or Leningrad with a single bomb at any time. In other words, the possible cost to the Soviet Union should they start a war would be too horrific for even Stalin to contemplate. However, given enough provocation, they *will* attack - or that is the Patton Group's theory. They intend to force the Soviets to initiate a war they cannot win and which would not only result in them being forced out of Eastern Europe, but would also inevitably entail the destruction of the Soviet Union itself, so that it would never again be a threat to the West. They believe that Berlin could be the flashpoint that starts this war.'

'So that's why it has to be here?' asked Cormack. 'Because the situation's on a knife edge as it is?'

'Partly, but it's also a matter of timing. The war that the Patton Group desires can only be fought in a situation in which only one side has the atomic bomb. The Soviets don't have one yet, but the signs are that they will have before long - quite possibly within the next couple of years. The Patton Group needs a situation like the Berlin Blockade in order to light the fuse, as it were, and there might never be another opportunity to do that before the Soviets develop their own atomic bomb. Once that happens, it would be too late, because the destruction on both sides would be too horrific for even the Patton Group.'

'So... this Patton Group thinks that assassinating Zhukov will be the spark that sets it all off?' asked Cormack. 'What if they're wrong? The last I heard, Zhukov wasn't exactly very popular with Stalin. Would they go to war over his death?'

'Zhukov *isn't* very popular with Stalin,' Guthrie conceded, 'but he is still a Hero Of The Soviet Union and idolised within the Red Army. I suspect even Stalin would not be able to withstand the demands of the Red Army to seek retribution - and there are other, very powerful, factions in Moscow who would want to see the Red Army take over Berlin by force, if nothing else - that would be their immediate objective.'

'Only it wouldn't stop there, would it?' Woodward interjected. 'We wouldn't take an armed occupation of the Allied Sectors lying down, would we? Not if there were casualties involved.'

'Exactly,' Guthrie agreed. 'And, remember, the Patton Group consists of very influential figures, who could ensure that we would take punitive steps to counter the Soviet aggression. Some of the generals in Germany have been champing at the bit to send in an armed relief column to Berlin as it is, so there'd be fighting all along the border between East and West Germany. The Patton Group's reasoning is that, once started, the confrontation will rapidly gather momentum and soon become unstoppable.'

'And they're prepared to accept the losses to our forces in Europe?' Cormack asked, appalled. 'They'll be horrendous.'

'They see it as a necessary price to pay,' Guthrie said, his voice sounding suddenly very tired. Cormack recalled that Guthrie had once been in a tank regiment; it would be his old comrades who would be in the front line, the first to be slaughtered. 'Easy enough to do if you're not part of that price, of course...'

'So this Patton Group is relying on America using the atomic bomb, yes?' asked Woodward. 'But suppose they don't? We'd lose Europe altogether.'

'Remember - they're influential people,' Guthrie replied. 'They will point out to President Truman that, inevitably, Europe *will* be lost unless he uses the atomic bomb. Alternatively, it might be used as part of an Allied invasion of Europe - but it *would* be used, one way or another, and the Soviet Union would be destroyed, both as a political unit... and as a country to live in.' He sighed and shook his head slowly, wearily; the thought came to Cormack that Guthrie must have been living with this information for some time now - how well did he sleep at night with what he knew?

Guthrie continued, 'The point is that the cost, in terms of human casualties, will be appallingly high - and not just for the Soviet Union. The most likely situation will be that Truman would not sanction the use of atomic weapons until heavy losses had already been inflicted on the Allies.'

'And if, despite all that, he still decides it's too horrifying a weapon to use, the Soviets will control virtually all of Europe,' Woodward said quietly.

'Quite. Not really what the Patton Group bargained for, but still not a desirable state of affairs, is it?' Guthrie commented.

Cormack thought for a moment, then asked, 'How sure are we that this will snowball into a full-scale war, though? The Soviets know the risks they'll be running. OK, so they might well take over Berlin, but suppose they decide that's it and don't go any further - would we invade East Germany just to get Berlin back?'

'Very probably, if only to save face,' Guthrie answered. 'You see, Berlin is seen as a litmus paper throughout Western Europe. The feeling is that if Berlin is not defended, then neither will the rest of Europe if it came to the crunch - and the Russians would come to exactly the same conclusion. Berlin *has* to be defended; it's part of the basic strategy of the Western Allies. In any case, Cormack, can we afford to take the chance? There are hardliners on both sides who want to start a war. There are those in Moscow who do not believe that the Americans would actually use atomic weapons in Europe, for example - they think that Washington would only use them if the United States itself were under threat. The point is that we cannot afford to take the chance that the Soviets will *not* react aggressively to Zhukov's assassination.'

Cormack looked at Woodward, then shook his head slowly, trying to fight off a sensation of being in the path of something unstoppable, a runaway boulder that was bearing down on him, gathering momentum all the while. *Because that's where we are all right, Tony and me...* 'So you want the two of us to stop Zhukov being killed, is that it?' he asked quietly. Out of the corner of his eye, he saw Woodward's eyes widen momentarily, saw his sudden nod of shocked realisation.

Guthrie stared intently at Cormack, then nodded slowly. 'I suppose it wasn't very difficult to deduce, really, was it?'

'Why else would you bring us here for a secret briefing?'

'Ye-es,' Guthrie said slowly. 'There *is* that to it.'

'OK,' Cormack said, leaning forward. He glanced momentarily at Woodward, then fixed his gaze on Guthrie. 'Why us?'

For the first time, Guthrie seemed hesitant, before he said, 'As you've probably guessed, I'm running an SIS operation to try and stop Kallmann from carrying out the assassination. It

- ah - it isn't going particularly well, to be perfectly honest. I know that Kallmann and his team are in the Soviet Sector, but not their exact whereabouts. I have also uncovered the main details of 'Carronade', the codeword for the assassination operation, and its rationale, and I also know the names of at least some of the members of the Patton Group, but that is all.' He hesitated again, then added, 'The reason I need your help is because the agent I sent after Kallmann has not reported back for over a fortnight - I have to assume the worst. In addition, his replacement was involved in a fatal road accident outside the RAF base at Wunstorf while on his way to take over in the field. Not only that, but there is a distinct possibility that a CIA agent has also been killed investigating this Patton Group.' He looked directly at Cormack. 'You worked with him during the War, apparently - Michael Easton.'

'Easton?' Cormack echoed, then nodded slowly. 'He was bloody good, as I remember.'

'One of their best,' Guthrie agreed. 'But he's been missing for nearly a month now - again, I have to assume the worst.'

Cormack nodded again, then said dully, 'You've got a security leak in London.' There was an air of weary resignation about him: he was being backed into a corner, and it didn't look as if he would be able to get out of it, the way things were going.

'I fear so,' Guthrie agreed.

'So we're all you've got left,' Cormack said sardonically. He shook his head slowly, disbelievingly and when he looked at Guthrie again, there was mockery in his eyes. 'You really are up the creek, aren't you? Rather scraping the bottom of the barrel, as it were.'

'On the contrary,' Guthrie said stiffly. 'I'm recruiting the services of an experienced team of proven ability.'

'Flattery will get you nowhere,' Woodward chipped in, with no trace of humour on his face or in his voice. 'Just cut out the flannel, will you?'

'I am speaking the truth,' Guthrie retorted. 'The two of you were involved in some of the most dangerous - and successful - undercover operations mounted during the War, so I'm hardly pulling in a pair of rank amateurs. On the contrary, I'm recruiting experienced professionals, a team with a proven track record.'

'That was three and a half years ago,' Cormack protested. 'We're out of practice. Look, let's be quite clear about this. You want the two of us, Tony and me, to go into the Soviet Sector to try and find Kallmann and prevent him killing Zhukov, right? You've already sent one man after him and he's dead or captured, you can't trust London any more, so you can't call up any support, and you want to use two has-beens to take on the Soviet MGB, the Red Army and Kallmann? Come off it, Guthrie - that isn't an operation, it's a complicated way of committing suicide.'

'I can't pretend the odds are exactly favourable-'

'You can say that again!'

'-but let me make one or two points. Firstly, you say you're out of practice, but, from what I've heard, you've lost little of your specialist skills when dealing with Mohrer, for example, or when escaping from the warehouse. Secondly, yes, I *do* have to assume the agent I sent in is either dead or captured, but the contacts I will be setting up for you will be unknown to him - he will not be able to betray them, even under torture. Thirdly, no, I cannot trust London, but the people to whom I am reporting are beyond reproach. With their help, I have succeeded in setting up a small network of contacts and sources in Berlin that is a highly effective one. Put it this way - I have generally had access to your reports within twelve hours, Cormack. And just to set your mind at rest, my source is *not* Frau Langemann.' He smiled briefly, then added, 'Perhaps that gives you some indication as to how well informed I am, Cormack.' The smile disappeared as he tapped his fingers absently on the table top; he did not seem to notice Cormack's startled reaction. When Guthrie spoke again, there was an edge to his voice. 'I too am not a complete amateur, after all. I would not be mounting this operation if I did not feel that it offered *some* hope of success. For one thing, as I have implied, I have been monitoring your activities ever since you arrived in Berlin - before that, even. Why do you think Major Metcalfe was recalled to the UK so suddenly?'

Cormack stared at him, then nodded in realisation. 'You set it up.'

'Indeed. I couldn't rely on him carrying out any sort of decent investigation so I wanted you here in Berlin both to take over from him and, if necessary, to form a back up team with Woodward here.' Guthrie gestured impatiently. 'Recruiting the pair of you has not been an off the cuff measure - it's been a contingency plan for some time now. Please bear that in mind.'

'Then why wait until now?'

'I needed to see what your investigation *would* turn up - whether you would trace Huber or Schell, for example, or how much you might uncover about Kallmann. I needed you in place, Cormack.'

'Until I got fired, you mean.'

Guthrie shrugged. 'I was about to approach you anyway once the Fairhurst lead was eliminated. Pallister merely speeded things up.'

Fairhurst... 'You *have* been well informed, haven't you? Who's your source in Unit B?'

Guthrie smiled faintly. 'You should know better than to ask that.' He raised his hand to forestall any further questions, then said, 'Shall we get back to the matter in hand? Your proposed operation in the Soviet Zone? As I have said, this has been thoroughly planned, even if it has been at short notice. Your support network will be first-rate and will have its security intact, because this operation will be entirely self-contained. Not even my superiors in London know about it, so there will be no risk of having your security compromised there.

'In addition, you will be given the necessary documents and identification papers to enable you to move around in the Soviet

Sector, as well as being provided with a safehouse, an efficient communications system and access to a source at Schonefeld airfield, the most likely arrival point for Zhukov. This is not just a seat of the pants operation, you see.'

'I *do* see,' Cormack murmured: Guthrie might be a stuffed shirt in many ways, but he was excellent at setting up this kind of penetration job, no two ways about that, That still didn't make this one any less hazardous, though... 'Aren't you missing something, though?'

'Am I?' Guthrie blinked rapidly. 'Such as?'

'Why don't you simply tell the Russians that Kallmann has been sent to kill Zhukov? Then they could step up their security precautions - they'd have a damn sight better chance than us of stopping Kallmann.'

'That has already been tried,' Guthrie said heavily. He leaned back in his chair. 'You see, originally, the visit was supposed to have been by Beria himself, not Zhukov.'

Lavrenti Beria: Stalin's Number Two. 'You mean, Kallmann was originally intended to assassinate *him*?' asked Cormack incredulously.

'Yes, he was, and while I tend to feel, on a personal level, that Beria's death would have been no great loss to Mankind, the point is that when we did send a warning to Moscow through unofficial channels, the only reaction was to substitute Zhukov for Beria.'

'But why?' asked Woodward. 'Why didn't they simply cancel the whole visit?'

'That's what we wondered,' Guthrie replied. 'Especially when, as far as my sources in the Soviet Sector can ascertain, security has not been stepped up at all. Why Zhukov? Beria's visit would have been purely political, but Zhukov's will be a military inspection tour. Add to that the fact that Zhukov is in official disgrace nowadays and has been given nothing but obscure postings in the Urals since nineteen forty five, and you have to ask why he's been chosen for this visit.'

'He's expendable,' Cormack said flatly.

Guthrie nodded. 'Exactly. There is a very strong likelihood that our warning only reached the pro-war faction in Moscow - Beria is one of their chief, if secret, supporters. They may actually *want* Zhukov to be assassinated, in order to start an armed conflict, as well as removing someone who is too popular for Stalin's liking - two birds with one stone. As a martyr, Zhukov would make a lot more sense than Beria - Zhukov's death would have the Red Army baying for revenge, whereas Beria's demise would probably only have produced a sigh of relief in some quarters.' He paused, then added, 'In *most* quarters, probably, come to think of it.'

'So Zhukov is being set up by the Russians?' Cormack asked.

'By the hard-line faction, yes. Or so it would appear - certainly, as I said, no extra security precautions seem to have been taken by the Russians to protect Zhukov.' Guthrie sighed. 'The point I am making is this: there are people over there in high places who would like to see Zhukov out of the way and who would also like an excuse to take over all of Berlin by force. If Kallmann succeeds, they would achieve both of these objectives.'

'So they're just going to let it happen,' Cormack said flatly.

'I don't know that for certain, but that's what it looks like at the moment.'

'Oh, great,' Cormack said slowly, his words dripping irony, but what he felt was a crushing sense of despair. 'So it's down to us, is it - Tony and me? We're the silly sods who've got to go and stop Kallmann, come what may?'

'I'm afraid so, Cormack. Obviously, I can't order you to do it, either of you, but I'm sure you can both see how important this is.' He paused, then added softly, 'Of course, I would quite understand if you were to refuse to take part.'

If we were too scared, you mean... You certainly know which buttons to press, don't you, Guthrie?

Cormack looked at Woodward, who pursed his lips, shrugged, and looked away. A heavy silence fell, lasting almost a minute before Guthrie rose to his feet. 'You'll probably want to talk about it,' he said quietly. He went over to the door. 'I'll leave you to it. Shall I return in half an hour? Will that be enough?'

Cormack glanced again at Woodward, who nodded briefly. 'Should be.'

'Right. Half an hour, then.' Guthrie went out, pulling the door closed behind him. Cormack rose slowly to his feet and crossed to the window; it was only when he saw Guthrie emerge onto the street and walk away that he turned and nodded to Woodward.

'He's gone.'

Woodward let out his breath slowly. 'Bloody frightening, isn't it?'

'You could say that, yes.'

Woodward stood up abruptly and went over to the kitchen area. He opened the larder door, then smiled triumphantly. 'Good old Guthrie,' he said and took out a bottle of schnapps and two glasses. 'I think I could do with some of this. You?' He held up one of the glasses and, in response to a nod from Cormack, began to pour out the schnapps into each glass. He brought the drinks over to the table and sat down; Cormack resumed his previous seat.

'Cheers,' Woodward said, raising his glass.

'Cheers,' Cormack echoed absently, but made no attempt to drink.

Woodward took a brief sip, then stared down at his glass. 'Right, Alan,' he said quietly. 'Are we in or not?'

Cormack rubbed his eyes tiredly, then blew out his cheeks as he let out his breath in a long sigh. Eventually, he said, 'It still sounds like a bloody complicated way of committing suicide. When it comes right down to it, it'll be our necks on the block, not Guthrie's.'

'It won't be for the first time, though, will it?'

Cormack smiled faintly. 'No, I don't suppose it is... His expression sobered. 'But things were different then.'

'Why?'

'We were at war then, remember? It was all very simple - in those days we knew who the enemy was so we shot at him. But this... Think about it, Tony. We're being asked to save the life of a Russian whose death has been ordered by British and Americans. See what I'm driving at? Whose side are we on, for God's sake?'

Woodward nodded heavily. 'Yes, I see what you mean, except that it wasn't the British and American governments who sent Kallmann, was it?'

'Wasn't it?' Cormack said, staring at Woodward as if to emphasise the point. 'I wish I could be sure of that... No, you're probably right, Tony, but... suppose this Patton Group is right? Suppose we *do* have to fight the Russians sooner or later - shouldn't it be now, while we have an edge on them? Only...' His voice trailed away and he turned his head so that he was staring out of the window.

'Go on,' Woodward prompted.

'I don't know...' Cormack said, his voice far away. 'I think it's the thought of those atomic bombs I can't take, Tony. And of another war.' His eyes swung slowly back towards Woodward. 'I mean, you've seen what happened here, and to Hamburg and Dresden - do we really want all that again? It's going to take years to put Europe back on its feet again as it is, but if we have another war... Jesus. And if they *do* use those atomic bombs...' He shook his head wearily, but there was a haunted look in his eyes.

'Just how bad are they?' Woodward asked. 'I mean, one reads in the press about these super-bombs, but the articles don't really say much about them at all.'

'They wouldn't,' Cormack said grimly. 'These bombs are probably the most closely guarded military secret ever. The trouble is, their security isn't as tight as London and Washington would like it to be - I saw some of the confidential reports on Hiroshima and Nagasaki. I shouldn't have, but I did. One bomb in each case inflicted several times more damage than a thousand bombers managed at Hamburg or Dresden. *One bomb*, Tony.'

'Good God.' Woodward's voice was appalled; he'd been in the Hamburg air raid during the night of 27/28 July, 1943, in which twenty thousand people had been killed and a firestorm created that had reached temperatures of a thousand degrees Centigrade. He had seen the flames engulfing the city; even from twenty thousand feet, the sight had been awesome. 'I knew it was powerful, but...' His voice died away as he stared at Cormack. 'You're right,' he said slowly. 'We can't afford another war. Not now.'

'Maybe not ever,' Cormack said bleakly. He looked down at his drink, then sipped absently from it, grimacing at its bite. He didn't particularly like schnapps, he thought vaguely...

'OK, so we agree Kallmann has to be stopped,' Woodward said quietly. 'I suppose the question is - are *we* the ones to do it?'

Cormack put down his glass and folded his arms, resting his elbows on the table top. His eyes still fixed on the drink, he said, 'Who the hell else is there, Tony? You heard Guthrie - we're his last shot, God help us. If he's right about the Russians not wanting to protect Zhukov, if they're only going through the motions, then if we don't stop Kallmann, nobody else will. Zhukov will die and if we're lucky, the Allies'll get booted out of Berlin and that'll be all that happens. Which'll be bad enough, of course, but, bearing in mind the alternative, I think I could settle for that.'

'But you don't think it'll stop there.'

Now, Cormack looked up and fixed his eyes on Woodward's. 'Do you?'

Woodward shook his head slowly. 'No, I don't.'

There was a heavy, ominous silence that lasted almost a minute, then Woodward said, 'Looks like it's tilting at windmills time again, doesn't it?'

Despite himself, Cormack grinned tiredly and shook his head in a gesture of wry amusement. 'You've changed, Tony - did you know that? Time was when you wouldn't have hesitated for an instant about this. What happened to all that King and Country bit?'

'Time was when I thought undercover ops were a bit of a lark - which was before I actually went on one, if you remember. I think my illusions about the romance of cloak and dagger work lasted about an hour after we landed on the Dutch coast, if I remember rightly.'

Cormack nodded grimly. 'You do indeed.'

'Now I know it isn't a lark, a bit of a whizz, dontcher know? It's dangerous and dirty and we could both end up dead or in a Russian prison camp somewhere in Siberia, so it scares the hell out of me. But do we really have a choice about this? Just think what's at stake.'

'I *am* thinking,' Cormack said tiredly. 'And that's exactly what's scaring hell out of me.' He sighed, then lifted his glass and downed his drink in one swallow, wincing at its taste. 'But you're right,' he said bleakly. Cormack paused, his attention apparently focused on the empty glass in his hand. He said, almost to himself, 'I don't think there's any way we can get out of this one, Tony.'

Chapter 13

Cormack paused outside the door to Elise's flat, momentarily hesitating, then knocked once on it, firmly. The door opened almost immediately, and she stood in the doorway wearing a white blouse and dark grey skirt, the mere sight of her enough to give him butterflies in his stomach - *and you say this is only infatuation?* 'Hallo, Elise,' he said, trying to smile and feeling that all he was achieving was a deaths-head grimace.

'Hallo, Alan, Do come in.'

He did so, feeling acutely awkward; she seemed to sense this, but, in any case, she did not appear to be entirely at her ease either, so that their kiss was perfunctory. *Is this the way it's going to be, a right washout?*

She stared at him, then said suddenly, 'I heard what happened today. With Colonel Pallister. One of the other girls told me - she's a bit of a gossip, but...' Her voice trailed away, as if she realised she was prattling on.

'Oh,' he said, nonplussed. 'What exactly did she tell you?'

'That you - you'd been suspended and that you were going to be transferred out.' She stared at him and he suddenly realised that she was holding back her emotions; that was why she seemed tense, ill at ease. 'Is it true?'

He nodded slowly. 'I'm afraid so,' he sighed.

'I see,' she said quietly; he sensed that she was doing her damnedest to keep her voice under control. 'When will you have to leave?'

He shook his head. 'I don't know. A few days, I expect.'

'I see,' she said again, but this time with a hint of frost. She stepped back from him and seemed about to say something else, but he held up his hand and said:

'Look, we need to talk. I've booked us a table for dinner. How does that sound?'

She stared at him disbelievingly but then seemed to see something in his eyes, a pleading perhaps, that made her nod her head slowly. 'OK,' she said softly, as if she herself could not quite believe she were saying it. 'Why not? I'll get my coat.'

***

Cormack brought the jeep to a halt next to the shore of the Havel, then reached forward and turned off the headlights. Elise looked suspiciously across at him, then said quietly, 'I thought we were supposed to be going to dinner?'

He did not answer at once, but, instead, stared through the windscreen out across the lake. 'I'm sorry about that, Elise. I - I needed to get you away from the apartment so that we could talk.'

'Away from the apartment? What for? Why-' She broke off suddenly and stared at him fearfully as realisation struck her. She shook her head slowly, then said, 'Alan, just what is going on? Were you afraid the apartment might have hidden microphones?'

He nodded slowly. 'Just a precaution. I don't think it is, but... well, I couldn't afford to take the chance.'

'Chance? Of what?'

He drew in a deep breath. 'I didn't want anyone listening in to what I'm going to tell you.'

'Alan, you're beginning to scare me. What's going on?'

'What you heard was perfectly true. I have been suspended and Pallister does want me out of Berlin. The thing is, something else has come up, so I'll be away from Berlin for a few days. I wanted you to know that, because otherwise you would just have heard that I'd disappeared and I didn't want you worrying about me.' *That's assuming that you would have done...*

She nodded slowly, but her eyes were unfocused, as if she had only been half-listening. 'Is it to do with Kallmann?' she asked suddenly.

He hesitated, then nodded. 'Yes.'

'And it's dangerous?'

Again, he paused before answering. 'A bit, I suppose, but I can't say any more than that, I'm afraid.'

'You're still looking for him, aren't you?' she said, persisting. 'Only you're going to do it undercover, yes?'

'Look, I really can't say any more-'

'You don't have to,' she said, her eyes fixed on his. She shook her head slowly. 'Does it have to be you? Can't it be somebody else?'

'Afraid not. I'm all there is, God help us.' He tried to make it sound flippant, but it all came out wrong: *frightened.*

'This isn't a joke, Alan. Why are you carrying on with this? Kallmann's a killer - why do you have to stick your neck out like this?'

'I've told you - somebody has to do it and there isn't anyone else.'

'Or is it that you can't let anyone else do it?' she demanded, and there was anger in her voice. 'It has to be you that finds him and nobody else?'

'It's not like that at all.' *Am I sure about that?* 'The thing is, I know what Kallmann is up to now - and he's got to be stopped, that's all there is to it.'

'Then let someone else do it. You still haven't told me why it has to be you.'

'I can't,' he said, aware of the inadequacy of his answer, but a part of him was feeling a warm glow of pleasure: *she actually seems to care what happens to me...* 'But put it this way - if I could get someone else to do it, I would - but I can't.'

'But why?' she pleaded. 'I still don't understand. What is Kallmann going to do that is so terrible that you are willing to risk your life to stop him?' She stared at Cormack, her face suddenly appalled. 'Dear God, who is he going to kill?'

'I can't tell you,' he said yet again. 'But we can't afford to let it happen.'

'I see...' she said slowly, then looked away. A heavy silence fell between them before she said, so low that her voice was almost inaudible 'I promised myself that I would never let this happen again, you know.'

'Let what happen?' Cormack asked, bewildered.

'I've already had one man go away and never come back again - I didn't want to be in that same situation again. But now it looks as if I am, like it or not.'

'Not if I can help it,' he answered. *Do I really mean that much to her?* 'This isn't the first time I've done something like this - I'm not exactly an amateur.'

'Neither was Heinrich,' she said wistfully, then shook her head. 'I almost wish you hadn't told me,' she said. 'No, I don't mean that... I'm glad you trust me enough to tell me the truth, or at least part of it.' She turned and faced him. 'But why did you? Wouldn't it have been easier for you to have just gone without saying anything to me?'

'Maybe it would,' he said softly, then shrugged. 'You deserved better than that, Elise. I thought... I thought you ought to know, because...' His voice trailed away uncertainly.

'Yes?' she prompted him gently.

'Because you mean a lot to me,' he said quietly. 'I couldn't just up and leave without some sort of explanation.'

She stared at him for several seconds, blinking rapidly as if she were holding back tears. 'Thank you for that, Alan. I appreciate that. It can't have been very easy for you.'

You can say that again. Guthrie had not wanted him to see her at all, but he had pointed out that he was going to have to see her before he left Berlin, even if only at work and there was no way that he was going to lie to her about what was happening. 'Not really, no,' he admitted. He took a deep breath. 'There's something else,' he said quietly.

'What?' she asked anxiously.

'I'd... I'd like you to go somewhere safe while I'm away.' He raised his hand to forestall her response. 'No, just hang on a minute. I don't *think* you'll be in any danger, but I'd sooner be safe than sorry. We've arranged a safehouse for you and I'd feel a lot better if you stayed there... just for a few days. Until this is all over.' He stared at her. 'Please say you will.'

Her eyes met his and he could see the fear in them. 'Maybe it would be for the best,' she agreed, her voice not entirely steady.

'Like I said, I don't think anything will happen, but...' His voice trailed away. But what? Viewed logically, there was no reason for the Patton Group to take any action against her, but you could not always rely on the opposition behaving rationally... In any case, this had been the condition he had stipulated to Guthrie - *I want a safehouse for Elise*; Guthrie had accepted without demur. 'I know it's an imposition, but-'

She shook her head. 'If you think it's for the best. I must admit I don't mind the thought of being hidden away, if things are as serious as you say.'

'I'm afraid they are,' he said grimly. 'Anyway, that's a weight off my mind, I must admit. I'd have been worried about you otherwise.'

'So... when does all this happen?' she asked, her voice brittle again, as if she were keeping it under control.

'Soon,' he said quietly. 'I don't think I'll be able to see you again before it starts.'

'I see.' She took a deep breath and turned her head towards the windscreen again, as if afraid to meet his eyes. 'So this could be the last time I ever see you?'

'I damn well hope not.'

She looked back at him. 'Me too. I just want you to know that... that you mean a lot to me as well. I wish... I just wish we'd had more time with each other.' She hesitated, then added, '*When* you come back... if you want me, I'll be waiting for you.'

He stared at her for several seconds. 'I'll hold you to that,' he said.

'I'm hoping you will.' And then, suddenly, she was in his arms, holding him tightly as their mouths pressed hungrily together. The kiss seemed to go on forever, until, eventually, she whispered tremulously, 'Promise me you'll take care.'

'I promise.'

'And... and come back to me.'

'I will.' The vehemence of his reply took him by surprise but then, as her lips sought his again, the realisation came to him: *I've got a bloody good reason to come back this time...*

Monday Night

Cormack sat with his back propped against the remains of a wall, trying to ignore an increasing numbness in his backside, caused by the fact that he had been sitting like that for almost half an hour now; several minor shifts of position had not really helped matters much. He lifted his arm to look at his watch, realised he had checked the time only a minute or so before, and let his arm fall back into his lap. Out of the corner of his eye, he caught sight of Woodward looking at his own watch; Cormack smiled to himself in the darkness, before the expression faded. What the hell was keeping them?

Patience, old son, patience... It was not yet midnight; there was still plenty of time. Better to wait until everything was ready than to go off half-cocked. But it was the waiting that was the worst... He looked around, more to stop himself brooding than anything else. At his back were the ruins that had once been the Reichstag, now little more than a pile of rubble behind the still imposing facade. To his left, perhaps a hundred yards away, was the barbed wire barrier that marked the beginning of the Soviet Sector; beyond that, every so often, he could see the movement of two-man Army patrols, policing their side of the demarcation line. In some places, Cormack mused, that was all it was - a line drawn on a map, with no physical barrier visible, but, even there, both Soviet and Allied patrols were very much in evidence. Increasingly, barbed wire barricades were being erected by the Red Army, both to keep the Allies out and their own people in: how permanent would these barriers be? He wondered. He wouldn't put it past the Russians to build a bloody great wall to divide up the city one day...

Despite himself, Cormack found himself checking the time again: he forced himself relax. Guthrie had told him they were in good hands tonight: the man who had identified himself as simply 'Karl' an hour earlier at the rendezvous specialised in clandestine crossings to and from the Soviet Sector. They had decided on a covert crossing because of the problems to involved in trying to bluff their way through a Soviet checkpoint; there was also a chance that there might be someone from Army Intelligence on duty at the British checkpoint who might recognise Cormack - and, officially, he was no longer in Berlin, as from four hours ago. He had turned up at Gatow in accordance with the order transferring him back to Hamburg (which had come through in less than forty-eight hours, suspiciously quickly). He had walked out to the plane, but had then kept on going until he reached the hole in the perimeter fence where Guthrie had been waiting with a car. By the morning, Pallister would know he had not left Berlin as planned, but, by then, they would be in the Soviet Sector.

If all went well...

Impatiently, he shook his head; how much longer was Karl going to be, for Christ's sake?

As if in answer to his unspoken plea, he heard a movement over to his left and, a few seconds later, Karl came into view, crouching low to stay below the level of the wall. He beckoned silently and Cormack and Woodward exchanged glances before they eased themselves into crouching positions and followed him.

The German led them through the rubble and shattered brickwork, the three of them bent almost double as they moved in a kind of scuttling run. Abruptly, Karl held out his hand and they came to a halt, crouching down behind a pile of bricks and masonry. Karl motioned them closer, then gestured into the darkness ahead. 'The barbed wire is about thirty metres away. We've cut through it for you. On the far side is another fifty metres of open ground before you reach some bombed-out buildings, but you'll find shell holes and craters if you need to take cover along the way. Keep an eye out for patrols, of course.'

Cormack shot him a venomous look - *Don't teach your grandmother to suck eggs, sunshine* - but it was wasted in the darkness.

'Now we wait for the signal,' Karl said, almost to himself.

Cormack sneaked another glance at his watch, then nodded slightly to himself. It was nearly midnight, which meant that the patrols were almost certain to be relieved in a few minutes; their vigilance would be at their lowest now. They'd be thinking about getting back to barracks, in front of a fire, or off to bed.

Lucky sods...

'Right,' Karl said. He was looking over to the right, towards the south, and, presumably, he had seen some signal. Cormack mentally chastised himself for having missed it - *really wide awake, aren't you?* - then forgot his momentary lapse as Karl motioned him forward.

Cormack looked around carefully, then nodded and moved past the German, still crouching low, with Woodward right behind him. It was only when they had reached the gap in the barbed wire that Cormack realised he had said nothing to Karl, no word of thanks or acknowledgment, nothing. Too late now... He dropped onto his stomach, and slithered through the gap, pressing himself flat to the ground on the far side as he looked around.

In front of him, as Karl had said, was a stretch of open ground, with a large shell crater twenty yards away, slightly to the right; their first objective. He looked to each side, taking his time, but there were no patrols in sight, so he nodded to

Woodward and the two of them began to crawl forward, commando fashion, eyes sweeping constantly to right and left as they headed towards the crater. Fifteen yards to go, ten...

And then, over to the right, a beam of light stabbed out into the darkness: a searchlight. Cormack hugged the ground, not moving a muscle as the cone of light swept towards them in a steady arc, closing his eyes a moment before the beam passed across them... Then, mercifully, it was moving away from them and Cormack began moving again, slithering across the ground in a frantic scramble until he virtually fell into the crater, Woodward sliding down in a heap next to him.

'Where the hell did that come from?' Woodward demanded in a hoarse whisper.

'God knows,' Cormack murmured tersely, peering cautiously over the crater's lip. The searchlight was about fifty yards away, mounted on the back of a Kubelwagen, the German Army equivalent of a jeep - and, beyond it, he could see four soldiers, moving in line abreast, spread out across the gap between the buildings and the barbed wire. They were advancing slowly, rifles held at the ready across their chests. They would reach the crater in about a minute, Cormack reckoned, certainly no more than two.

Shit. Had there been a leak somewhere? Those bastards looked as if they knew someone was coming across tonight. Cormack looked desperately around and saw a low wall thirty yards away that would provide cover almost all the way to the skeletal shell of a building; once there, they could vanish into the shadows.

It would have to be a sprint from here to the wall, but it'd be suicide now because they'd be silhouetted against the illuminated ground beyond; they'd have to wait for the searchlight beam to swing back past again so that it was between them and the soldiers. Cormack looked over to the left, and saw the beam beginning to move back towards them, but slowly, agonisingly slowly. A glance to the right, the soldiers only forty yards away now, going to be too damn close for comfort... For a moment, he thought about shooting out the searchlight and running for it, but that would be suicidal as well, because he'd have to hit the bloody thing first time, no mean feat with a silenced handgun and even if he did, he'd be giving their position away anyway... *No; keep your head down, wait... and cross your fingers.*

The beam of light was only feet away now, sweeping towards them; Cormack and Woodward ducked down out of sight as it moved past, then, the moment it was dark again, they came up out of the crater in the crouching run that was almost instinctive now, ten yards gone and no warning shout, twenty and flick a glance to the right, the searchlight beam between them and the soldiers, probably affecting their night vision, making them less likely to see anything in the darker area beyond, *twenty-five yards* and then Cormack hurled himself forward, behind the wall, Woodward slamming into the ground next to him. Now, it was back to scrambling forward on their stomachs, but they still couldn't afford to hang about, because those bastards would still look behind the wall when they reached it...

Cormack came to a halt as the wall petered out, staring longingly at the space between them and the nearest building. The gap had once been a street, he realised with a vague feeling of surprise, but now the road surface had been twisted and shattered by shellfire. And the soldier at that end of the line was walking along what had been the pavement, no more than twenty yards away now - and coming straight towards their hiding place... He sensed Woodward's sudden tension next to him, knew that he had seen the approaching soldier, and reached out a restraining hand, motioning Woodward down into cover.

Sighing, Cormack took out his Browning pistol and lined it up on the soldier, sighting carefully along the silenced barrel as he aimed for a point between the eyes: there was no alternative now, not any longer. If they stayed where they were, he'd very likely trip over them and if they made a dash for it, he'd see them anyway, so the only way out was to silence him before he could give the alarm - and it had to be the gun because he was facing them and so they could hardly sneak up behind him.

But it was still murder...

It's him or you.

All right, I bloody know it is. Doesn't mean I have to like it, does it?

Carefully, steadying his wrist with his left hand, Cormack held the gun unwaveringly on the soldier as he came closer. Who was he, this man he was going to kill? Some farm boy from the Ukraine who had been called up and sent to some place he had probably never even heard of before and who would not have time to know what had happened to him, let alone wonder why? Would his parents have to spend the rest of their lives trying not to look too often at the black-lined photograph on the mantelpiece, thinking about how he would have taken over the farm eventually and would *they* wonder why?

Stop thinking like this - it's got to be done!

Poor bastard... He was only five yards away now and he'd see them any second now...

It's time. Cormack's finger began to tighten on the trigger - *forgive me* - and he knew that he would not miss, that the bullet would smash through the soldier's skull and brain, probably dead before he hit the ground...

A shot rang out in the night but it was over beyond the soldiers, beyond the barbed wire and it was followed a second or two later by another. Cormack froze as the soldier turned his head towards the sound. A third shot, *Go on, Ivan, go and see what's going on*, then there was a shout from one of the others in the line and the soldier broke into a run, heading towards the gunshots. *And maybe he would get to take over the farm one day...*

He was still only twenty yards away when Cormack gestured urgently to Woodward and they scrambled to their feet, sprinting across the road, disappearing into an alleyway. Yet, even then, Cormack paused for a moment at the alley's entrance and looked back at the Reichstag, still gaunt and forbidding, silhouetted against the lights of the British Sector beyond.

That way lay safety...

And Elise.

Cormack stared across the gulf for a moment longer, then turned away to follow Woodward into the shadows.

Part II

Chapter 14

The address Guthrie had given was in Biesdorf, at 27, Gleiwitzerstrasse, and, as he approached, Cormack could see that it was a semi-detached house that had a small garden in front with rows of winter cabbage across it - almost *de rigeur* on either side of Berlin these days, Cormack decided. The neighbourhood reminded him of suburban London: Harrow, perhaps, or Surbiton, with houses built in the Thirties, a lower middle-class area. Or it had been once, but now several of the houses that were relatively intact were liable to have gaping holes in the roof or boarded-up windows. In fact, the Soviet Sector seemed little different to the Allied sectors, when it came down to it; apart from the fact that the power cuts were less frequent and, by all accounts, food and fuel not quite as scarce, he could just as easily be in Spandau or Reinickendorf in West Berlin. Cormack had heard that the people in the Soviet Zone were little better off than in the Trizone sectors, but he had been inclined to dismiss the stories as propaganda - until now. Although, perhaps, had he really thought through the implications of the various reports that had crossed his desk over the past weeks, he should have realised just what a hole the Soviet authorities had dug for themselves. Since the end of the War, they had stripped something like two-thirds of the total industrial capacity of East Germany and trans-shipped it to the Soviet Union, along with raw materials and manufactured goods; as a result, industrial production was running at an appallingly low level that was made worse by the Allies counter-blockade, that deprived the Soviets of coal and steel from the Ruhr. Food was running short because the Soviets had stripped shops and warehouses to provide extra rations as a bribe for people to vote for the SED, the Socialist Unity Party, in the City elections - unsuccessfully, as it turned out - but now, the shortages were beginning to bite; rumour had it that the harvest had been taken early this year, before the crops were fully grown. Cormack had known all this, but only in a vague, abstract way - it had no direct bearing on his own work - and it was only now that he was beginning to understand the reality of the situation. Win or lose in the Blockade, the Soviets were going to inherit one hell of a problem when it was all over.

Always assuming there's any Berlin left to administer, of course. If Kallmann succeeds...

He pushed the thought aside and checked his watch; it would be curfew in a few minutes. There were few people around at the moment, except for those hurrying home so as not to be caught by any patrols before the deadline. Darkness had fallen an hour or so ago when he had left Woodward in the apartment in Lichtenberg where they had holed up overnight; it belonged to one of Karl's network. There had been one brush with a Red Army patrol, but his papers had evidently passed muster, mainly, Cormack felt, because the soldiers had only been going through the motions, perhaps resentful of being given the duty. An MGB checkpoint might have been more painstaking, but, so far, the only one he had seen had been in the distance and he had been able to use the back streets to detour around it.

Cormack paused in front of Number 27, looking around, apparently casually, then pushed open the rickety gate and walked up the path. He hesitated a moment, then knocked on the door.

After no more than four or five seconds, a stockily-built man appeared in the doorway, blinking rapidly at Cormack through metal-rimmed spectacles. 'Yes?' he asked.

'Herr Schoemann?' Cormack asked, giving the intentional mispronunciation that was the coded introduction. 'I beg your pardon - it's Herr Schoerner, not Schoemann, isn't it?'

'Indeed it is. You must be Herr Beitzen.'

'Yes, I am.'

'Come in, please.' Schoerner led Cormack through into a room at the back of the house that was evidently a study-cum-office, with a filing cabinet in one corner and a battered desk in front of the French windows. There was a yard behind the house containing three lorries of various sizes and a closed van: Schoerner's cover was that of a proprietor of a small haulage firm. 'I thought there were supposed to be two of you?' Schoerner asked, a hint of suspicion still in his voice.

'There are - myself and Josef Zagorski.'

Schoerner nodded and seemed to relax. 'But there is no need for me to meet Zagorski - is that your reasoning?'

Cormack nodded.

'Very wise,' Schoerner commented, nodding in approval.

Cormack watched the other man thoughtfully. Schoerner seemed more like a bank clerk than a dealer in the black market, but then he looked still less like an MI6 contact. It was certainly a good double cover, because any suspicious activities on his part - night-time visits, clandestine meetings - could be explained away by his black market involvement, which would also afford him some protection from investigation, because his clients would include high-ranking members of the Soviet hierarchy. Did he gain a sense of quiet satisfaction whenever he charged them an exorbitant price for their goods? Quite possibly; it would only be the Russians, or their collaborators, who would be able to afford a lot of the luxuries Schoerner could provide. Even so, it required a good deal of nerve to carry on two such illegal lifestyles at once. When the knock came on the door in the middle of the night - as it almost certainly would, sooner or later - he wouldn't know whether it was the police - or the MGB...

Rather him than me, Cormack decided.

Schoerner went over to the desk and unlocked one of the top drawers. He took out a large envelope, which he handed to Cormack. 'These are your papers, made out in the names of Reinhard Beitzen and Josef Zagorski, as arranged, along with priority travel permits, which will allow you to move around during the curfew. I suggest that you dispose of your old papers as soon as possible.'

Cormack nodded. 'Will do.'

'Secondly, the safehouse.' Schoerner reached into the drawer again and took out a key ring. 'You wanted somewhere close to Schonefeld and Adlershof?'

'Yes.' These were the two airfields in south-east Berlin; Schonefeld was the most likely arrival point for Zhukov, but Adlershof was less than five miles away from it, so it made sense to have a safehouse that was conveniently situated for both.

'Eighteen, Taucherstrasse,' said Schoerner. 'It's in Grunau, roughly four kilometres from each airfield. Flat Number Seven - it's on the top floor. Don't worry about the *blockwart* - he's on my payroll and will ask no questions.' He passed the key ring to Cormack. 'There is enough tinned food and other provisions to last several days - please don't go out unless absolutely necessary.'

'We've got nosey neighbours, you mean?'

'No more than anywhere else, but it's best not to push your luck. The large key opens a lock-up garage, which you'll find just around the corner. There's a motorcycle and sidecar combination in there. Rather old and battered, I'm afraid, but the best I could do. In any case, it will suit your cover as an electrical engineer - there's an electrician's toolbox in the sidecar.'

Cormack nodded. 'Sounds fine.' In fact, anything else would be too conspicuous, in all probability, because petrol was as heavily rationed here as in the British Sector and motorcycles tended to attract far less attention than a car.

'You'll find the keys in the flat. The relevant documentation is in the envelope.'

Cormack nodded, his face impassive, but in reality, he was impressed. Schoerner clearly knew his business - but then Guthrie would not have chosen him otherwise.

'Finally, you wanted to talk to my source at Schonefeld, I understand?' Schoerner asked.

'Yes, I do.'

'Very well. His name is Korotkov and he is one of the permanent security staff at Schonefeld. A word of warning, however. He is a mercenary, who provides me with information in exchange for money or black market goods, not for any ideological motives. Of course, I do have some leverage over him as regards blackmailing him if I have to, but you ought to know the manner of man you will be meeting.'

'Thanks. I'll bear it in mind.'

'I'll arrange a meeting with him,' Schoerner said, then looked questioningly at Cormack. 'I think that covers everything, doesn't it?' He seemed anxious for Cormack to go, which was hardly surprising; if the MGB were to storm in now, battering the doors down, neither of them would have a hope in hell of talking their way out of it, not with all these documents around.

'That's about it, yes,' Cormack agreed.

'Good.' Schoerner hesitated, then held out his hand. 'I don't suppose we'll meet again, Herr Beitzen - or we shouldn't do, if all goes well - so... Good luck.'

'Thank you,' Cormack said, surprised. Maybe Schoerner had picked up enough clues from the document requirements to realise that 'Herr Beitzen' was on an extremely dangerous operation. *Damn right it was...* 'I think I might be needing it.'

Soviet Sector

Lieutenant Yuri Pankov gasped and climaxed, thrusting urgently at the woman underneath him, his face contorted as if in pain before, gradually, his motions slowed to a halt. He opened his eyes and looked down at her, grinning exultantly. 'You are some woman, Monika,' he said hoarsely.

'And *you* are some man,' she replied, grimacing as he withdrew from her and rolled onto his back next to her.

'Terrific,' he murmured, his chest still rising and falling rapidly from his exertions; he failed to notice that the woman beside him was not even breathing heavily. 'Terrific,' he said again, then sat up, reaching for a packet of cigarettes from the bedside cabinet. He took two from the pack, lighted them both, then offered one to her.

'Thanks,' she said, taking a long draw from the cigarette. She smiled up at him. 'It was good, then?'

'You know it was.'

She nodded, unselfconsciously. 'You did seem to get carried away at the end. I'm glad you enjoyed it.'

'I did. What about you?'

'It was wonderful,' she sighed. 'It always is, with you, Yurya.' She reached up and touched his cheek gently. 'You're such a *man*.'

Pankov grinned. There was more than a hint of complacency in his expression, despite the nagging doubts that occasionally surfaced about her feelings for him. It was just that she was so damned attractive: long, blonde hair that cascaded over her smooth shoulders, big blue eyes, a generous mouth that seemed to be made for kissing, a tall, slim figure that she kept in superb trim, she said, with regular exercise... beautiful. He was no oil painting, he had to admit that, although some women found the scar on his cheek 'intriguing', and he knew damn well that the silk stockings and cigarettes he supplied her with contributed to his attraction as far as she was concerned, but, on the other hand, there were others she could have chosen at the officers' dance - she had certainly not been short of partners, he recalled, but she had left with him... True, he had embellished his job at the airfield to some extent, saying that he was second in command of the security squad there, where, in fact, he was merely only responsible for the perimeter patrols, but she had not appeared to be interested at all in what he did at Schonefeld;

in fact, that first night, there had seemed to be only one thing on her mind... Back here, at her flat, in the wide double bed, she had introduced him to the joys of oral sex, amongst other delights... OK, so she was a few years older than he, and he was realistic enough to admit that she might only be interested in the stockings and the cigarettes, but she still made him feel ten feet tall when he was with her... *You're such a man.*

'What time is it?' she asked, her voice dreamy.

'Nearly midnight,' he said, looking at his watch; it was Swiss-made, bought from that fellow Korotkov for only twenty roubles - worth at least twice that, Korotkov had said.

'How long can you stay?'

'I'm on duty at six, I'm afraid.'

'Pity.' She drew on her cigarette, then blew a perfect smoke ring that drifted up towards the ceiling; she seemed oblivious of his eyes on her body. He had never known anyone like her: the light still on and he could see... everything. Nor had he ever been in a situation like this, with a woman's naked body there for him to look at - or touch - whenever he wanted. Anya, the only girl who had ever completely undressed for him, had insisted on the light being off and that they would both be under the blankets... Monika was glorious: long, slim legs, the mound of pubic hair below the flat stomach, the smooth breasts. Hesitantly, he reached down and cupped her breast, kneading it gently, savouring the feel of it against his hand. He felt a stirring in his groin...

'When can I see you again?' she asked, her eyes fixed on his, as if unaware of his hand.

'Thursday?' he said, still stroking her breast.

She thought for a moment, then shook her head. 'I can't manage Thursday,' she said and he felt a sudden stab of jealousy: was she seeing somebody else then? 'What about Friday?' she asked.

It was his turn to shake his head. 'I'm on duty.' He moved his hand down, over her belly, towards her pubic mound.

She took hold of his hand and gently restrained it; not removing it, just preventing it from going any lower. 'Couldn't you swap with someone else?' she asked, her voice husky, persuasive.

'No, I'm afraid I can't. All security personnel are on duty on Friday.'

'All of them?' Her voice was icy, heavy with disbelief - and she firmly lifted his hand away from her body.

'Everybody,' he insisted. 'We've got some VIP coming in-' He broke off, appalled. 'Look... I shouldn't have said that,' he said, flustered. 'Don't tell anyone I told you, for God's sake. It's supposed-' Again, he stopped himself, belatedly realising he was only making things worse.

Her voice softened. 'Of course I won't, Yurya. I just thought... Well, never mind what I thought.'

'You thought I was just making excuses?'

'Well, you might have been.' There was contrition in her eyes and voice now.

'Monika, I hate having any day go by without seeing you.' The compliment sounded awkward, even to his own ears, but she smiled.

'I'm glad to hear it.' She reached down and touched his erection, stroking it very gently. 'So when *can* I see you?'

'Saturday?' he asked, breathlessly; his entire groin area seemed to be tingling exquisitely, the sensations almost unbearable in their intensity...

'Saturday it is.' She turned onto her side, looking down at his erection, which she was still caressing. 'You're so *big*,' she breathed. 'Would you like me to do something about that?'

'I'd love you to,' he gasped hoarsely.

She moved astride him, guiding him expertly into her, and he almost sobbed with relief as she lowered herself onto him; it was less than a minute since he was convinced he had made her angry and now... He closed his eyes again as she began to move to and fro on him. God, she was wonderful...

It was only when he reported for duty the following morning, hollow-eyed through lack of sleep, that he remembered telling her about the VIP visit, but, short of reporting his lapse to his superior, there was nothing he could do about it by then - and there was no way at he was going to blight his career by saying anything, not when it couldn't possibly matter anyway. Monika had shown no interest in the information at all - and she wasn't a spy, after all, was she?

*****

'Kallmann here.'
    'This is Monika. It's Friday.'
    'Friday. You're certain?'
    'Positive.'
    'Excellent. Any idea of his ETA?'
    'No, but they're on duty all day.'
    'Good... Well done, Monika.'
    'Any time. See you soon.'
    'I look forward to it.'

Chapter 15

Wednesday Evening

'OK,' Cormack said. 'It's time to go, Tony.'

'Right.' Woodward levered himself out of the battered armchair, glancing at his watch before grinning sheepishly at Cormack, as if apologising for doubting his word. He lifted a donkey jacket off the back of a chair and put it on while Cormack quickly checked the living room, more out of habit than out of any real fear that they were going to leave anything incriminating behind. It wasn't much of a room, Cormack thought, not for the first time - the armchairs did not match the sofa, nor, indeed, each other and the faded wallpaper was peeling away from the wall - but, like the apartment itself, it would suffice. All they wanted was a roof over their heads and beds to sleep in, when all was said and done, but he knew why he was paying so much attention to it: it might be the last place he would ever live in.

For Christ's sake, stop being so bloody melodramatic and get on with the fucking job!

They left by the back door, letting themselves out through a gate that gave onto a path beside the Teltowkanal: the towpath was only a few feet below, at the bottom of a grassy incline. To the right, the direction in which they turned, was a metal footbridge about two hundred yards along the towpath, while on the far side of the canal were the forbidding silhouettes of factories and warehouses, mostly disused nowadays; the phrase 'satanic mills' drifted across Cormack's mind as they walked along the path, looking carefully around. There was no sign of any surveillance - there shouldn't be, of course, not with a safehouse, but a safehouse only remained one until it was blown...

The row of lock-up garages was about fifty yards along the path; theirs was the third door they came to. Woodward unlocked it and they went inside, Cormack shining his torch on the machine. It was an ex-German Army combination, sturdily built and probably capable of a fair turn of speed, but its use by an electrical engineer on an emergency call-out would not excite too much comment: electrical engineers were worth their weight in gold these days. The tool box Schoerner had mentioned was stored in the compartment at the back of the sidecar and contained the kind of tools an electrician would carry - but God help them, Cormack reflected, if they ran into anyone who knew anything about electrical installations or circuits, because he knew sod all about them. He knew just about enough to change a fuse and that was it...

Cormack mounted the motorcycle, then kick-started it, taking it out onto the path as Woodward closed the lock-up's door and locked it before climbing into the sidecar. Cormack turned the headlamp on and drove away carefully; it had been some years since he had last ridden a motorcycle and it showed. Woodward had had far more experience, but the machine's documents were in Beitzen's name - another not-so-minor blemish in the planning.

That was the trouble, Cormack decided, gingerly negotiating the corner that took them into the track that led to the street itself: despite what Guthrie had said, this whole thing had been set up in too much of a rush. OK, he had got them into the Soviet Sector and Schoerner had found them Korotkov and a safehouse, but it only needed one slip, no matter how slight, to blow the whole thing sky high - like a patrol stopping them simply because Cormack was clearly unused to riding a motorbike...

After a few minutes, however, he began to relax as it all came back to him; you never really forgot it, he realised, it was like - like riding a bike. He grinned at the thought, then remembered how much he had enjoyed riding a motorbike when he was younger, opening up the throttle and letting it rip... But not tonight, he reminded himself soberly.

'Next right,' Woodward said suddenly; he had memorised the route to the rendezvous.

'OK.' Cormack turned into the indicated street, then muttered, 'Oh, shit...'

Ahead of them, just beyond the next intersection, was a roadblock, a jeep parked sideways on that blocked off half the road, and a wooden pole resting across two oilcans that accounted for the rest. For a moment, Cormack thought about turning round and diving down one of the streets they had just passed, but that would be utter folly, because the soldiers manning the checkpoint must have seen the headlight already. Even if they did manage to evade pursuit, they would not be able to use the combination again, because an alert message would go out telling all checkpoints and patrols to watch out for exactly that. No; they would just have to bluff it out.

Unhurriedly, Cormack slowed to a halt at the barrier, reaching inside his jacket for his papers, a resigned expression on his face. There were four soldiers at the roadblock, a corporal and three privates - and they were Red Army, not MGB, which was all to the good. They'd be less used to this sort of thing. The corporal took the documents and thumbed rapidly through them. 'Where are you going?' he asked, in poor German.

'Buhtzelstrasse,' Cormack replied. 'It's in Falkenburg. They've had a power cut.'

The corporal nodded, then looked at the documents again. 'When and where were you born?'

'Potsdam. May the seventh, nineteen eighteen.'

'Mother's maiden name?'

'Heidemann.' Cormack allowed the merest hint of impatience into his voice; he was a highly prized professional on his way to do an important job and he was being held up. These were no more than routine questions anyway: the corporal had probably been told to ask everyone that passed the same ones.

'Very well.' The corporal returned the papers, then held out his hand imperiously to Woodward, who had his ready.

The Russian glanced through them, then suddenly stared at Woodward. Cormack felt his shoulders beginning to tense; what the hell had gone wrong?

'Polish?' the corporal asked Woodward.

'Er - *ja*.'

The corporal abruptly unleashed a barrage of guttural consonants at Woodward, his voice rising at the end as if asking a question. He stared expectantly at Woodward.

Oh fuck, he's talking in Polish... Cormack's right hand dropped down onto the throttle: the engine was still running, *slam it into gear, knock the pole out of the way, zig-zag along the street before slewing around into a side-street, not a hope because one of them's got a machine-pistol so he'll just let us have it with a three second burst, but better than just sitting here...*

'*Bitte?*' Woodward asked, a puzzled frown on his face. 'I - I don't understand Russian,' he added, in broken German.

'Russian?' the corporal demanded. 'I'm speaking Polish to you!' Instantly, the machine-pistol came up, covering Cormack and Woodward. *Too bloody late to do anything now,* Cormack thought bitterly. *The end of the fucking line...*

'Polish?' Woodward echoed incredulously, then shook his head with such emphasis that the corporal seemed taken aback. 'That was not Polish - *this* is Polish.' He reeled off a string of words just as incomprehensible to Cormack as the corporal's had been, but which undeniably sounded different. 'See?' Woodward finished triumphantly.

The corporal stared at him, then muttered something under his breath and handed the papers back. As Cormack watched, still not quite daring to believe it, the corporal signalled to the two soldiers by the oil cans and the pole was lifted out of the way. 'You can go,' the corporal said tersely to Cormack, who nodded as if he had expected nothing else and rode away, resisting the impulse to go roaring off into the night, get the hell out of it...

As soon as they were out of sight, however, he pulled over to the side of the road and came to a halt. He stared across at

Woodward. 'How the hell did you know he wasn't speaking Polish?'

'I didn't,' Woodward admitted bluntly. 'I just thought that the chances of a mere corporal whose German was even worse than mine knowing Polish were pretty remote. I figured he was just trying a bluff, hoping to panic us.'

'He didn't do a bad job of it,' Cormack commented dryly. 'But supposing he *had* been speaking Polish?'

'Then we were sunk anyway, weren't we? Calling his bluff wasn't going to make it any worse, was it?'

'True,' Cormack conceded. He shook his head slowly, forcing himself to relax. That had been too bloody close: if Woodward hadn't kept his head... And what about himself? He'd fallen for the bluff, hook, line and sinker, had been on the point of blind panic: it had been Woodward who had got them through it, no two ways about it... 'Well done, old son.' A thought struck him. 'What language were you using, then? Or was it just gobbledegook?'

'It *was* Polish, actually. We had some Polish officers attached to our squadron for training during the Battle of Britain, and I picked up a few phrases along the way. Most of them weren't exactly polite, though.'

'I can imagine... So what *were* you saying, for God's sake?'

'Nothing much, really... just some comments about his ancestry, along with an instruction telling him to do something rather obscene and anatomically impossible,' Woodward said, poker-faced.

Cormack chuckled, shook his head wryly, then set the bike in motion again.

They still had to meet Korotkov.

***

'OK, Tony, wait here. If I'm not back in thirty minutes, don't come looking for me, just get the hell out if it, right?'

Woodward nodded reluctantly. 'And if I hear shooting?'

'What are you trying to do - cheer me up? I'd tell you the same thing applies if I didn't know damn well you'd come charging in like the Fifth Cavalry.'

'Very probably,' Woodward agreed wryly. 'I'll - ah - use my discretion, right?'

'Right,' Cormack echoed emphatically. 'OK, let's get this show on the road.' He nodded to Woodward, then went to the end of the workmen's shed behind which they had parked the motorcycle. In front was a strip of wasteland separated from a road fifty yards away by a wooden railing fence, but it was to the left that Cormack turned, keeping to the shadows until he emerged onto a street. Cautiously, he looked around, listening for any sound of an approaching patrol, because now he was separated from the motorcycle, his cover story was rather less watertight. Apart from a crying baby somewhere up in the tenements above him, and the far off sound of a goods train, however, the night was silent, disquietingly so; as if the entire city's population had simply vanished in the night. A city under occupation, Cormack thought distantly: the citizens had learned to keep their heads down during years under, first, the Gestapo, then the NKVD and now its successor, the MGB.

He walked slowly along the street for about fifty yards, then crossed a bridge over a narrow canal that passed somewhere behind the shed where he'd left Woodward. On the far side was a flight of steps leading down to the towpath and Cormack descended them cautiously before turning into the stygian blackness under the bridge itself.

'Herr Beitzen?' a voice said from the shadows.

'Yes,' Cormack replied quietly, coming to a halt as a tall, thin man came into view, silhouetted against the light coming from beyond the bridge.

'I am Korotkov,' the other man said gravely, in heavily accented German.

'And I could have been anybody,' said Cormack icily, 'Didn't Schoemann teach you anything about giving out names?'

'He taught me enough to know that it is Schoerner, not Schoemann,' Korotkov replied levelly, with no hint of apology in his voice.

Cormack stared at him in the darkness, then sighed inaudibly: *what the hell, let it go.* 'Schoerner said you could provide me with information about Schonefeld.'

'I can, yes - for a price, of course.'

'Naturally,' Cormack hesitated, then said bluntly, 'When is Zhukov coming?'

Korotkov did not answer at once; he seemed to be eyeing Cormack up speculatively. After several seconds, he said slowly, 'Zhukov's visit, eh? That's what you want to know about, is it? Well... that might cost a little extra.'

Cormack sighed, more loudly this time, and nodded resignedly. 'How much extra?'

'Double. It *is* rather more important information, after all.'

'Yes, I suppose it is,' Cormack said thoughtfully, nodding again as if considering the situation. The next moment, he slammed Korotkov up against the wall behind him, his left forearm clamped across the Russian's throat. 'Now listen, Korotkov,' he hissed. 'I don't have time to piss around. You get the normal payment - if I'm feeling generous - but if you carry on playing games, I'll make you wish you'd never been born.' He pressed his forearm into Korotkov's neck. 'Do you understand me?'

'Yes! Yes!' Korotkov gasped. 'Friday. Oh eight hundred hours - that's when he's arriving.'

'Good. How long is he here for?' Cormack relaxed his grip - but only fractionally.

'Just one day - he flies out at eighteen hundred.'

'What's his itinerary?'

'I don't know - nobody does!' he added frantically as Cormack began to exert more pressure again. 'Nobody at Schonefeld, anyway.'

Cormack thought for a moment; unfortunately, it made sense. Probably only Sokolovsky, the Military Governor, and Rudakov, the head of the MGB in Berlin, knew Zhukov's full itinerary; the COs of the units Zhukov was scheduled to visit would know their own timetables, but that would be all. 'What security arrangements are being made at Schonefeld?' he asked.

'I don't know,' Korotkov said again, desperately. 'Colonel Borisenko is in charge of them.'

'Borisenko?'

'He's been sent out from Moscow. He arrived last week - he's running all the security arrangements.'

'What, just on the airfield, or for the entire visit?'

'The entire visit.'

'Have there been any reinforcements drafted in?'

'Not so far, no.'

Cormack stared at Korotkov, then nodded and stepped back, releasing the Russian. Korotkov rubbed his throat and Cormack thought that it was probably just as well that the darkness was concealing the other man's expression. Cormack reached inside his jacket and took out an envelope, which he tossed at Korotkov's feet. 'Your money's there,' he said indifferently. 'A word of warning, though - don't ever try that again. You're only an amateur, Korotkov - you wouldn't last five seconds.' He spun on his heel and strode rapidly away.

***

'So it's Friday?' Woodward asked, peeling off his jacket and throwing it carelessly across a chair. He checked his watch, then went over to the small gas stove and turned it on experimentally, nodding as he heard the hiss of gas. 'Great - now maybe we can have some coffee.' He lighted the stove and put a saucepan of water on it. 'Friday?' he said again, turning back to Cormack.

'Yeah. Oh eight hundred arrival, eighteen hundred departure, no idea what he's doing in between.'

Woodward nodded. 'Would Kallmann be able to find out how he'll be spending the day?'

Cormack shrugged. 'Who knows? Depends entirely on what sources he's got. If he's got someone in Borisenko's unit-'

'Borisenko? Who the hell is Borisenko?'

'Yeah, that's an interesting angle,' Cormack replied thoughtfully. 'He's a colonel from Moscow who's handling all the security for Zhukov's visit. Rudakov has apparently been left out of it.'

'I don't imagine he's too pleased about it,' Woodward observed, but a trifle absently; his attention seemed to be focused on the saucepan.

'I don't suppose he is, but that's not the point - *why* has he been left out of it? He's the MGB commander for Berlin, remember, responsible for all security, yet they've brought in this Moscow colonel to handle security for Zhukov's visit. Why not use one of Rudakov's subordinates, or Rudakov himself? They're the ones who know Berlin, after all.'

'Maybe Borisenko is a specialist at this sort of thing.'

'Yes, but-'

'Look, I know what you're thinking, Alan. You're wondering if Guthrie is right when he says that some Russians want Kallmann to succeed, so this Borisenko has been sent in to make sure the security arrangements for the visit allow enough of a chance for Kallmann to bring it off, right?'

'It's a possibility.'

'I'm not saying it isn't, but another possibility is that, as I said, Borisenko is an expert at this sort of thing. The Russians could be doing their damnedest to protect Zhukov and Borisenko is working hand in glove with Rudakov to make it impossible for Kallmann to get anywhere near Zhukov. True?'

'Korotkov said they hadn't brought in any reinforcements... and what the hell would he know about it?' Cormack sighed, suddenly deflated. 'He's only in Air Traffic Control, after all... In any case, Borisenko could be holding extra troops in reserve, ready to bring them in on the day.' He stared glumly at Woodward. 'Talk about letting your imagination run away with you.'

'At last,' Woodward said, as the water boiled. He began to make the coffee. 'You're not necessarily wrong, Alan - you could have the right of it. The trouble is, we just don't know for certain, do we? And we can't afford to assume the Russians will have it all sewn up from the security angle - we've still got to find Kallmann.'

'You're right, as usual, old son,' Cormack said, nodding in thanks as he took the mug of coffee that Woodward brought over. He sipped at it, scarcely noticing that it was only *ersatz*: like most people who had been in Germany for any length of time, he'd become accustomed to it. 'OK, so we know when Zhukov is arriving now, but we don't know where he'll be going in Berlin. Maybe Kallmann will find that out, maybe he won't, but... Where's the one place we *know* Zhukov is going to be?'

'The airfield.'

'Right.' Cormack unfurled a large-scale map of Berlin and the surrounding districts. 'Schonefeld airfield,' he said, indicating its location on the map. 'Right on the outskirts. Trees here, here and here - and a huge perimeter to patrol. You could carry out the assassination and either escape into the country or head back into Berlin.'

'You think that's where Kallmann will make his move?'

'Well, let's face it, it's the only place in Berlin where he can be certain Zhukov will be, isn't it? No matter what itinerary they work out, Zhukov could change his mind, or it could run late, or something else could crop up - but he's got to be at Schonefeld. If I were Kallmann, I'd go for the airfield.'

Woodward nodded. 'Makes sense, I suppose. So - what's our next move?' He held up his hand, and added heavily, 'Don't tell me, let me guess. We take a look at the airfield, yes?'

Cormack nodded. 'Got it in one.'

Chapter 16

Cormack shifted position slightly to ease a cramp in his leg, then lifted the powerful Zeiss binoculars to his eyes again, carefully surveying the scene before him, traversing slowly from left to right until a tree obscured the view. He sighed and lowered the glasses before handing them to Woodward beside him, without comment. Woodward began examining the scene in turn, but Cormack knew that there was very little left to be learned now; they probably had seen all they needed. He flicked a rapid glance around to make sure that no Russian patrols were sneaking up behind them through the trees, but there was no sign of anyone at all. Even if there were any soldiers approaching, they would still not see the two of them until they were within ten yards or so: Cormack had chosen the depression on the fringe of a small wood, concealed from view from every angle but ahead - and there was only the airfield itself in that direction. The perimeter fence was about thirty yards away, made of wire mesh, with barbed wire along the top, but it was not electrified. It was not, by the looks of it, even patrolled very frequently and what patrols there had been had gone past at regular, predictable intervals, all but one of them inside the fence. The only external patrol - three men - had passed by fifteen minutes before, but without so much as a glance in their direction. Not especially heavy security, to be honest, or even markedly vigilant, not the kind of thing you'd expect to be seeing on a military base that had been tipped off about a possible assassination attempt...

Cormack made a rapid naked eye surveillance. They were on the southern perimeter, so that the runway, which ran from east to west, was at almost ninety degrees to them. The Administration Building and the Control Tower were on the far side of the airfield, with a long concrete apron in front of them -

that would be where Zhukov would almost certainly step down from the plane. The main entrance gate was concealed beyond the buildings, while there was a large hangar to the left of the apron, from their viewpoint. The only aircraft visible were eight fighters and two transport planes parked on the concrete: add a few maintenance vehicles, three or four sheds, several stacks of oil drums and half a dozen anti-aircraft guns scattered around the airfield, and you had about all there was to see.

Woodward put down the binoculars and stared thoughtfully at the line of aircraft in the distance. 'What do you reckon?' he asked, not looking around.

Cormack shrugged. 'He's going to have to get inside the fence,' he said, lifting the binoculars to his eyes again.

'You think so?'

'He' s got no choice, not if-'

'Patrol,' Woodward said abruptly, touching him on the shoulder. He pointed over to the right, to where three soldiers were heading their way, inside the fence. Cormack nodded, and the two of them slithered backwards on their stomachs, into the undergrowth behind. They lay very still, watching as the soldiers went past, with only a cursory glance beyond the fence. Cormack glanced at his watch; in fact, they had been two or three minutes early, which might have been intentional - or they might simply have taken a short cut earlier on. Either way, the three soldiers had seemed no more vigilant than any of the others they had seen.

Once the Russians were out of sight, Cormack and Woodward inched forward again. 'You said Kallmann would have to get inside the fence?' Woodward prompted.

Cormack nodded. 'He won't get in a clear shot otherwise. The only part of the perimeter that's close enough to the concrete apron has no line of sight to it - the Admin Block and the Control Tower are in the way. Anyone outside the fence who does have a clear line of sight is going to be too far away, half a mile at least. Kallmann's a bloody good marksman, I know that, but even he wouldn't be able to guarantee hitting Zhukov at that range, let alone get in a killing shot. The only way he's going to get close enough and have a clear shot will be from inside the perimeter.'

'But then how would he get out? Sounds pretty risky to me.'

'Tony, we got in and out of a Luftwaffe airfield in Holland, remember? It *can* be done, you know.'

'Yes, but we had an air raid laid on as a diversion, if you recall - and we flew out. Do you think Kallmann's going to steal a plane, the same as we did?'

'He'll have *some* escape route worked out, that's for sure. He's no amateur, don't forget that.'

'Assuming this is where he's going to do it.'

Cormack sighed, conceding the point. 'True. If he's got hold of Zhukov's schedule, he could make his move anywhere.' That was the real fear that was nagging away at the back of his mind, he realised. Kallmann had had almost a fortnight in which to gather information, and if he knew where Zhukov would be going, he probably would *not* set up the kill here at the airfield, because there would be a high amount of risk involved for him, as had become apparent. And if that happened, if he chose somewhere else, then there wasn't a hope in hell of doing anything to stop him; it would be down to the Soviets. There had never been enough time, really, to have had a genuine chance against Kallmann, not when they had only gone into the Soviet Sector a mere four days before Zhukov's visit, not when their only source of information was a greedy Air Traffic Control officer. Their only chance would be if Kallmann was going to make his attempt here...

'Bloody hell,' Woodward exclaimed suddenly; he had the binoculars pressed to his eyes. 'It's him. Kallmann.'

'Where?'

Woodward handed the glasses back to Cormack. 'One o'clock, to the left of that orange runway marker, in amongst the trees.'

Cormack followed the direction of his pointing arm, then raised the binoculars to his eyes. All he could see was a green blur, but a touch on the focus adjustment brought the view leaping into sharp reality. Nothing - only trees... Slowly, he traversed to the left and froze as he saw the back view of two men walking away into the trees. The leading one, the taller of the two, turned his head to say something to his companion and both men looked back at the airfield for two or three seconds before turning away again. Within seconds, they had disappeared from view.

'You're right,' Cormack said slowly, disbelievingly, trying to keep any hint of the excitement he felt out of his voice. 'It's Kallmann and Schell.' He combed to the right and left, on the off chance that they would reappear, but there was no sign of them. It was pointless to think of using the motorbike hidden in the woods behind to try and intercept the two Germans because they'd been right over on the far side of the airfield, probably a mile and a half as the crow flew, at least twice that once they'd gone around the airfield: Kallmann and Schell would be long gone by then. 'What were they doing when you saw them?' Cormack asked, putting the glasses down.

'Just getting to their feet - that's what attracted my attention,' Woodward replied. 'They'd been lying flat on the ground, by the look of it. They just sort of appeared, as if they'd been lying in a hollow, or behind a bank.'

'And Schell was carrying a pair of binoculars,' Cormack grinned. 'They were doing the same as us - reconnoitring.'

Woodward nodded. 'Which means they're going to do it here.'

'It means they're probably going to, yes. I can't see them wasting time the day before if they're not.' Not quite true, Cormack decided; Kallmann might just be sizing up the airfield as an alternative, but he still didn't think Kallmann would be carrying out a reconnaissance at this late stage for a fall-back operation. The chances were that this was to be the killing ground... 'Come on,' he said. 'We've seen enough. Let's get out of here.'

The next moment, Cormack froze as he heard a sound over to his left - a snapping twig, followed by a muffled curse as someone stumbled. Cormack lay absolutely still, his head turned to the left now and, a few seconds later, he saw them, three figures about forty yards away, moving slowly through the trees, each one holding a rifle across his chest. Shit... How the hell had they got so close without his hearing them? Simple; he had been too distracted by Kallmann's appearance, but that was still no excuse. Jesus, his old instructor would have crucified him if he'd seen that... His eyes met Woodward's and he gestured behind him; slowly, carefully, Cormack began to ease himself backwards on his stomach, Woodward following suit, both of them watching the three men intently.

Evidently, the guards had not yet seen them because they were looking all around them, moving in almost complete silence, but with no sign of alarm - this was obviously a routine precaution, rather than an indication that someone had spotted any intruders and had sent these men out specifically to deal with them. On the other hand, they were heading straight towards their hiding place in line abreast, about five yards apart - the left hand one would probably have tripped over them if they had not moved. Cormack flicked a glance behind him and slid behind a tree, where he rose silently to his feet. A few yards away, Woodward had taken cover behind a bush, his eyes fixed on the Russians.

A few seconds later, the three men came slowly past, still looking all around them. The nearest one seemed to stare directly at the bush, but then he turned his head away without a break in his step. As the men moved by, Cormack let out a long, silent sigh of relief. That had been close, too damned close for comfort and it was all down to carelessness on his part. He was going to have to do one hell of a lot better than this...

The three men were well past now, but he waited until they were fifty yards away before he looked around and rose slowly to his feet, signalling to Woodward. He stepped out of his hiding place and in that moment a fourth soldier appeared from behind a tree only ten feet away from Cormack. The newcomer came to a halt, his face registering utter astonishment but Cormack was already in motion, launching himself forward in a headlong rush. The Russian tried to bring his rifle round into a firing position, but Cormack's left hand chopped downwards, knocking it away a split second before his right hand exploded into the other man's solar plexus. The guard let out a gasp as the breath was driven out of him but then the rifle fired as his finger tightened reflexively on the trigger. Only one shot and it was directed down into the ground but the sound was deafening, echoing around the trees.

The Russian was doubled up now, clutching at his midriff as he fought vainly for breath and Cormack stepped forward to bring the edge of his hand chopping down on the back of the soldier's neck. The man pitched heavily forward but Cormack had already spun on his heel and was running through the trees, up a slight slope, pushing aside branches and twigs as he crashed through the undergrowth after Woodward.

There was a shout from over to the left then someone opened fire, the bullet carving chips out of the branches above him. He ducked as a second shot rang out, but then he had reached a ridge and was plunging down the slope on the far side. His foot caught a root and he sprawled headlong but he was up on his feet in an instant, still sprinting downhill as he heard gunfire again behind him - a sustained burst of fire this time. *Jesus Christ, they've got fucking automatic weapons back there...* He began to zig-zag, leaping over fallen branches and roots, crouching low as the bullets zinged all about him. How much further was the bloody motorbike, for Chrissake? He was only dimly aware of Woodward ahead of him, arms flailing as he pushed branches out of the way, not looking back, concentrating on staying on his feet... More shots, but only single ones this time.

There it was, the clearing where they had left the combination covered by underbrush; Woodward was already hurling the camouflage aside as Cormack skidded to a halt, hauling the motorbike bodily out onto the track, trying to ignore a second burst of automatic fire. It sounded closer this time... He straddled the bike and stamped down on the starter pedal, the bike lurching as Woodward jumped into the sidecar. *Nothing happened*; Cormack kicked downwards a second time - still nothing. *Come on, for Christ's sake!*

The engine roared throatily into life and Cormack slewed the bike round in a tight turn, spitting out stones and dirt from the tyres as he pointed it down the narrow track. A line of bullets churned up the path behind but he crouched low over the handlebars, hurling the bike from side to side as it picked up speed, putting distance between them and the guards. A final shot rang out from behind, but then they rounded a corner and were finally out of sight behind a low spur of trees.

Thursday Evening

It was nearly dark by the time Cormack and Woodward returned to the safehouse; they had followed a roundabout route from the airfield, partly to avoid checkpoints, but also to make absolutely certain that they had not been followed. Neither man said much as they polished off a rapid meal of baked beans on toast, more in the interests of building up protein than out of any hunger, but it was when they were washing the meal down with coffee that Woodward said quietly: 'OK, Alan, will you say it, or shall I?'

'Be my guest.'

'What the hell do we do now?'

Cormack smiled crookedly. 'You mean, after our so-called covert reconnaissance this afternoon?'

'Exactly. I mean, if we're actually going to stop Kallmann, we're probably going to have to get inside the airfield ourselves, right?'

'Right.'

'Only they'll be on their toes now, won't they?'

Cormack did not answer at once; instead, he stared at his coffee mug. 'Unless Guthrie was right and they're trying to make it easy for Kallmann. If that's the case, they might step up security a bit, but not by very much.'

'They certainly didn't look as if they were going all out on their security precautions this afternoon,' Woodward agreed. 'But it might be a different story tomorrow.'

'True,' Cormack conceded. 'On the other hand, if they are going to draft in extra security personnel, it'd make more sense to have them patrolling the airfield for several days beforehand so they'd get to know the layout. Think about it - if, say, they draft in a hundred new MGB troops tomorrow, or during the night, the new ones won't have a clue where everything is, or what the procedures are.'

'And with all those new faces around, it'd be less difficult for Kallmann to sneak in,' Woodward pointed out.

'Right.' Cormack nodded thoughtfully. 'Right,' he said again. 'The point is that, either way, security is not going to be as well organised as it could be tomorrow. Even if it's something no more sinister than slipshod security work, there are still going to be loopholes for Kallmann to slip through.'

'But what if it is *more* sinister?' Woodward asked. 'Suppose Guthrie is right and they *do* want Zhukov dead?'

Cormack looked intently at Woodward. 'What are you getting at, Tony?'

'Maybe we're going about this the wrong way. If there is a conspiracy amongst the Russians to kill Zhukov, it can't involve all of them, can it? The Red Army wouldn't be involved, would it? Zhukov is their big hero, after all. I doubt if very many MGB people are, either, because it'd be hellish difficult to keep secret if too many people were in the know. There might be only one or two people in Berlin who are involved. Borisenko, for example.'

'Right.'

'But that doesn't mean to say that Rudakov is, does it? I mean, if he is, then they wouldn't have had to go to all the bother of appointing Borisenko, would they?'

Cormack nodded slowly. 'Very true.'

'So Rudakov *could* be doing his damnedest to find Kallmann. The thing is, if the assassination takes place *inside* the airfield, there'd be damn all Rudakov could do about it - unless he knew beforehand.'

Cormack nodded again. 'You're saying we should tip Rudakov off, right?'

'Why not? If he's not in on this, then, with any luck, he'll be able to do something about it. I imagine his nose has been put out of joint by Borisenko's appointment, so this will be his chance to get his own back - and to take all the credit for saving Zhukov's life.'

Cormack thought for a moment, then shook his head slowly. 'It's a nice idea, Tony, but we can't afford to take a chance on it. Suppose we've got it all wrong and Rudakov *is* involved in the conspiracy? Or even if he isn't, would he dare stick his neck out? We're talking about some pretty powerful people in this conspiracy, from Beria downwards - does he really want to upset people like that? He's got an easy get-out if we do manage, somehow, to get a message to him - all he has to do is ignore it, or simply pass it on to Borisenko. The point is, if he stays out of it, then no matter what happens to Zhukov, he's in the clear. He might take some action, but... well, we can't guarantee it, can we?'

'No,' Woodward said heavily. 'I suppose not. But what about Sokolovsky? He's Red Army - he wouldn't want Zhukov killed, would he?'

'Not on a personal level, no - but he's the Military Governor, remember, a political appointee. Which way is he going to jump? Again, we can't afford to assume he'll act, can we?'

Woodward sighed. 'No, I suppose not.' He shrugged. 'It was just a thought.'

'And not a bad one either but even if we decided to follow it through, how would we get a message to either Rudakov or Sokolovsky in the time we've got left? Not only that, would you really be happy having to trust the Russians to pull our irons out of the fire?'

'Not really, no.' Woodward finished off the last of his coffee, grimacing as he set the mug down on the table. 'So we still have to go in and stop Kallmann ourselves?'

'Unless we can think of something better,' Cormack said grimly.

'Oh, terrific...'

'I know,' Cormack said heavily. 'Whatever we do, we're going to need transport, though - and we can't really use the motorbike again after this afternoon. '

'We could unbolt the sidecar and just use the motorbike itself,' Woodward suggested.

'We could do, I suppose,' Cormack said thoughtfully. 'We might have to, of course, but I'll try giving Schoerner a ring to see if he can lay on anything else for us.' He stood up abruptly and reached for his coat. 'Won't be long.'

***

In an action that was almost entirely unconscious now, Cormack checked the street in each direction before pulling open the door into the phone booth. He placed a handful of coins on the shelf below the cradle and checked the time on his watch: fifteen minutes since he had left the apartment, longer than he had anticipated because the nearest phone box, just around the corner from the apartment, had been inoperative. In the normal course of events, the extra time and distance would not matter, but he did not want to be out on the streets any longer than he had to, especially if the incident at the airfield that afternoon had caused street patrols to be stepped up. The last thing he wanted to do at the moment was to bluff his way through another document check, not when his nerves were still jangling.

Nerves... You'd forgotten about them, hadn't you, old son? Forgotten how they would became stretched wire taut, so that he was ready to jump at the slightest sound, the merest glimpse of movement. He was getting too old for this sort of thing, getting past it...

Bollocks.

Cormack dialled the number and waited, still watching the street through the glass partitions. This close to the curfew, with darkness settling in, it was almost deserted, apart from a raincoated man hurrying along on the far side of the road.

'Hallo?' a man's voice said on the other end of the line and Cormack froze.

It wasn't Schoerner.

Cormack stared sightlessly at the telephone cradle, then said, 'Is Hans-Peter there?' *Say 'There is nobody called Hans-Peter here,' for Chrissake...*

'Not at the moment, I'm afraid. Can I-'

Cormack crashed the receiver back down on the cradle and pushed the door open with his shoulder, looking around him as if checking for traffic before he crossed the street, resisting the impulse to break into a run. Instead, he pushed his hands into the pockets of his donkey jacket and settled into a brisk walk, his face carefully expressionless.

Schoerner had been blown - and arrested.

There could be no other explanation: the correct code reply had not been given. OK, so it was possible, just possible, that there had been a slip up at the other end of the line, but Cormack doubted it, because Schoerner was a professional, and in any case, Cormack knew that there was no way that he could afford to take a chance. He had to assume that Schoerner was under interrogation - and that the safehouse could be blown at any minute. Woodward and he would have to get the hell out of it, go to ground.

How had it happened? Cormack pushed the thought aside; it was irrelevant at the moment - and he would probably never know the answer, anyway. Of far more pressing urgency was where it left Woodward and himself. *Up shit creek,* to put it bluntly. On their own in the Soviet Sector, with no transport they could safely use, no back up facilities at all to draw on, no way of contacting Guthrie, no useable documents, because Schoerner could give the MGB the names on them... *Jesus Christ.*

Forget about Kallmann: their chances of even getting out of the Soviet Sector had just about vanished, never mind anything else...

Watch it! Cormack suddenly realised he had been on the point of breaking into a run and forced himself to slow down. A hurrying walk was OK - he was trying to get home before the curfew - but a running man would attract immediate attention. And suspicion... If the alert had gone out to stop and detain Reinhard Beitzen and Josef Zagorski and a patrol were to spot him now...

Don't even think about it!

Only he had to, because if it happened, it would come down to two choices: the last, desperate throw of the dice, the zig-zagging run along the street while they shouted *Stop!* then the first shots while he tried frantically to find cover before the bullets ripped into him, end of story, with maybe time for a last thought that at least Tony might get away; or the attempt to bluff it out and if it didn't work, the drive to MGB headquarters, the bright lights and rubber truncheons and it wouldn't make the slightest bit of difference if he told them why he was here because they wouldn't believe him and they'd go for the groin or the kidneys, put the electrodes on, inject the pentathol, turn him into the husk of what had once been a human being...

He knew damn well which choice he'd take.

Slow down. He'd reached the junction into Taucherstrasse, and slowed, crouching down at the corner to adjust his shoelace, looking carefully towards the apartment block. No cars outside, no overt signs of surveillance. He'd been away nearly twenty-five minutes, of course, so they *might* have arrived in the meantime, grabbed Woodward, taken him away and left the flat under observation, a trap - but the chances were against it, to be honest. It would be pushing coincidence a bit too far.

He hoped.

Cormack crossed the street and walked unhurriedly into the lane that led to the track behind the rows of houses, next to the canal. Again, he paused as he reached the track, looking intently each way into the darkness, trying to peer into the shadows cast by the virtually full moon, then across the water at the disused factory yard opposite, finally checking the narrow barge that was moored to the far bank, fifty yards to the right. There was nobody in sight, but that proved nothing: they could be standing in the shadow of that pile of crates, for example, and he would not see them. Or at a window behind him, standing well back, the light turned off...

He drew in his breath and turned to the left, heading along the track towards the gate behind the apartment block. As he passed the lock-ups, the thought came to him that he could just go in there, take the motorbike combination and get the hell out of it: he shook his head in self-disgust and carried on without a break in his step until he reached the gate. He stood for a moment with his hand on the catch, straining his ears for the slightest sound from beyond the wooden door, then unlatched it and pushed it open, moving rapidly through the entrance and pulling the door closed behind him. A quick check around the yard, then he was at the back door, opening that in turn before going inside. He moved stealthily up the stairs, his gun in his right hand now as he took out the door key with the left.

Once more, he hesitated, with the key in the lock, then, with a shrug, turned it and pushed the door open. Woodward was sitting in the armchair, his eyebrows arching as he saw the Browning automatic in Cormack's hand. 'Everything all right?' Cormack asked.

'Everything's OK,' Woodward replied carefully.

Cormack let out his breath and finally relaxed: if Woodward had said *anything* else, it would have meant that there were Russians hiding in the bathroom or behind the door, ready to leap out. But everything was OK... *Talk about a bloody anti-climax.*

Except everything was *not* OK, he thought suddenly. 'Come on, Tony - grab your things. We're moving out.'

Woodward was on his feet in an instant, reaching for his jacket. 'What's up?'

'Schoerner's been blown, by the looks of it.'

Woodward simply nodded as he pulled on the jacket. 'Right.' He scooped his pistol off the sideboard, checked it, then pocketed it. 'How much do we take?'

'Papers, weapons, duffel bags.'

'Right,' Woodward said again, slinging his bag over his shoulder. 'Let's go.'

Cormack grinned, despite himself - good old Tony, nothing ever seemed to throw him - and was just about to pick up his own bag when he heard the sound of an approaching car. Three rapid steps took him to the window and he peered out. 'Shit...' he murmured, as he saw headlights speeding towards them along the street.

Woodward was just behind him. 'Trouble?'

'You bet. Come on, let's move!' They ran for the door and out on to the landing. 'The window!' Cormack hissed and they headed for the sash window at the end of the landing. Cormack lifted the lower sash and Woodward scrambled through, dropping down onto the corrugated iron roof of the coal shed, eight feet below. Cormack followed, letting himself fall just as he heard the front street door open downstairs. Jesus, they were bloody close...

Woodward was sliding down over the edge of the roof, lowering himself down into the yard; Cormack followed him, dropping lightly to the ground. He went to the gate, pulled it open, then peered through the opening, checking each way along the track. Nothing. Although the shadows could conceal anything, of course...

'Come on!' he hissed. 'The bike!'

They came out in a run and darted off to the right, heading for the lock-ups, but then there was a shout from behind them. Reacting instinctively, Cormack hurled himself to his left as a shot rang out; he hit the ground and rolled, paratrooper fashion, ending up on his stomach, the Browning gripped in both hands as he squeezed off three rapid shots at the shadowy figure behind - *where the hell had he come from?* The Russian seemed to stagger, clutched at his shoulder, then fell heavily sideways, but that was all Cormack had time to see because he was up on his feet again and running. The gunman had been further along the track than the gate - he'd obviously been sent round the back, but the gunshots would bring more pursuers from the apartments.

'Get into cover!' he yelled to Woodward and the two of them dived behind a line of dustbins as another shot came from behind them. Cormack twisted round and brought up his gun as he saw someone come diving out of the gate, but Woodward was still faster, firing twice, resting his gun hand on a dustbin lid. The gunman jack-knifed convulsively, then pitched heavily forward. A third man stuck one eye round the corner of the gate and fired three shots; Cormack and Woodward ducked down.

'Get the bike,' Cormack said tersely to Woodward, pulling his duffel bag over his head and throwing it aside; Woodward did the same. 'I'll keep them pinned down. Count of three, right?'

'Right.'

'One - two - three - go!' Cormack moved into a firing position again, loosing off shots over the dustbins as Woodward broke into a low crouching run behind him. The man at the gate fired back, one of the bullets ricocheting off the dustbin lid with a loud clang! and as Cormack involuntarily ducked momentarily, another gunman came lunging out of the gate, firing a quick snapshot on the run before he skidded into cover behind the incline down to the towpath.

Cormack bit his lip. Two to one: not good odds and likely to get worse, because there was no knowing how many more there were, either coming through the apartment block or circling around in the lane beyond the lock-ups. He reckoned he and Woodward had about thirty seconds at most to escape - and he ducked again as a bullet smashed into one of the dustbins. The situation was deteriorating rapidly: the two gunmen could keep him pinned down while a third or fourth could move into a firing angle from which they could get in a clear shot at him, probably long before Woodward could even get the bike started...

Better do something about it, then, hadn't you?

Another shot and Cormack fired back, shooting at random before he came out from behind the dustbins at a dead run, heading toward the canal, firing again - *eight shots gone, five left* - hurling himself forward as he heard another shot, felt it pluck at his sleeve, then he was over the edge of the incline, rolling and tumbling downwards until he hit the towpath. He twisted round, lining up the Browning on the second Russian, who was bringing up his own gun as Cormack fired, the bullet slamming into the MGB man's chest, throwing him backwards, arms outflung, but before he had hit the ground, Cormack was scrambling up the grassy bank to the track, because he could hear the motorbike as it came roaring out of the lock-up. As he reached the top of the bank, he heard the gunman at the gate firing again, but he was clearly visible as Cormack brought the Browning up and firing, counting off the shots as Woodward came up behind. *Twelve, thirteen* - and the hammer clicked on an empty magazine as Woodward slewed the bike round next to him, tyres spitting gravel. Cormack jumped into the sidecar, crouching down as Woodward opened the throttle, the bike lurching and swaying on the uneven surface. Shots from behind, but Woodward was hurling the bike to left and right, zig-zagging and the range was opening rapidly now... sixty yards, seventy... he'd have to be one hell of a marksman now - or bloody lucky... Ninety, a hundred - nearly at the lane now...

And the Mercedes came screaming out from the lane and skidded to a halt directly in front of them, blocking the track...

Woodward swore and wrenched the handlebars to the left, towards the incline. They roared past the car, missing it by no more than six feet, and plummeted down the slope at an angle, Woodward fighting to retain control before they hit the towpath, the impact nearly throwing Cormack along the towpath and for a few seconds there was a respite, no shots, but then they started again and there was no room to zig-zag, not with the incline on one side and the canal on the other... Something hit the bike at the back and the rear end lurched to one side - *blowout* - and Woodward tried to correct but it was too late and the bike hurtled over the edge, towards the dark water of the canal. It seemed to hang in mid air for an endless moment, then it smashed into the water and flipped over in a welter of spray, hurling the two of them over the handlebars. Cormack had just enough time to draw in his breath before the canal came up to meet him.

The impact, and the shock of the icy water, nearly drove the air out of his lungs, but he managed to hold it in, knowing that it was his only chance of survival. The water was pitch-black, but he kicked downwards, diving down to the bottom as he wrestled his jacket off. He swam powerfully away, before surfacing to take in another breath and to look around.

There was an expanse of seething water thirty yards behind, where the bike had gone in and he could see torch lights on the towpath. There was a sound over to the right and Woodward broke surface, but gradually, not causing any more disturbance than necessary. He saw Cormack, then gestured towards the barge, which was now only forty yards or so away; Cormack nodded and the two of them slid below the surface again as the torch beams began to play on the spot where the motorbike had disappeared. They won't do that for long, Cormack thought, swimming through the darkness - they would soon start widening the search. He surfaced again, five yards from the barge, then ducked his head under rapidly as a torch beam headed towards him. A few moments later, he had reached the barge's hull, Woodward's head coming up a few yards further along. Carefully, keeping an eye on the searchers on the opposite bank, they made their way along the hull.

Shit. The Russians were beginning to spread out along the towpath - and there were about half a dozen of them now. They'd be calling in reinforcements and... Cormack plunged his head underwater again to avoid a torch beam. He stayed down, working his way along the hull until his lungs felt as though they were going to burst, then came up again, sighing with relief as he saw the blunt prow in front of him. Woodward had already rounded the bow and Cormack joined him, so that, for the moment at least, they would be out of sight from the opposite bank, in the narrow V of water between the barge's bow and the side of the canal. But, again, they could not afford to stay there; it was only a matter of time before the Russians came across the footbridge further along and started combing this bank as well.

Cormack gestured up at the barge; Woodward nodded. Cormack reached up, grabbed hold of the thwart and hauled himself up out of the water, rolling onto the deck and lying flat before he eased himself into cover behind the deckhouse.

Woodward followed, his chest heaving, like Cormack's, from his exertions. Cormack looked around. Next to the towpath were the remains of a wire fence, with the disused factory yard beyond. The factory itself, no more than a gutted, roofless shell, was about fifty yards away.

Cormack turned back to Woodward. 'Did you manage to hang on to your gun?' he whispered urgently.

Woodward shook his head. 'Afraid not.'

Cormack nodded. 'Me neither.' His own gun had been empty in any case and it had been a pretty forlorn hope that Woodward would somehow have managed to keep hold of his, even assuming the bloody thing would have fired after its immersion, but... He tensed as Woodward tapped him on the shoulder and pointed towards the footbridge: Cormack muttered an oath under his breath as he saw some of the Russians running towards it. 'The factory,' he murmured to Woodward and the two men moved off immediately, scrambling onto the towpath, then clambering over what was left of the mesh fence before they headed across the yard, crouching low. They reached the cover of a pile of crates and looked around again. Four men were already on the footbridge, with another two heading towards it - and there were still another seven or eight Russians on the opposite bank of the canal, shining their torches into its dark waters, but less frequently now. They were beginning to direct their torch beams across the canal and Cormack pulled his head back as the pile of crates was abruptly illuminated. There had to be at least four cars involved now and it would only be a matter of minutes before further vehicles arrived on this side of the canal...

The beam of light passed on and Cormack and Woodward were off again, flitting silently from cover to cover, constantly flicking glances over to their right, where the Russians who had crossed the footbridge were moving closer. Then, suddenly, Cormack and Woodward were plunging through what had once been a doorway, into the main factory building. They skidded to a halt, then flattened themselves against the wall and flicked rapid glances around the interior. The place had been completely gutted; whatever machinery had been here had been ripped out and, presumably, shipped to the Soviet Union. All that was left was an empty shell, whose walls cast shadows of almost Stygian blackness. Cormack snatched a momentary glance through the doorway and his lips set themselves into a grim line as he saw two men heading straight towards them. Each Russian held a torch in one hand - and a gun in the other.

Cormack gestured to Woodward, who nodded and moved soundlessly into position on the other side of the doorway, pressing himself against the wall once more. Then they waited, absolutely motionless, as the light from the approaching torches grew brighter... Cormack tensed as he heard a footstep that sounded as though it came from only just beyond the entrance. There was a pause and Cormack was aware of his pulse rate accelerating: they would have to search the factory interior, but how would they do it? If the Russians had any sense, only one of them would come in while the other held back for a few seconds; it would be too much to ask that they'd both come blundering in...

Then, without any warning at all, a dark figure came leaping through the doorway, landing in a low crouch as he swept the torch round in a rapid arc. For a split second, Cormack's torso was transfixed by the beam of light, but then Woodward's hand came scything down onto the back of the Russian's head in a vicious rabbit punch as Cormack pivoted through the doorway and launched himself at the second Russian, his left hand chopping down at the other man's gun hand, slamming into the wrist. The gun fell from the Russian's suddenly nerveless fingers but before it had fallen more than three or four inches, Cormack's right hand came whipping forward in a straight-fingered strike that speared into the MGB man's solar plexus, the impact driving the breath out of him in a *whoosh* of air. The Russian doubled up, his face contorted as he fought to draw precious oxygen into his lungs, powerless to resist as Cormack stepped forward, grabbed him by his collar and the back of his coat and threw him, almost contemptuously, through the doorway, so that he fell in a sprawling heap on the concrete floor, Cormack scooped up the gun and torch, and darted back into cover.

Woodward had already retrieved the other Russian's gun and was searching him rapidly, thoroughly; he took a spare magazine clip from a pocket as Cormack passed him and bent over the second man, bringing his right hand down onto the Russian's neck with carefully controlled power, enough to render him unconscious, but no more than that. Cormack also found an ammunition clip and stuffed it into his pocket before he began to remove the Russian's coat, gesturing to Woodward to do the same; they were both soaking wet and the night was not very far above freezing.

As he pulled the coat on, Cormack glanced back across the yard. None of the other Russians seemed all that close; they were searching along the towpath, or to the left or right. Clearly, the factory had been the search area for the two men now lying on the floor: with a bit of luck, Cormack realised, they might actually get away from here...

He picked up the gun and torch and put them into each of the coat pockets, then nodded briskly to Woodward, who had done the same. 'Come on, Tony,' he said quietly. 'Let's go.'

Chapter 17

Thursday Night

Cormack and Woodward found the warehouse at a few minutes before midnight, a disused building in the Falkenberg district that had once been a grain depot but was now, like too many buildings in Berlin, nothing but an abandoned shell. They searched carefully through it, before finally settling down next to a window on the upper level from which they had a good view; they could see anyone coming from that direction a hundred yards away. For all the good that would do, Cormack thought sourly as he sat down with his back propped against the wall next to the window, because if the MGB took it into their heads to search the warehouse, then all that he and Woodward could do would be to make another run for it - and if they were spotted, he did not give much for their chances of escaping a second time. Even if they did, they'd still only have to find another bolt-hole like this one...

Or try getting out of the Soviet Sector, of course, make a run for it across no-man's land, when every patrol would be on maximum alert now after what had happened back at the canal... *Forget it...*

He looked across at Woodward, who had volunteered to take first turn on watch and was sitting on the far side of the window, looking out; like Cormack himself, every so often he would begin shivering again and would huddle down in his coat to summon up what little warmth was left. The coats had helped keep them warm for a while but now they had become almost as wet as the clothes that had been soaked in the canal - and there was no way to dry any of them. *If it gets much colder,* Cormack thought distantly, feeling himself starting to shiver in turn, *we won't have to worry about finding our way back to the Allied sectors*

- we'll sodding well freeze to death. Still, at least they had found somewhere to hide, if nothing else.

It had taken over an hour for them to make their way here through the darkened streets, moving carefully from cover to cover, peering cautiously for any sign of Army or MGB patrols before moving on. Twice they had been obliged to make lengthy detours to avoid Russian troops, but they were relatively safe now they were off the streets. There had not been much chance for conversation along the way, not when you had to be constantly alert, ready to dive flat at the merest hint of trouble, but... Well, things needed to be said now, decisions made.

'OK, Tony,' he sighed, then blew into his hands to try and warm them. 'I don't think we can put it off any longer. What the hell do we do now?'

Woodward did not answer for a moment, and when he did, his voice was so low that Cormack had to strain to hear him. 'I've been wondering about that myself, to be honest.'

To his surprise, Cormack found himself grinning slightly in the darkness: *typical Woodward understatement...* 'Did you come up with any ideas?'

'Oh, plenty... well, some, anyway.'

'How many?'

'Two, actually. But I imagine you've thought of them as well.'

'Go on.'

'We decide that discretion is the better part of valour and all that and get the hell out of it while we still can. Make a bee-line for the American Sector - it's only three or four miles from here, isn't it?'

'About that, yes.' Cormack stuffed his hands into his coat pockets to try and warm them: *Jesus, it was cold...*

'Or we go ahead with the original operation. Try and stop Kallmann ourselves. Full speed ahead and damn the torpedoes, all that sort of rot.' He shrugged. 'They're the only two options, aren't they?'

'But then they always were,' Cormack reminded him gently.

'I know,' Woodward said, almost wistfully, then pulled his coat more closely about him. 'Whatever we do, let's try and get some dry clothing, for God's sake.' He rubbed his hands together vigorously.

Cormack nodded absently in sympathy. 'OK... Let's take a long look at this.' He paused for a moment, then said, 'How much does Schoerner's arrest actually affect our chances of carrying out the original assignment?'

Woodward stared incredulously at him. 'Are you joking?'

'No - think it through.'

Woodward rubbed his chin, thoughtfully. 'Well, we're on our own now, because the only contact we've got has been arrested, for God's sake - which means that Guthrie's security wasn't as tight as he thought... Schoerner could tell them we talked to Korotkov, who in turn could then tell them we were interested in Zhukov's visit, which might mean they step up security at the base, but if Guthrie was right and they want Zhukov dead, that won't make any difference...' He was half talking to himself, mulling the ideas over. 'OK,' he said reluctantly, 'I don't suppose either Schoerner or Korotkov can tell them anything vital about our actually getting into Schonefeld, and it isn't as though we were going to need either of them again to get in - but what about getting out again? Schoerner's arrest is going to make a hell of a difference there.'

Cormack nodded, almost approvingly. 'Go on.'

'Look, even assuming that we can get into the base without being spotted, which is probably only a fifty-fifty chance, all hell is going to break loose in there if we actually have to take Kallmann on inside - I'd say the chances of our getting out again are pretty remote, but, after that, we've got to try and make our way back out of the Soviet Sector, without any back-up, no papers we can use, nothing. If Schoerner were still around, he could probably have done something for us, or contacted Guthrie, but now...' His voice trailed away and he was silent for several seconds before he said, very softly, 'I imagine the sensible thing to do would be to run for it while we still can.'

Cormack stared intently at Woodward. 'Is that what you want, Tony?' he asked, quietly. 'You're in this up to your neck the same as I am. You've got a vote too. Which way do we jump?'

Woodward sighed in the darkness, before he said softly, 'To be perfectly frank about all this, the whole thing scares me. It's not just the danger to the pair of us, although I can't pretend that doesn't come into it... It's more the thought of what's at stake, the consequences if we get it wrong. It's not like the other times, is it? I mean, the first time, we brought back a radar set that might have affected one part of the war for a few months, and the second time, we brought back an agent who had information that probably helped capture a few escaping Nazis. All right, valuable results in themselves, but hardly vital, to be honest. But this... I tell you, Alan, I get the shakes whenever I think about it. If we mess this up...' He shook his head slowly and seemed to shudder; Cormack suspected it was not just from the cold. Woodward continued, 'That's why the thought of running away from it all is so appealing. I don't want this bloody great responsibility. I didn't ask for it - I mean, dammit, I've probably spent most of my adult life avoiding responsibility, one way or another... Part of me wants to run away and hide and let someone else sort it out.' He paused, then added softly, 'The trouble is, there isn't anyone else, is there?'

'No, there isn't,' Cormack agreed heavily. 'We're all there is. Two shit-scared amateurs with a single handgun apiece holed up in a clapped-out warehouse, freezing to death and wondering if we've got the guts to carry on.'

'But we've got to, haven't we? We can't just let it happen, or take the risk that Rudakov or Borisenko will do the job for us.' Woodward shook his head. 'And, like I said, if we get it wrong...'

'World War Three, quite possibly,' Cormack said grimly. 'We still don't really have any choice, do we?'

'I don't think we do, no.'

'OK... We'd just better make damn sure we *do* get it right,' Cormack said, his voice deliberately brisk. 'We've managed to get this far, so we must be doing something right.' *Whistling in the dark...*

'God knows what.'

Cormack heard the ghost of a chuckle in Woodward's voice and was suddenly aware of a lessening of tension in the room. They had a job to do and could now concentrate on carrying it out - even if it did scare the living daylights out of both of them... But it had to be done, Woodward was right about that - and not just for the reasons they had discussed. Because, for Cormack, those motives were important, yes - but there was one other consideration that made it impossible for him to turn back now...

Elise.

If the Soviets invaded West Berlin, she would be in the front line...

More than that, was she safe anyway? Schoerner had been blown, but what about Guthrie? If they had got to him as well, he knew where Elise's safehouse was... *Dear God, was she their prisoner? Were they questioning her right now?* Pointless to tell himself she didn't know anything, that if they were professionals, they'd know that they would accomplish nothing by interrogation because there was no way that he would have told her anything useful... Because they might *not* be professionals...

Impatiently, Cormack rubbed his eyes, using the action to cut off that train of thought. *There's damn all you can do about it right now anyway, so stop worrying about it...* 'OK,' he said slowly, 'We'd better sort out what we're going to do. Which is where we came in, I think...' He thought for a moment, then continued, 'As you said, we'll need to get some clothes from somewhere, but in addition to that...' He fought down another shivering fit, then added, 'I think I might just take you up on your earlier idea, Tony. Before, there was no way that we could make contact with Rudakov, but now, we've got almost a direct line to him, haven't we?'

***

Cormack experienced an undeniable sense of *déjà vu* as he dialled Schoerner's number; he even found himself checking the street in each direction as he had done the previous time, even though he could see Woodward standing in the shadows only a few feet away from the phone box, ready to signal if he saw anyone approaching. Yet again, Cormack had to fight down a fit of shivering and knew, somewhere deep down in his mind, that it was not just down to the cold: at this time of night, the only people around would be soldiers - and they would be looking for two men in wet clothing. They were taking one hell of a risk...

So what's different?

'Yes?' the voice over the line said suddenly, startling Cormack out of his reverie, but his voice, when he spoke, was crisp enough.

'I want to speak to Colonel Rudakov,' he said in precise German; he wanted there to be no misunderstanding.

There was a momentary delay at the other end of the line, as if the other man had been taken aback, before he demanded, 'Who is this?'

'I'll call back in exactly one hour,' Cormack continued. 'My name is Beitzen. B-E-I-T-Z-E-N. I imagine that name will mean something to you by now. What I have to say is for him alone - tell him to be there.' Cormack reached up and pressed down the cradle to break the connection before he replaced the receiver. He let out his breath slowly, blowing out his cheeks, then turned and pushed the door open, nodding briefly to Woodward. 'OK,' he said quietly. 'That should stir them up. Now let's get hold of some transport - and some clothes.'

***

Silently, Cormack dropped down from the top of the wall and landed in a crouching position, pivoting round rapidly to survey the scene before he slowly straightened up. He was in the yard behind a backstreet garage, one that specialised in motorcycle repairs, and he was surrounded by the paraphernalia one would expect to find there: motorbikes in various stages of dismemberment, wheels and tyres propped up, pieces of exhausts and various components scattered around, along with oil cans, jerry cans, air hoses, tools and, incongruously, the remains of a brown leather armchair, left exposed to the elements and almost disintegrating now. Cormack stared at this last, wondering how the hell it had come to be there, then pushed the question out of his mind; it was not exactly important, after all.

He crossed the yard, treading carefully over any obstacles on the ground - there was enough moonlight to see by - until he came to the back of the workshop. The door was locked, so he turned his attention to the window next to it. He took out the gun he had taken from the MGB agent, a Tokarev TT33 automatic, and, holding it by the barrel, rapped the butt sharply against one of the panes of glass. There was a tinkling sound as the glass shattered and he froze, listening for any sound of alarm, but the night was silent. He reached through the broken pane and undid the catch, pulling the window open; a few moments later, he was clambering inside, scrambling over a cluttered workbench, then down onto the floor. Now, he took out the MGB man's torch and shone it carefully around the interior until he found what he was looking for, a bunch of keys hanging from a hook on the wall. He found the key to the rear door at the second attempt and opened it, before going over to the back gate, which was fastened with a heavy padlock. Again, it only required a few moments to unlock this and open the gate, whereupon Woodward slipped silently into the yard from the back alley beyond. Cormack pulled the gate closed and the two of them went back to the workshop.

There were five motorbikes in the workshop, but two had been largely dismantled; they ignored these and went on to the other three. One had a flat tyre, but the other two were intact, as far as Woodward could tell after examining each of them by torchlight. Of course, they wouldn't know for certain until they tried to start the damn things, but they couldn't do that here, of course... Working in utter silence, Cormack filled each bike's petrol tank with fuel from the cans, while Woodward took a crowbar and forced open the metal lockers along the side wall, grinning in triumph as he found two pairs of overalls; he held them up towards Cormack, who nodded approvingly. They'd look a bit strange under the coats, but people were wearing whatever they could lay their hands on these days - and at least they were dry, for God's sake... He finished filling the petrol tanks then he and Woodward carefully wheeled the bikes out into the yard. Finally, Cormack took a large pair of bolt cutters from the workshop and locked the workshop door behind him, tossing the keys in through the broken window pane. They pushed the bikes out through the gate, then Woodward pulled it closed before, still without a word being spoken, they wheeled the bikes along the alley towards the warehouse, a quarter of a mile away.

***

Carefully, Woodward peered around the corner. About thirty yards away was a jeep, presumably one of those sent to the Soviet Union during the War, while standing just beyond it was a single soldier, whose attention seemed to be focused on a derelict building on the far side of a stretch of rubble-strewn wasteland that lay between Woodward and the jeep. Woodward eased back into cover, then nodded to Cormack beside him, before he glanced back around the corner, saw that the soldier's back was still turned, then darted out from the corner and into the piles of rubble that dotted what had once been a square. Crouching low, Woodward flitted from cover to cover, pausing every so often to check on the soldier, but he still seemed engrossed in the abandoned building; he had not looked round at all. Woodward paused when he was within ten yards of the jeep, and examined the last few yards, realising that he could get almost within touching distance of the vehicle by crawling along a narrow gulley; dropping down onto his stomach, he slithered along the channel, watching the soldier's feet under the jeep, but still the Russian did not turn round.

Slowly, Woodward came up into a crouching position next to the jeep, peering over the bonnet at the soldier - what the hell was so fascinating about that bloody building? Then he heard them, the rhythmic groans and gasps that came from the darkened building, gradually increasing in tempo and volume... Smiling faintly, Woodward began to search the jeep's interior, keeping one eye on the soldier, but he seemed far too interested in what was happening in the ruins to bother about the jeep; it might well be his turn next if, as Woodward suspected, the patrol had picked up a local prostitute...

There. A pair of binoculars, still in their case, lying on the back seat; Woodward removed the case, slipping it into his coat pocket, then moved away from the jeep, back into the gulley. In less than a minute, he had rejoined Cormack, holding up the binocular case.

'We're in business,' he murmured.

***

'This is Beitzen. Am I talking to Rudakov?'

'Rudakov here. Who are you?'

'What is your mother's maiden name?'

'What-'

'Answer the question.'

'Malenskaya. What-'

'Date of your promotion to Colonel?'

A pause. 'Seventh of July, nineteen forty seven.'

'Right. Listen carefully. An assassin named Dieter Kallmann is going to try and kill Zhukov when he arrives at Schonefeld tomorrow morning. I suspect he will have to be inside the perimeter fence to carry it out, and given the virtual lack of any effective security patrols at Schonefeld, he won't find that too difficult to accomplish. He's going to do it, Colonel, believe me.'

'Who are you?' Rudakov asked. 'Am I supposed to take this seriously?'

'You'd damn well better. Zagorski and I have been sent in from the British Sector to try and stop Kallmann any way we can - but you're getting in the way. Now either take some positive action yourself to stop the assassination or step aside and give us a clear run at Kallmann ourselves. I don't care which you do - if you want to take the credit for saving Zhukov's life, that's fine with me - but if *someone* doesn't stop Kallmann, we'll have World War Three on our hands. Am I getting through to you? Kallmann has to be stopped.' Cormack broke the connection, then replaced the receiver. Quickly, he pushed open the door of the call box and nodded to Woodward, standing in the shadows about five yards away. They walked rapidly up the street towards the alleyway where they had left the motorcycles.

'Did you talk to Rudakov?' Woodward asked.

'If it wasn't him, then it was someone he had briefed.'

'And?'

Cormack shrugged. 'Who knows? Maybe he'll do something, maybe he'll just sit on the fence. There's damn all we can do about it either way now.'

***

Kallmann lighted a cigarette and drew the smoke deep into his lungs before looking at each of the faces gathered around the table. Schell was his usual impassive self, but Bruckmann, the fourth member of the team, was undeniably tense, expectant; for a moment, Kallmann wondered how he would perform - he had never worked with him before, but Bruckmann had come with the highest recommendations - then dismissed the thought. It was too late now for doubts or reservations; they were committed. In any case, Bruckmann would be with Monika and she would keep him in line. Kallmann's gaze shifted to Monika's face, opposite him, and he smiled faintly to himself as he saw her eyes, bright, shining: of them all, she was the one who was actually relishing tomorrow.

'Right,' he said quietly, tapping the large sketch-map of the airfield that was spread out on the table top. 'One more time, then we'll get some sleep. Klaus?' he asked, nodding to Schell beside him.

Schell cleared his throat, then said, pointing to the map, 'Dieter and I will be in position *here* at oh seven thirty. Sunrise will be at oh seven forty three and Zhukov's plane should land at exactly oh eight hundred. Dieter should be able to get in at least one shot from a range of four hundred metres when Zhukov emerges from the aircraft.'

'Quite possibly four or five,' Kallmann interrupted. 'But, of course, each one will be correspondingly more difficult. The first shot is always the easiest.' He noticed Bruckmann nodding unconsciously and suppressed a taut smile; Bruckmann seemed almost to hero-worship him and certainly was inclined to hang onto his every word when he was discussing marksmanship. He probably saw himself becoming an assassin in his own right in the not too distant future... Kallmann brought himself back to the matter in hand. 'Monika?' he said, looking quizzically at her.

She nodded. 'Bruckmann and I will be waiting in the lock-up here.' She pointed to a location on the map a few hundred metres from the airfield's northern perimeter. 'Bruckmann will be watching from the roof. The minute the plane touches down, I get the Volkswagen out of the lock-up. And yes, we will be giving it a final check tonight,' she added, smiling faintly, an expression mirrored by the others around the table; the maintenance work that had been done on the car had become something of a standing joke amongst them. From the moment Schell had taken delivery of it from a black market operator ten days before, the Volkswagen had not emerged from the lock-up in which it had been hidden; it had, however, been given a thorough overhaul by Bruckmann, including a complete engine re-bore and would be able to perform considerably better than its shabby exterior indicated. Monika continued, 'When the plane comes to a halt, we get moving, heading along the road here until we reach the hole in the fence *here*, ideally just when Zhukov is emerging from the plane, but that will be largely guesswork - we won't be able to see him from the fence, of course.'

Kallmann nodded. 'Right. If there is no firing by the time you reach the hole, keep going - we don't want to arouse any suspicions. The moment you do hear any gunfire, turn the car around and come back. You *have* to be there, because Klaus and I will be heading for that gap like bats out of hell. We'll be there within fifteen seconds of opening fire, I would estimate, twenty at the most, so make sure you're there.'

'We will be,' Monika said firmly. 'Bruckmann and I will lay down covering fire if necessary. Once you and Klaus are in the car, we get out, fast, and head back here.'

Kallmann nodded and turned back to Schell. 'Klaus?'

'Once we're back here, we change clothes and documents,' Schell said, smoothly taking over. 'We should be at the Rudowerstrasse crossing point within an hour and, although we anticipate that security there will be extremely tight, we have MGB verified passes so the chances of us being stopped and detained are remote. Once we're in the American Zone, we split up and resume our previous identities.'

Kallmann nodded again. The plan was for Bruckmann to remain in Berlin, until contacted again, but he, Monika and Schell would be flying out that same afternoon, if all went well - and they were not relying on the Patton Group for that, either. Schell had used his old *Kamaradenwerk* contacts, because neither he nor Kallmann trusted the men who had hired them. True, the information and planning had been first rate so far, including providing the two MGB uniforms that were hanging on the wall facing him at the moment, but this was only going to take them as far as the actual assassination; after that, they were very much on their own. Given the identity of the target and the likely consequences, the Patton Group might well decide to cut off all leads back to them - by killing the killers.

But first, they'll have to find us...

'Excellent,' Kallmann said. 'You all know your parts. If everything goes to plan, we should not have too many difficulties.'

'Indeed not,' Schell agreed, then addressed the others. 'Most of the planning is behind us, we're in position, we have access to the target and we have an escape route. We're almost there.'

'Exactly,' Kallmann said. He looked at the others. 'Any questions?'

Monika and Bruckmann shook their heads. Kallmann had not anticipated any queries, not when they had already been through the plans countless times already, ironing out the flaws, modifying it where necessary, but sticking to a premise that Kallmann had come to regard as virtually sacrosanct over the years: *Keep It Simple.* 'Right.' He looked at his watch. 'It's zero one hundred. We start at zero five hundred. Grab some sleep while you can. I want you all alert in the morning.'

Bruckmann nodded and stood up immediately, heading towards the door, but, just before he reached it, he stopped and turned back. 'Herr Major?' he said.

Kallmann looked up from the map. 'Yes?'

Bruckmann snapped into a parade ground Nazi salute. 'Heil Hitler!'

Kallmann nodded gravely and rose to his feet, along with Monika and Schell; the three of them snapped rigidly to attention. 'Heil Hitler!' they chorused.

Bruckmann looked at each of them in turn, then spun on his heel and left.

Kallmann, Monika and Schell exchanged glances, then Kallmann nodded again. 'He was right to do that,' he said quietly. 'We must not forget why we are doing this.'

'No,' Schell agreed somberly, then, with sudden briskness, he reached for his coat. 'There's still a lot to do. I'd better get on with it.'

Kallmann smiled. 'Indeed, Klaus. But try and get some sleep.'

'I will,' Schell replied. There was a faint grin on his face as he said, 'Don't over-do it, you two, you have to be alert as well.'

Kallmann smiled lazily. 'We will be, don't worry.'

Schell nodded briefly and went out, leaving Monika sitting facing Kallmann; she gave no sign that she had even noticed the others leaving.

Kallmann studied her. 'I get the distinct impression you are about to ask me something.'

'You're right, as always. You and Schell seem very confident that you will be able to get into the airfield without too much difficulty.'

'Don't worry about that - that part of it's been laid on.'

'You mean Borisenko won't be making it awkward.'

'Exactly. The security precautions will be less than perfect, shall we say?'

'So how is Borisenko going to get himself off the hook afterwards? Won't he be held responsible?'

Kallmann shook his head. 'No. Rudakov is being set up as the scapegoat.'

'How?'

Kallmann looked at his watch. 'Round about now, Borisenko should be boarding a plane back to Moscow. Rudakov will be appointed head of security for the visit as from midnight tonight - only, because of an unfortunate lapse in communications, he will not find this out until tomorrow morning, after Schell and I are inside the base, and so will not have time to do anything to stop us. No doubt he will try, because he will realise that his only chance of survival will be to protect Zhukov, but even if he orders every security unit in Berlin to the airfield, they will not arrive in time to make any difference. Moscow will hold him responsible for Zhukov's death - Beria will say that he was informed twenty-four hours ago and should therefore have had ample time to step up security. I imagine Borisenko will claim that he left specific instructions that Rudakov failed to implement, and so on. Rudakov will be shot or sent to Siberia and Borisenko will be in the clear.'

Her eyes widened in respect. 'Ingenious.'

'Indeed. One can almost feel sorry for Rudakov.' He smiled briefly. 'Almost.'

She nodded slowly, her eyes fixed on his face, then lighted two cigarettes, passing one to him. 'How do you feel?' she asked quietly.

He shrugged. 'How do you think I feel? Tense. Nervous.'

'Excited,' she said huskily. 'You're looking forward to it, aren't you? You have been for weeks and now we're almost there.' She reached out and touched his cheek. 'The man who killed Marshal Zhukov,' she said softly, her eyes glowing. 'And who avenged the Fuhrer.'

'The Fuhrer,' he echoed, his eyes rapt. He nodded slowly, as if in satisfaction.

She reached out her hand to him, her eyes shining in anticipation and excitement. 'Come to bed,' she said throatily.

***

Cormack came awake with a start, glancing rapidly around before he realised where he was - in the warehouse where he and Woodward had taken refuge. For a moment, he wondered what had awoken him before the sound played itself back in his mind: it had simply been Woodward shifting position slightly at the window, no more than that, but it had brought him awake instantly, which showed just how wire-taut his nerves were, for God's sake... He looked over at Woodward, the pilot's face no more than a pale blur in the darkness.

'Can't sleep?' Woodward asked gently.

'Doesn't look like it,' Cormack replied. He stretched and mimicked a yawn, affecting nonchalance before it dawned on him that the gesture was wasted: Woodward could not see the expression on his face in the almost complete darkness and even if he could, he would not be fooled for a moment. They knew each other far too well... 'Want to grab an hour's kip while I stand watch?'

'Not much chance of me sleeping either, to be honest,' Woodward admitted. 'Too many butterflies in the old stomach.'

Cormack stared at him, then nodded. 'Makes two of us.' He shifted position so that his back was propped against the wall and, for the first time ever, wished that he had taken up smoking - *just for something to do, for Christ's sake, anything at all rather than sit here waiting for the minutes to tick away...* 'Tony?' he asked suddenly.

'Yes?'

Cormack hesitated as he wondered what the hell to say: he had spoken without any conscious volition. 'Just how did we get ourselves into this?'

Although he could not see Woodward's face clearly, Cormack had the distinct impression that the pilot was giving him a very intent look. 'Seemed a good idea at the time, I suppose,' Woodward replied, his voice deliberately off-hand. 'Perhaps we would have been better off staying at home.' There was a pause before he added almost wistfully, 'Actually, the idea of managing the Huntsbrook estate does have a certain attraction just now, I must confess.'

'You?' Cormack riposted, grateful for the conversational opening. 'You'd go bonkers inside six months.'

'Very likely,' Woodward agreed. 'I'm not exactly the settling down type, am I? But then I don't think either of us exactly fits the bedroom slippers and pipe mould, do we?' Woodward paused, then asked gently, 'Or are you serious about Elise Langemann, Alan?'

Cormack did not answer at once; the question had taken him by surprise, not so much because it revealed the extent of Woodward's knowledge - he must have had some inkling of what was going on by the way Cormack had insisted on a safehouse for her - but more because it was totally unlike Woodward, who normally respected other people's privacy. If you wanted to tell him your secrets, fine, but he would not dream of asking a question like that under normal circumstances. *Normal circumstances... what am I saying?* Cormack shook his head slowly, then realised that Woodward was waiting for an answer. 'I think I am, yes.'

'Bully for you - she's absolutely smashing. Much too good for the likes of you, of course, but I have to say I admire your taste.'

'She *is* quite something.' Cormack said wistfully.

'Frankly, I envy you,' Woodward said quietly. 'At least you've got someone to go back to...' There was an undeniable sadness in his voice, a regret that brought a chill sensation into the pit of Cormack's stomach; that didn't sound like Woodward at all... 'It's about time you settled down, anyway,' Woodward continued suddenly, his voice cutting across Cormack's thoughts. 'Maybe I should have done as well instead of getting involved with the likes of Sarah or Jennifer.'

The Past Tense; Jesus, he really is feeling morbid... 'You?' Cormack said again, forcing a note of joviality into his voice. 'Settle down? That'll be the day. Anyway, what woman would be daft enough to have you?'

'Very true,' Woodward agreed dryly. 'You may very well be right at that.' He sounded more like the real Tony Woodward now, Cormack noticed with relief: ironic, flippant. 'Although how you have managed to get your hooks into someone like Elise is beyond me. Has she had her eyes tested lately? Whatever does she see in you?'

'It's my magnetic personality,' Cormack replied lightly, pleased that Woodward's mood of gloomy introspection had seemed to be short lived; the humour might be forced, heavy-handed, but at least it was there...

'And she seemed such a sensible, sane young woman when I met her,' Woodward chuckled. 'Not the sort to part company with her marbles the way she evidently has done.'

'You're just jealous.'

'Damned right I am... Seriously, though, Alan, like I said, she really is a stunner. I hope you realise just what a lucky sod you are.'

'I do indeed,' Cormack replied fervently. 'She is rather special, I've got to admit that.'

'How serious is it?' Woodward asked gently.

Cormack hesitated, considering the question, then replied, 'Pretty serious, I reckon. Put it this way, I've been thinking of asking her to come back to the UK with me once this is all over.' *Assuming I'm still around to ask her, of course...* 'It's that serious.'

'So I see.' There was a pause, then Woodward said softly, 'Like to tell me about her?'

Again, Cormack was taken aback by the bluntness of the question but then realised why Woodward had asked; partly, it was genuine interest, but there was also the undeniable fact that talking about Elise would take their minds off what they would almost certainly have to do a few hours from now... 'She's quite something, Tony,' he said again, dreamily. 'I mean, OK, she's pretty good looking - or, at least, *I* think she is-'

'You and the vast majority of the male sex as well, I should imagine,' Woodward interjected archly.

'If you say so... Would you believe it took me quite a while to realise how attractive she was? Anyway, it isn't just that, or the fact that she's intelligent, fun to be with and a wonderful lover - all of which is true - it's just...' His voice trailed away as he tried to collect his thoughts, before he said, 'It's just that it... I don't know, it feels right being with her somehow. She's easy to talk to, but even if we're not saying anything, it doesn't seem to matter - we're not frantically trying to find things to say just to appear clever.'

'Just as well, really, seeing as how you're a taciturn son of a bitch at the best of times, aren't you?'

'Very probably, now you come to mention it... I don't know, Tony... It's just that...' He shrugged. 'She makes me happy - that's all there is to it. The thought of losing her scares the living daylights out of me and that's the honest truth.'

'You *have* got it bad,' Woodward murmured. 'She must be quite a remarkable woman.'

'That's what I've been trying to tell you, for God's sake.'

'I'd like to meet her properly one day.'

'You will, Tony.' *Assuming we get through the next few hours...*

It was as if the same thought had struck Woodward simultaneously, because both men fell silent, alone with their brooding reveries once more. It was only then that Cormack realised how much he had opened himself up just now. He and Woodward had never spoken like this before, not even when they had been in some pretty hairy corners in Holland or Germany during the War. Mind you, there had not really been time then, he supposed, but... Maybe it was only when you were right up against the wire like this that the barriers came down and you could finally unburden yourself.

And one decision had crystallised in his mind while he had been talking to Woodward: he *was* going to ask Elise to go back to the UK with him. Never mind about not having a career or any prospects - they'd manage somehow - the basic fact was that he needed her to be with him more than anything.

Dammit, he loved her...

Which meant that it was suddenly vitally important that he *did* survive today - and the thought filled him with a sudden chill sensation of fear. He couldn't die, not now, not when he had so much to live for...

'Alan?' Woodward said suddenly, slicing across Cormack's thoughts,

'Yes?'

Woodward seemed to hesitate, then said quietly, 'I'm not sure how to say this.'

'Say what?'

Cormack heard Woodward draw in his breath. 'Listen... No matter what happens today...' He paused, then went on slowly, 'It's been a privilege knowing you, Alan.' He shrugged, as if in disbelief at his own words. 'I just wanted you to know that.'

Cormack stared at him in the darkness. Just what the hell did you say to something like that, for God's sake? 'The feeling's mutual, Tony,' he said awkwardly, aware of the utter inadequacy of his words: was that the best he could do? Frantically, he tried to think of a further response that would not sound trite or hackneyed, but then Woodward let out an ironic chuckle.

'Getting a bit serious, aren't we?' he demanded; Cormack could picture the sardonic grin on Woodward's face. 'We're going to be horribly embarrassed when we look back on all this, won't we?'

Cormack shook his head slowly. 'No, Tony, I won't be. Not ever.'

Woodward stared at him, then nodded slowly. 'Thanks, Alan,' he said quietly. 'I appreciate that.'

An unspoken message seemed to pass between them and the thought came to Cormack that he was doubly lucky, because there was no one he would rather have with him to do what had to be done today than the man sitting across from him. One in a million...

So why the hell can't I tell him that? Even now, some reticence, some inhibition, was holding him back: the realisation saddened him.

As if to push away the sudden self-awareness, he looked at his watch and it was almost with a sense of relief that he saw it was nearly time to go. He was about to say so when Woodward beat him to it:

'I know. It's time to get the show on the road, right?'

'Afraid so.'

'Once more unto the breach...' Woodward rose to his feet, then paused. 'One more thing, Alan,' he said slowly.

'Yes?'

'Look... If anything happens to me...' He swallowed, then continued, 'If I don't make it... Will you go and see my father?'

Cormack nodded. 'Of course.'

'Thanks.' Woodward began to turn away, but then Cormack said:

'And if I don't get back... you'll see Elise?'

Woodward nodded slowly in his turn. 'Yes. I'll do that.'

For a long moment, the two men stared at each other, then, as if by a predetermined signal, each one turned away and began to gather up his meagre equipment.

It was five o'clock.

Chapter 18

Friday Morning: Schonefeld Airfield

Carefully, Cormack leaned his motorcycle against a tree trunk, then peered cautiously around, watching for the slightest sign of movement in the darkness, his ears straining to hear the far-off snapping of a twig that might betray an approaching patrol, but the night was empty. The only sound was the far-off rhythmic thumping of machinery, probably from a factory beyond the airfield, and the occasional hoot of an owl. Without looking back, Cormack gestured with one hand and heard Woodward approaching, pushing the other motorbike. Once the other man was beside him, Cormack pointed ahead of them, at the wire mesh fence just visible in the darkness, forty yards away. Woodward nodded an acknowledgment, then looked around in his turn.

Cormack compressed his lips into a thin line as he looked eastwards. They had seen the first hint of grey there when they had started to push the motorbikes through the undergrowth, fifteen minutes earlier, but the sky was quite definitely lightening now. Vaguely, he recalled reading somewhere that the Muslim definition of dawn was when you could distinguish a white thread from a black one and, although it wasn't light enough for that yet, he reckoned they probably had no more than a quarter of an hour before it became impossible to use the darkness itself as cover.

Better get moving then... He tapped Woodward on the shoulder and gestured towards the fence, receiving a silent nod in return before he crouched down and began crawling forwards, until he had reached the base of the fence. Taking out the heavy bolt cutters, he began to snip through the thick mesh, opening up a large enough gap for the bikes to be pushed through, before he gave a thumbs up sign to Woodward, who raised a hand in acknowledgement; Cormack saw that he had lain both bikes on their side. Cormack glanced around, then slithered through the gap, moving over to take cover in a shallow depression that sloped down to the fence. From there, he could peer over the lip of the hollow with only the top part of his head exposed.

He looked carefully around again. In the distance, he could see the lights of the Control Tower and the Administration Block on the far side of the east-west runway; at the moment, he and Woodward were in the south-east sector of the airfield, perhaps three-quarters of a mile from the airbase's main buildings. To his right, about four hundred yards away, was a flat-roofed shed, twelve feet by eight, that probably housed tools and equipment for runway maintenance: that was their immediate objective, but first they had to get there...

What was that?

Cormack's head snapped round in the direction of the sound he had heard, over to the left, and he tensed as he saw two uniformed soldiers approaching, side by side, fifty yards away, about five or six yards inside the fence. He looked back and saw Woodward, still by the tree. Urgently, Cormack made a downwards gesture and Woodward disappeared behind the tree. OK, so he was out of sight, but what about the bikes? Little chance of their being spotted, to be honest - lying flat on the ground as they were, they'd just look like shapeless mounds in this light.

Unless the guards had torches... If they were carrying them, they weren't using them at the moment, but that could change any time... Slowly, Cormack took out his gun and, steadying his right wrist with his left hand, lined it up on the soldier on the left, the nearest one to the fence.

The seconds seemed to crawl by with an agonising slowness as the two sentries advanced; it did not help that they were in no apparent hurry, but seemed almost to be strolling. They were nearly level with Woodward now... The left hand guard was only about fifteen feet inside the fence, so all he had to do was to turn his head and he would be looking straight at Woodward's tree from a range of no more than forty-five yards. *But you're not going to turn your head, are you?* Cormack thought desperately, willing the sentries to keep walking, there's no danger, no intruders, everything is fine... just keep on walking.

There was a sound and the two guards looked suddenly to their right, through the fence and Cormack almost squeezed the trigger in pure reflex, but it hadn't been Woodward, it had come from the trees beyond. One of the sentries unclipped a torch from his belt and shone it through the fence but it was aimed to one side of the tree. Slowly, the sentry traversed the beam, moving it towards the bikes, which suddenly looked anything but shapeless mounds to Cormack - and in the full beam of a torch, it would be only too obvious what they were... Ten yards, then five... three... *two* and Cormack's finger began to tighten on the trigger.

Abruptly, a young deer stood transfixed in the light at the edge of the trees, its eyes gleaming, before it bounded away. The torch beam followed it for a few yards, then it disappeared into the woods. The sentry with the torch said something to his companion, who laughed and added some remark of his own, then the light was extinguished and the two men passed on, passing Cormack without so much as a glance in his direction.

Cormack lowered the gun, feeling his arms trembling in reaction as, slowly, he let the air out of his lungs in a heartfelt sigh of relief. He waited until the two sentries were some distance away before he headed back towards Woodward.

'Bit close for comfort that, wasn't it?' Woodward murmured as they began wheeling the bikes towards the fence.

'Just a bit,' Cormack agreed. 'But we're still in business.'

Within two minutes, they had pushed the bikes through the hole in the wire mesh, patching it up as best they could - it would be unlikely to be spotted straight away - and were heading towards the shed.

They were in.

***

It was 7.25 when the guards on duty at the main gate saw a Mercedes staff car come driving up at speed, skidding to a halt in front of the double gates. The sergeant on duty stepped forward, saluting smartly as he saw the uniformed MGB major in the back of the car. The driver wordlessly passed out a sheaf of documents that the sergeant took, but did not study, because he was nerving himself for what he had to say next.

'I'm sorry, Comrade Major, but Colonel Borisenko left strict instructions that nobody was to be allowed into the airfield without further orders.'

The major pushed the door open impatiently and emerged from the car, glaring angrily at the sergeant. 'Then contact Colonel Borisenko and tell him that Major Ostrovskiy is here to see him on a matter of State Security,' he said icily.

The sergeant licked his lips nervously. 'Colonel Borisenko is not available at present, Comrade-'

'Then get me whoever is available, idiot!' Ostrovskiy barked, then shook his head suddenly. 'No, that'll take too damned long. Read those documents, sergeant, then open those damned gates!'

The sergeant hesitated and, with a snort of disgust, Ostrovskiy grabbed them from him, taking out a manila envelope, which he handed to the sergeant. 'Read what's in there and you'll realise why I cannot afford to be delayed. I assume you *can* read?' he added scathingly.

The sergeant flushed. 'Yes, Comrade Major,' he muttered, hurriedly opening the envelope. He took out the sheet of paper inside, unfolded it, then drew in his breath sharply as the name at the bottom of the page seemed to leap out at him.

Beria. Lavrenti Pavlovich Beria. *Son of a bitch...* Desperately, the sergeant tried to focus his attention on the contents of the document, but could only take in a few scattered phrases - personal representative, utmost priority, full co-operation -

253

because all that mattered was that this Ostrovskiy had orders direct from Beria himself. Of course, the sergeant had never actually seen Beria's signature before, but it never even crossed his mind to query the document: that would be a quick way into the Gulag Archipelago.

'At once, Comrade Major,' he said, signalling to the guards at the gate. He replaced the document in its envelope and returned it to Ostrovskiy, saluting again as the major climbed back into the car. The Mercedes shot forward, through the opening gates, and accelerated away. It turned a corner and, for a moment at least, was lost to view from the gate behind the guardhouse itself; the sergeant blew out his cheeks in a heartfelt sigh of relief.

***

Slowly, Kallmann began to relax, letting out his breath as he lifted his foot off the accelerator. His eyes met Schell's in the rear view mirror and he saw the momentary, half-ironic grin on the other man's face; Schell had been on edge as well. Hardly surprising, of course, although the chances of a mere sergeant having the balls to stop a major carrying documents with Beria's signature on it were remote: Schell's icy tone of command, as well as his almost accentless Russian, had tipped the scales, as they had expected - but it had still been a nerve-racking affair.

Nevertheless, they were inside the base now... Kallmann drove the car past the front entrance of the Administration Block, then turned the corner of the building and kept on going, along the narrow track between the two rows of workshops. Several men glanced at them as they passed, including a couple of airport security men, but they all tended to look away hurriedly when they saw the uniform of an MGB major in the back. Kallmann drove on beyond the end workshop, towards a stack of oil drums. These were laid out in an untidy 'L' shape, with the longer arm running parallel to the runway, the shorter, which was at the end nearest to the Administration Block, at roughly right angles to it, pointing towards the concrete apron. Kallmann drove the car around to the opposite side of the main arm to the runway and brought it to a halt, looking around. The car would be hidden from view from most angles because of the drums - they were set further back from the apron than the workshops and so nobody would spot the car from them - and the only arc of view that might be a problem, in the direction of the perimeter fence itself, to their left, had a grassy mound that had once been an air-raid shelter that obscured a good deal of the view of the fence itself; in any case, Kallmann felt that the chances of the black Mercedes being seen at any distance against the black oil drums were pretty remote. Even if it was, the fact that it was a Mercedes would probably deter most patrolling soldiers, because only an officer would have a Mercedes and soldiers the world over knew better than to interfere with officers. There was a slight risk leaving it there, but it had to be nearby, for their escape.

Or if they had to go over to the contingency plan...

Kallmann pushed that thought aside and climbed out of the car, followed by Schell, who lifted out the leather briefcase that had been sitting alongside him on the rear seat. They walked quickly around the oil drums, then took up position in the interior angle of the 'L'. Kallmann and Schell exchanged glances, then nodded in mute satisfaction. The longer line of drums concealed them from the fence, while the shorter arm hid them from the buildings; Kallmann could not have arranged things better himself. He went to the far end of the longer arm and peered cautiously around it, focusing on an old anti-aircraft emplacement just inside the perimeter fence, a hundred and fifty metres away. That was their landmark, because directly beyond that was the hole in the fence he and Schell had cut the night before, carefully replacing the strands of wire mesh so that it would not be detected. That was their escape route: the moment Zhukov had been shot dead, they would jump in the Mercedes and drive hell for leather towards the fence, where Monika and Bruckmann would be waiting.

Kallmann nodded again, then moved back to rejoin Schell. He crouched down and opened the briefcase, pausing for a moment to stare, almost lovingly, down at its contents.

Inside, carefully packed in foam rubber padding, were the various components of a Mauser high-powered rifle, along with a silencer and a telescopic sight.

***

Cormack lowered the binoculars, then turned away from the window to look across at Woodward, who was stationed at the opposite window, watching the direction from which they had come. Woodward glanced at him and shook his head: Cormack nodded acknowledgment, then checked his watch. Seven thirty-five. Twenty-five minutes before the plane was due to land and it was only too evident that Borisenko had not stepped up the security measures at all. Ten minutes before, Woodward had reported a three man patrol moving from right to left, just inside the perimeter fence, almost exactly twenty minutes after the previous one, the same frequency as had been in force the day before. Similarly, Cormack had detected no sign of any security reinforcements around the Control Tower and Administration Block; it looked as though Guthrie had been right all along... Not only that, it was also only too apparent that Rudakov had not taken any action in response to the telephoned warning; it had only been a forlorn chance at best, but worth a try - anything was at the moment... But it meant that he and Woodward were going to have to go the whole hog after all, like it or not...

Shit.

He sighed and let his eyes wander slowly around the interior of the shed, a lesson he had learned long since while on passive surveillance. After minutes on end of watching the same, unchanging scene, there was a risk of semi-hypnosis setting in, a kind of day-dreaming that prevented one from noticing slight changes in the pattern - you saw what you expected to see. The best way to prevent this was to take a break every few minutes, let the eye see something entirely different, so that when it returned to the original scene, it was more likely to note any developments or alterations. Not that there was much to look at in the shed: apart from the two motorbikes on their stands in the middle of the floor, there were spades and pick-axes propped up against three of the wooden walls, several fire-extinguishers and a mobile oxy-acetylene welding apparatus against the fourth, next to a cupboard containing wires and leads of all sizes, and a large drum with insulated cable coiled around it in the centre of the floor. Cormack guessed that the shed was used for the maintenance and repair of the runway lights - not that it really mattered, he decided, turning back to the window and raising the binoculars to his eyes. The only reason they were here anyway was that the shed provided a useful vantage point, no more than fifty yards from the runway, from where they could observe the concrete apron where Zhukov would disembark, five hundred yards away.

Slowly, Cormack traversed the glasses, taking in the details once more. At the western end of the apron - to his left - was a large hangar, whose main door was open, with a single fighter aircraft parked outside. Two twin-engined aircraft a few yards to the right, both unattended, a small shed of some sort, a larger four-engine job that was being refuelled - they'd started on that before seven - then a single-engined plane before there was a large gap in front of the Control Tower and Administration Block. Presumably, they were reserving that for Zhukov's aircraft - but it also left a clear field of fire for any marksman. Another twin-engined plane in front of a line of low buildings, probably workshops, then a large stack of oil drums at the eastern end of the apron, then nothing until the perimeter fence curled round to the south. Carefully, taking his time, Cormack brought the binoculars back again, then lowered them once more, staring at the lay-out with his unaided eyes. He had been right, he decided, in that Kallmann would have to take his shot from inside the perimeter fence if he were to get close enough for accuracy. And if he wanted to shoot from cover - and give himself a fighting chance to escape - there were really only two options, the small shed to the left of the Tower Block, approximately three hundred yards from the target area, or the oil drums to the right which were about a hundred yards further away in terms of range. Four hundred yards would be no problem with a high-powered rifle, a telescopic sight and an expert marksman like Kallmann, but the hut would provide better cover if the gunman could break into it. Once inside, the chances of being spotted would be lessened considerably and it would be an easy matter to use the small skylight window for the shot itself. On the other hand, the shed was no more than a hundred yards from the hangar, which would almost certainly have some armed sentries on duty. True, Kallmann could make a break for it straight towards the fence, but he wouldn't be giving himself that much of a head start... The oil drums were more isolated and would offer cover in terms of concealment from the concrete apron, but there seemed to be nothing to prevent a perimeter patrol from spotting him from behind. In addition, the oil drums were about twice the distance from the fence as the shed was... *Swings and roundabouts,* Cormack decided. There was not really very much to choose between them. So which one would he go for in Kallmann's place?

Simple. If I were Kallmann, I'd take whatever money was paid in advance and get the hell out of it to South America... Only Kallmann would have disappeared long before yesterday if that had been his intention. The bastard looked as if he were determined to see it through. How much was he being paid, for God's sake, to take such a risk as this?

Unless...

Cormack felt a chill run down his spine: *suppose he wasn't doing it for the money?* OK, so he would have been paid by the Patton Group, but what if he were playing his own game? Kallmann had been in the SS, after all, and had been ordered to join the Werewolves - how did anyone know he hadn't? If he killed Zhukov, then the very countries who had defeated Nazi Germany would be at each other's throats, plunged into a war of unparalleled ferocity, unleashing weapons of terrifying power. Hitler's own *Gotterdammerung* brought into reality... Was that why Kallmann was here? If he was, if he was motivated primarily by Nazi fanaticism, then Cormack knew that he was being confronted by that most dangerous of opponents, a suicide killer, a man who would take any risks to achieve his objective. If that was what Kallmann was intending, a last defiant gesture to ignite a funeral pyre for the Third Reich, then he wouldn't have to worry about escaping; he could drive a car right up to Zhukov, for example, and cut him down with a burst of machine-gun fire from point-blank range. He would be ripped apart by Russian bullets within seconds, of course, but that would not matter to him, not once Zhukov was dead... A glorious death for the Fuhrer and the Fatherland.

Jesus fucking Christ. If that was what Kallmann planned to do, there wasn't a hope in hell of stopping him, short of getting in close - *on a pair of motorbikes, for God's sake* - and killing him in a short-range shoot-out... and then hoping that the Russians would say thank you and let them go afterwards. Assuming they hadn't just mown down all the combatants in the meantime...

Fat chance.

Cormack tensed suddenly, then lifted the binoculars to his eyes once more. 'Uh-oh,' he said softly. 'We've got trouble, Tony.'

'What?' Woodward was at his side in an instant. Cormack handed him the glasses, still staring intently at the Administration Block. A Kubelwagen, the ex-German Army equivalent of a jeep, had emerged from beyond the building, with two men in it, one driving, the other positioned behind the tripod-mounted machine gun in the back; it was followed almost immediately by a second, similar vehicle. Even without the binoculars, Cormack could see others coming into view - four, five, six of them, heading out in different directions to disperse themselves around the airfield. Maybe Borisenko was stepping up security after all, he thought - except that an extra dozen men, none of them deployed on the apron, were hardly going to make any significant difference...

'One of them's coming our way,' Woodward murmured, as calmly as if he were discussing the weather.

'Oh, terrific...' Cormack said grimly; he could see that for himself now. Perhaps the Kubelwagen would just go on past, with the perimeter fence its objective... *And maybe pigs will fly.*

Cormack watched as the Kubelwagen approached, lurching and swaying across the grass; along with Woodward, he dropped into a crouching position, peering over the sill when the car was fifty yards away. It slowed and came to a halt ten yards from the shed. Cormack ducked down, out of sight, as the machine gunner looked his way, but risked a second peek as he heard the gunner jump down. The Russian had his back to the shed now as he took a machine pistol from the back of the car - a Schmeisser, probably one of the thousands captured from the Germans during the War. The driver was looking idly around, but neither man seemed especially alert or vigilant. Clearly, this was simply routine, which would make them all the less ready to handle any surprises.

Silently, Cormack moved to the door, flattening himself against the wall next to it, signalling to Woodward to take up position on the other side of the doorway. There was silence from outside for three or four seconds, then a voice sounded just on the other side of the door: he'd probably noticed it wasn't locked, Cormack thought, but there was no hint of any anxiety in the Russian's voice. Perhaps this happened all the time...

Suddenly, the door flew open and would have slammed into Woodward had he not already had his foot pushed forward to catch it; the door rebounded and began to swing slowly back, quivering. This time, the Schmeisser's barrel came into view, to push the door gently open again. Cormack's hands snaked out, grabbing the weapon before he pivoted round and yanked at the Schmeisser, dragging the Russian through the door, the soldier's momentum throwing him off-balance as Cormack threw him across the shed, wrenching the Schmeisser from him. The Russian spun round and cannoned backwards into the opposite wall as Woodward sprang at him, his foot kicking upwards into the soldier's groin. Cormack spun on his heel and launched himself through the door, into a headlong sprint towards the Kubelwagen. The driver was staring at him, astonishment on his face, but before he could react, Cormack threw himself forward in a flying drop kick, his right leg straightening convulsively an instant before it pistoned into the driver's ribs. The impact of the blow sent the driver reeling, falling heavily onto his back as Cormack landed and rolled to his feet, all in one movement. He took two steps towards the driver as the Russian rolled over and hauled himself up onto all fours, shaking his head groggily. There was time to spare for Cormack to bring the edge of his right hand chopping down onto the back of the driver's unprotected neck; the Russian slumped forward, unconscious.

Cormack turned and saw Woodward standing in the shed doorway; the pilot made a thumbs-up sign, then Cormack looked quickly around to see if anyone had observed the incident. Nothing: the nearest Kubelwagen was still heading towards the fence, oblivious to anything amiss. Cormack beckoned to Woodward, who came over, and between them, they dragged the driver into the shed. The other Russian was sprawled in an untidy heap on the floor, also unconscious.

'Right,' Cormack said, his chest still heaving from his exertions. 'They're about the same size as us, aren't they?'

'More or less.'

'OK - let's get these uniforms off them. Anything's better than these sodding overalls.' Cormack looked around doubtfully. 'We'll need to tie them up, though.'

'Plenty of wiring in the store cupboard,' Woodward said, nodding towards it.

'Of course there is,' Cormack said wonderingly, shaking his head. 'Now why the hell didn't I think of that? OK - let 's get moving, then.'

It was 7.45.

***

'I think I can hear it,' Schell said softly. Kallmann became suddenly still, then he too heard it, very faintly, the sound of an aircraft approaching from the east. He was aware of a sudden increase in his heart rate and took several slow, deep breaths to calm himself. He nodded to Schell and they moved out from where they had been waiting - on the opposite side of the drums to the runway so that they would not be spotted - round to the firing position. Kallmann took another long look round; the light was good enough to see clearly now, he noted with satisfaction as he focused his attention on the concrete apron.

Nothing much had changed since his last look, five minutes before. The military brass band was still in place, lined up in neat rows, sideways on to the Administration Block, and facing Kallmann himself, while there were four lines of soldiers on parade facing the runway; presumably, Zhukov would inspect them when he arrived. Kallmann had a pretty good idea of where the plane would come to a halt and knew that he would be able to get in a clear shot from where he was - had the band been formed up facing in the opposite direction, they would have been in the way, which would have meant him shifting position, but everything was fine.

He looked over at Schell, who had sat down with his back propped against the oil drums as he checked a machine pistol. A sensible precaution, but Kallmann knew that if Schell had to use it before he himself had fired, then something would have gone terribly wrong...

But nothing would. Not now.

The sound of the aircraft was increasing and Kallmann turned his head towards the eastern end of the runway, to his left. Almost immediately, the aircraft seemed to materialise out of the overcast sky, its undercarriage already lowered, a four-engined plane - Kallmann had no idea what type it was and couldn't have cared less anyway. The plane came in over the perimeter fence, bounced once as its wheels hit the runway, then hurtled past, its engines screaming. It slowed, then turned at the far end of the runway and began to taxi back. As it approached, Kallmann felt his pulse rate accelerating again in anticipation and this time he did nothing to stop it: he would need the extra adrenalin that was being released into his bloodstream in a few minutes' time. This was it, he told himself, as the aircraft turned off the runway and onto the concrete apron. The moment when History would be changed forever - and by his hand...

Carefully, forcing himself not to hurry, Kallmann placed the barrel of the Mauser on the top of an oil drum, steadying it, then fitted the stock comfortably against his shoulder and pressed his eye to the telescopic sight. At once, the view seemed to leap towards him, the plane looking as if it were about to run over him. The image was slightly blurred; he twisted the focus adjustment, then smiled faintly to himself as the outlines became sharp, well-defined.

The aircraft came to a halt, almost exactly where he had predicted, and, immediately, the hatch opened in the fuselage. A set of steps was lowered from the hatch and manoeuvred into position, then an officer emerged, a lieutenant, probably one of Zhukov's aides. Another lieutenant - then Zhukov himself, unmistakeable in his uniform, with its impressive array of medals across the chest. As Zhukov descended the steps, Kallmann centred the sight on the Hero of the Soviet Union award, but made no attempt to squeeze the trigger, because Zhukov was still in motion; he had reached the ground now and was walking briskly forward. Kallmann took his eye from the sight and saw, as he had expected, the tall figure of General Sokolovsky, the Soviet Military Governor, waiting in front of the troops, ready to greet Zhukov. *Scheisse*, what a pair they would make - and it was entirely possible that he would be able to shift aim to Sokolovsky once he had dealt with Zhukov... Kallmann peered through the sight again.

Zhukov was still coming forward, ahead of his aides now, his face grave. Kallmann traversed the rifle slowly, keeping Zhukov in his sights, breathing rapidly, shallowly now and, yes, even aware of a stirring in his groin, a sudden mental image of Monika, naked, *push it aside, no time for that*, lining up the cross-hairs on Zhukov's head, waiting for the moment when he came to a halt. He was almost up to Sokolovsky now...

There. Zhukov and his aides came to attention, staring impassively into the distance as the band struck up the Soviet national anthem. Zhukov was absolutely motionless, and would remain so for the next minute at least while the anthem was being played, so Kallmann had plenty of time to centre the crosshairs on Zhukov's right temple, to steady the gun - and then to pause, to savour the moment, to picture the path the bullet would take once it slammed into the skull at over six hundred metres per second, its soft nose opening out like the petals of a flower, ripping through the brain tissue and creating a hole the size of a fist as it exited, blowing the side and back of the head away... Zhukov would almost certainly be dead before he hit the ground.

Now. Slowly, Kallmann's finger tightened on the trigger.

***

'It's coming in,' Woodward said quietly.

Cormack removed his eyes from the binoculars and stared into the distance, concentrating on auditory input, then nodded slowly. 'I hear it,' he said, then sighed: deep down, a part of him had been hoping that Zhukov would be diverted to another airfield, or that the plane would develop engine trouble - anything, really - but it hadn't happened and so they were going to have to go through with it after all, were going to have to put their lives on the line. Again.

So where the hell *was* Kallmann? The plane was just about to land and there was still no sign of the bastard. There had been no suspicious activity around either the small shed or the oil drums, as far as either one of them could see. They had been taking turn and turn about with the field glasses, but it was entirely possible that at the very moment they were watching, say, the oil drums, Kallmann might be slipping unobserved into the shed. So where...

'Trouble,' Woodward said succinctly and, reacting automatically, Cormack ducked out of sight, then looked at Woodward.

'Where?'

'Mobile patrol, heading this way,' Woodward replied. He was next to the window, pressing himself flat against the wall, but peering around the edge of the window frame. 'On the other side of the runway,' he added.

Cormack desperately wanted to take a quick look over the sill, but resisted the impulse: Woodward was in a far better position to keep an eye on the approaching car. 'Still coming our way?' he asked, having to pitch his voice louder now, because the aircraft noise was increasing rapidly as the plane came in to land.

'They're paralleling the runway... No, turning away - they probably don't want to be too close when the plane lands... They've stopped.' Woodward was virtually shouting now as the sound of the approaching aircraft reached a deafening crescendo; to Cormack, it sounded as if the bloody thing was coming straight at him... But Woodward never took his eyes from the car, not even when the plane hurtled past along the runway. 'Moving again,' he said, pitching his voice lower now that the noise level outside was decreasing. 'Paralleling the runway again... Oh, bugger.'

'What?'

'They're coming our way again.'

They'd seen the Kubelwagen parked outside, Cormack thought detachedly; seen the car, but no sign of the crew and were wondering what the hell was going on - and all the while they were hanging about, that *bloody* plane was moving closer to the concrete apron and the moment when Kallmann would have Zhukov in his sights...

Cormack stood up abruptly and went towards the door, saying tersely, 'Cover me, Tony. Though what good it'll do, God only knows.' He opened the door and walked out, taking half a dozen steps towards the Kubelwagen before he came to a halt facing the oncoming car, raising an arm casually in greeting, seemingly totally unconcerned. For two or three seconds, the car kept on coming, then the man behind the machine gun lifted a hand in reply and the other Kubelwagen turned away, heading along the runway to the right. Cormack watched it go for a moment, then turned and walked back to the shed, forcing himself not to hurry, but blowing out his cheeks in a grimace of relief. As he pushed open the door, he glanced across at the aircraft and swore under his breath: the plane was already taxi-ing towards the apron.

Woodward had the binoculars to his eyes, traversing them slowly from left to right, slowly because he could not afford to miss anything, not now when there were probably only two or three minutes left before Kallmann made his move. Cormack knew all this but it was all he could do not to yell at Woodward to get a fucking move on or to snatch the glasses from him and...

'There he is,' Woodward said suddenly. 'The oil drums,' he added succinctly, handing the binoculars to Cormack, who found a moment to admire the other man's self-possession before he peered through the eyepieces. *Where-?*

Shit. There he was - and he was already lining up the gun. From that range, he could hardly miss...

Cormack threw the binoculars aside and launched himself into a run towards the door and out, sprinting towards the Kubelwagen, Woodward right behind him, a glance across at the plane - it had only a few more yards to go - then he was skidding to a halt in front of the car, seizing hold of the starter handle as Woodward leaped into the driver's seat, wrench the handle round and nothing happened and yank it round again *and still nothing* and *fucking start, will you, for Chrissake!* as he tried a third time and the engine caught, a beautiful sound as Woodward revved the engine and Cormack jumped into the back, bracing himself behind the machine gun as Woodward let out the clutch and the car leaped forward, swaying and lurching as it picked up speed across the grass. There were a few seconds of relative smoothness as they raced across the runway and Cormack flicked another glance at the aircraft - *Jesus, it was stationary*, how long had it been? Had Zhukov come out yet? The Kubelwagen seemed to rear up in the air as it hit the grass again, Woodward's foot flat to the floor as he squeezed every last ounce of speed out of the car. Cormack clung on to the machine gun, feeling the wind buffeting him, trying desperately to retain his balance as he took another look over to his left and *Oh God*, Zhukov was coming to a halt and the band conductor was raising his baton and that would be when Kallmann fired, while Zhukov was at attention for the national anthem and they were still too far from the oil drums to have a hope in hell of hitting anything...

But there was sod all else to do so Cormack swung the gun round and loosed off a two second burst of fire, knowing that the bullets would be sprayed anywhere, the way the car was leaping around, but then Kallmann's head snapped round in the direction of the gunfire. For perhaps a second, his attention was distracted, then he turned back towards Zhukov as Schell, beside him, opened up with a machine pistol, firing at the oncoming car. Woodward swerved, the sudden motion almost throwing Cormack out of the car, but, out of the corner of his eye, he could see everyone on the apron throwing themselves flat to the ground in an instinctive reaction to the gunfire, which wouldn't make Kallmann's job any easier, but the bastard was lining up his rifle again and so Cormack fired another burst and saw Kallmann duck out of sight as the bullets slammed into the oil drums around him. Schell fired again and Woodward yanked the wheel over, steering straight at Schell as Cormack squeezed the machine gun's trigger again, the range now no more than forty yards. The oil drums behind and on each side of Schell were suddenly peppered with holes and a line of scarlet exploded across his chest. He pirouetted around, arms outflung, then, slowly, toppled to the ground.

Woodward slammed on the brakes and the Kubelwagen skidded to a halt, narrowly missing the drums; Cormack leaped out, the Tokarev in his hand. He ran up to Schell, but a single glance at the staring eyes and the gory ruin that had once been his chest was enough - *where the hell was Kallmann?* He wasn't where Cormack had last seen him and...

The sound of a car engine made him spin round even before Woodward's shout and, a second later, a Mercedes came screaming out from behind the drums, slewing round as its driver - Kallmann - spun the wheel to turn it towards the apron. Cormack loosed off two rapid shots at it, then turned on his heel as Woodward came slewing round in the Kubelwagen: Cormack leaped into the back again and took up position behind the machine gun, ramming another ammunition clip into place as Woodward raced off in pursuit of the Mercedes.

Because it was obvious what Kallmann intended now: this was a suicide run, the thing that Cormack had most dreaded. Kallmann was going to drive the Mercedes straight at Zhukov, either to run him down or get close enough to use whatever weapons he had with him. And he could probably do it, because all hell had broken loose on the concrete apron. Most of the soldiers were still lying flat on the ground, while others were running for cover: Cormack saw one, in his full parade uniform, raise his rifle to aim at the Mercedes as it came straight at him - but the car smashed straight into him, hurling him high into the air before he slammed back down onto the ground and rolled over and over, a crumpled rag doll.

And *there* was Kallmann's objective: Zhukov and his aides, a group of about half a dozen, the aides hustling him towards the safety of the Administration Block, but they would never get there, not with fifty yards still to go... and Cormack couldn't shoot because they were in his line of fire, directly beyond the Mercedes...

As if reading his mind, Woodward swerved to the left, opening up an angle, and Cormack fired a long burst that chewed up a line of concrete chips behind the speeding Mercedes, then slammed into the car, shattering the rear window and ripping through the interior. The Mercedes swerved violently, the rear end slewing sideways before it whipped back again, but too late: the car hurtled past Zhukov and his aides and kept on going. Cormack had a momentary impression of Kallmann slumped over the wheel, then the Kubelwagen raced past Zhukov's group on the other side, their faces registering shocked incomprehension.

It was only then that Cormack realised what was going to happen: the Mercedes was careering straight towards a fuel tanker, its speed undiminished. Woodward hit the brakes and the Mercedes seemed to leap ahead, the motionless figure still hunched over the wheel - and in those last few yards, Cormack saw Kallmann's head come up, as if watching his death coming straight at him. A moment later, the Mercedes slammed into the tanker and was engulfed in an incandescent fireball as the aviation spirit exploded, hurling a sheet of flame directly across the path of the Kubelwagen. There was an instant of indescribable heat and agony and then they were through, skidding sideways,

Woodward wrestling frantically with the wheel to bring it back under some sort of control but then they hit something and the car flipped over. Cormack felt himself sailing through the air and had just enough time to position his arms and legs to break his fall; he rolled over and over, paratrooper fashion, finally coming to a halt.

He came up onto one knee, shaking his head to clear a momentary blurring of his vision before he looked round and saw Woodward lying a few yards away, blood pouring from a wicked-looking gash on his temple. He was lying very still, ominously so...

'Tony!' Frantically, Cormack scrambled over to the motionless figure. 'Tony!' He placed his hand to Woodward's head, just behind the ear, then closed his eyes momentarily in relief as he felt a pulse, fast and regular. There were no other signs of injury as far as he could see - with any luck, the wound was superficial and...

And what? he thought tiredly. It wouldn't make any difference how badly injured Woodward was, not any more... He turned his head and his shoulders slumped in defeat as he saw a Russian soldier standing only five yards behind him, aiming a rifle directly at him. Beyond the first soldier, at least a dozen more were running towards the little group on the concrete, shouting excitedly: within seconds, Cormack and Woodward were surrounded.

This is it, chum... the end of the line.

Slowly, Cormack rose to his feet, taking his time, because he was dreadfully aware that the whole situation was balanced on a knife edge. The Russians were keyed up, ready to shoot at a moment's notice: the only reason they hadn't opened fire yet was because the two of them were wearing Russian uniforms, but none of them knew what the hell had happened apart from the fact that someone had tried to kill Zhukov and none of them had fired a shot so far and all it needed was for one of them to lose control and pull the trigger for them all to join in and he and Woodward would be ripped to shreds by a hail of bullets... Slowly, careful to do nothing that might panic them, Cormack raised his hands, feeling his stomach muscles tensing involuntarily in a nervous response. *Come on, comrades, I'm harmless, can't you see I'm surrendering, for Christ's sake? Shit, if only I knew some Russian...*

Suddenly Woodward let out a loud groan and rolled over onto his side and some of the rifles moved, lining up on him, fingers tightening on the triggers and Cormack began to turn, because he could probably kick the nearest rifle away if he moved fast enough, bloody futile, wouldn't make any difference, but you had to try *anything* if you possibly could...

'*Nyet!*' a voice bellowed, followed by a volley of commands in Russian; the soldiers snapped to attention, holding their weapons across their chests. Cormack turned slowly, breathing rapidly, shallowly, still ready to explode into violent action, and saw Zhukov striding rapidly towards them; the Russian Marshal came up to within two yards of Cormack, studying him intently, then he said something to one of his aides. The aide said, in fair German:

'Who are you?'

'We're British,' Cormack replied, still breathing rapidly: *calm down!*

The aide translated and Zhukov spat out another question, but before the aide could speak, the sound of a car approaching at speed made them all turn round. A Mercedes staff car was roaring across the concrete towards them and even before it skidded to a halt, the rear door was opening. Although he had never seen the man who emerged in person, Cormack identified him at once from file photographs: Rudakov. *What the hell was he doing here?*

As soon as he was out of the car, Rudakov's eyes sought out Zhukov; he seemed to relax slightly before switching his attention to Cormack. He nodded briefly, as if in recognition, then turned back to Zhukov, saluting him smartly. Zhukov snapped a question at him - *who the fuck are you?* Rudakov made a lengthy reply, pointing once at Cormack; Zhukov seemed startled, then stared levelly at Cormack: *what the hell was going on now? Jesus, was Rudakov trying to pin the whole fucking thing on him?* The thought sent an icy chill through Cormack and he licked his lips, his mouth suddenly dry.

Abruptly, Rudakov turned towards him and said, in German, 'Captain Cormack?'

Cormack hesitated momentarily, then nodded. *Not much point denying it really - the bastard's obviously seen my file as well...*

'And you are also Beitzen?'

'Yes.' Cormack stared suspiciously at Rudakov, who turned back to Zhukov and spoke again to him; Zhukov nodded several times, then peered intently at Cormack once more, frowning slightly. Cormack waited, his nerves at screaming pitch now, hardly daring to breathe as the seconds crawled by, suddenly, incongruously aware of a bird singing somewhere off to the left, as though it might be the last time he would ever hear one.

Maybe it damn well will be... Come on, what the hell are you waiting for?

Abruptly, Zhukov nodded as if he had come to some sort of decision, then turned to the soldiers and spoke again, his voice terse, accustomed to command. Cormack watched, incredulously, as the soldiers formed a line and marched away, leaving Woodward and himself alone with Zhukov, Rudakov and the staff officers. Zhukov began to speak again; the aide translated.

'The Marshal says that Colonel Rudakov has explained the situation to him and has decided it would be inappropriate for you to be detained under the circumstances. He says he can probably arrange for the security patrols to be diverted for the next couple of hours, but he can't guarantee anything beyond that. We will leave you a field dressing for your colleague's wound. The Marshal offers you his best wishes.'

Cormack stared dumbly, wonderingly at him, not trusting himself to speak; he simply nodded slowly.

'Marshal Zhukov asks me to say this to you. We were allies once. Perhaps one day we will be again.'

As soon as the aide had finished speaking, Zhukov said, in heavily accented English, 'Thank you.' He came to attention, his heels clicking together, and saluted.

Cormack returned the salute, then, with a further brief nod, Zhukov turned and walked away, the others following him. He did not look back.

Cormack shook his head slowly, only now allowing himself to believe what had happened, then crouched down next to Woodward, whose eyes were flickering open.

'Alan?' Woodward said shakily, then tried to sit up, wincing with the effort. He shook his head to clear it. 'What happened?'

Cormack stared down at him, then said softly, his voice trembling in awed incredulity, 'We did it, Tony, old son. We did it...' He shook his head again disbelievingly and looked around, his eyes wide as if seeing their surroundings for the first time; the bird was still singing, the most beautiful sound he had ever heard... *We're still alive, for Christ's sake... And there's at least a fighting chance that I will see Elise again...* He felt a lump rising up in his throat and forced it down.

'We bloody well did it...'

Also from the *Cormack and Woodward* Series

The Dutch Caper

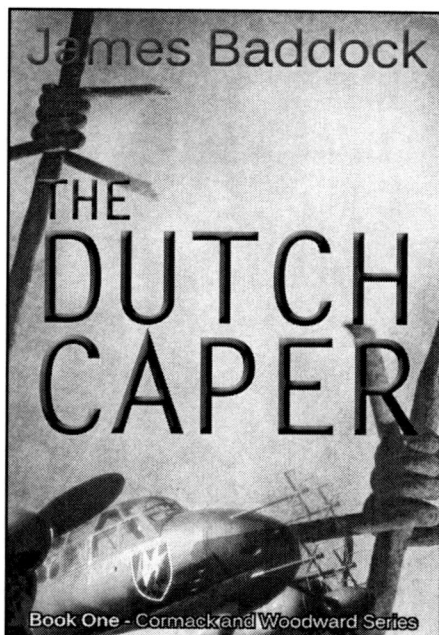

The First in the acclaimed Cormack and Woodward series. On May 9, 1943, while World War II raged in Europe, a German Ju88 night fighter landed at Dyce Airfield, Aberdeen, Scotland, equipped with the new FuG202 Liechtenstein airborne radar. The authorities have never disclosed the story of where this plane came from and how it reached the UK.

Also from the *Cormack and Woodward* Series

Emerald

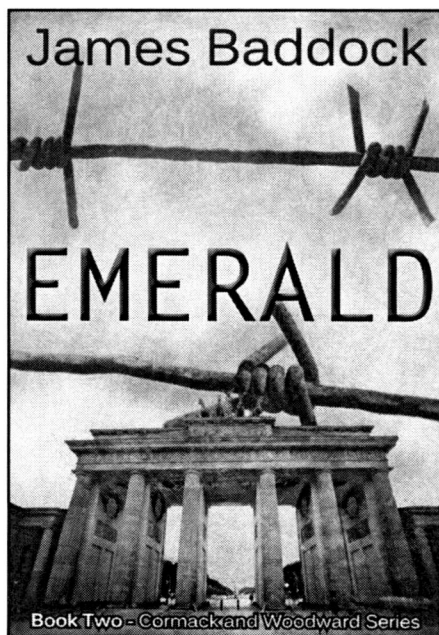

Second in the Cormack and Woodward series. Based on a true story, Emerald is the fast-moving sequel to The Dutch Caper, showing Cormack and Woodward being flown into Berlin in order to bring out 'Emerald', the mistress of a high-ranking member of Hitler's staff in Berlin but also a long-standing British undercover agent.